Remnants of Tomorrow

Also by Kassy Tayler

♦

Ashes of Twilight

Shadows of Glass

Remnants
of Tomorrow

.

Kassy Tayler

St. Martin's Griffin 🦁 New York 〰

This is a work of fiction. All of the characters, organizations, and events portrayed in this novel are either products of the author's imagination or are used fictitiously.

REMNANTS OF TOMORROW. Copyright © 2014 by Kassy Tayler. All rights reserved. Printed in the United States of America. For information, address St. Martin's Press, 175 Fifth Avenue, New York, N.Y. 10010.

www.stmartins.com

LIBRARY OF CONGRESS CATALOGING-IN-PUBLICATION DATA

Tayler, Kassy.
   Remnants of tomorrow / Kassy Tayler.—First edition.
      p. cm.
   ISBN 978-0-312-64177-1 (trade paperback)
   ISBN 978-1-250-03269-0 (e-book)
  1. Survival—Fiction.   2. Government, Resistance to—Fiction.   3. Social classes—Fiction.   4. Coal mines and mining—Fiction.   5. Science fiction.
I. Title.
   PZ7.T211487Rem 2014
   [Fic]—dc23

                      2013046430

First Edition: March 2014

10 9 8 7 6 5 4 3 2 1

Do not look for me in the morning, for I will not be there.

Do not seek me at the table or by your side, but know I care.

For you will find me in the wind that rushes through the trees.

You will find me in the bird song as it carries on the breeze.

You will see me in the ocean, as it tosses upon the shore.

You will hear my voice at sunset as I whisper your name once more.

For I will always be with you as long as you remember me.

I will wait for you on the other side, until your face I see.

Then we will journey together, to the world that awaits us there.

Do not look for me in the morning, for I will be elsewhere.

Dedicated to the Memory of

Chad Hudnall

Acknowledgments

There are so many people who contributed to the publication of a book. Believe me when I say it is a team effort. Thank you to my wonderful agent, Roberta Brown, who is always there, no matter what. Thank you to Holly Ingraham, my editor, who pushes me to write the best story possible. Also huge thanks to the team at SMP, who work behind the scenes telling everyone that my books are awesome. Thank you to the art department for giving me great covers that I love so much that I have one on my phone case. I write a story, everyone else turns it into a book, and I cannot do it without them.

Also heartfelt thanks to my dear friends Lucy Connors and Mari Mancusi, extraordinary writers who share this journey with me. Thank you for being there and making it so much fun. You lift me up when I am down and you give me honest answers. I love you both to pieces.

· Remnants of Tomorrow ·

• 1 •

I have always had a fear of falling. Heights do not bother me at all. It is the thought of having no control, of spinning through the air with my arms and legs flailing about as I scream in terror that terrifies me more than anything. Especially when I think about the chasm that was discovered in the tunnels where I used to live and the knowledge that the bottom was way past where any light filtered down. Not knowing where the bottom was, when I would hit, yet knowing that eventually it would come . . . I shake off the chill that rattles my spine as I look down from the windowsill I crouch upon.

Here I can see the bottom. It is the streets of the dome twelve stories or more below me. I really don't want to know how far it is as I am reminded of my fear with the same impact as a punch to my gut. Instead of looking down I turn my face to the wind whistling in through the hole in the roof of the dome. It carries with it the smells that became so familiar to me in my time outside. I take a deep breath of sea and evergreen to steady myself as I try to decide my next step.

I am two floors below the roof of the government building. The floor above holds my father's office and his quarters, I think. I don't really know, as I'm not privy to my father's personal life. I perch like a bird on the sill of the small window in the water closet attached to my room. Even though my accommodations are luxurious I still consider them a prison because I have been locked inside for the past two weeks, ever since I surrendered to my father with Levi and Pace so that James and Lyon, and hopefully our other friends trapped inside the dome, could get away. This is my father's building, and from here he rules the people of the dome with an iron fist and outdated notions.

I have no idea what has happened to any of my friends, as I have had no contact with them since the night we came into the dome through the hole in the roof. I can only hope that they are faring better than I at this moment. Down is definitely not an option. I must go up if I am going to escape.

It took me two weeks to remove the bars that kept me imprisoned. Two weeks of scraping at the bricks with a spoon I managed to conceal from my tray. I worked at night when I knew I would have long hours alone. Two weeks of hiding the scrapes and bruises on my fingers from Ellen, who brings my meals three times a day with a sullen face and a sense of resentment. Two weeks of praying that my father's man, Findley, will not notice the disturbance around the window.

Finally, I was able to remove the bars and squeeze through to the outside. It is the middle of the night and the buildings that surround me are dark. A few lights flicker down by the street, nothing more than a couple of candles sitting behind windows because there is no power in the dome now. It does not matter to me that there is no light. I can see quite well with my shiner eyes without it.

There is a window above me, but it is as small as the one I came through, and the sill is too far above me. There must be another water closet above mine. There is a tall window six feet to my right. I think it is one that lights the staircase that is next to my room, if the memory of the night of my capture is true. It is the only way to go because to my left is the corner of the building and around the corner the window to my room. All the windows I can see have bars, but the one to my right is tall enough that I can use it to get to the top floor, where there are no bars. From there I hope to make it to the roof, and from there down to the streets and then to the tunnels below that used to be my home. It feels like several lifetimes have passed since I lived there. In reality several lives have passed. I hope mine is not the next.

Most of the windows are tall enough for me to stand on and set deep into the bricks, with wide spaces on the bottom and narrower ones on top. Unfortunately the one I am occupying at the moment isn't. Still, I stand as best I can and stick my right foot into the corner of the window between the bricks and a bar and grab on to the same bar with my right hand as I try to gage the distance.

I am going to have to jump. There is no way around it. Still it takes me a while to gather my courage. If I miss I am dead. My only hope is in catching the bars. I place both feet on the edge of the sill while holding on with my right hand. I crouch and push off and drag my right hand along the way with a wish that it will give me some purchase as I reach out with my left.

I catch the bar with my left, and my upper body jerks to a stop as my legs thump against the brick and I hang sideways with my face to the wall. My cheek burns where I scraped it against the wall and my shoulder cramps with my effort to hold on. I pry my fingers into the mortar and scratch my right hand up to grab on to the bar.

Don't look down . . . My heart is pounding. I hold on tightly as I try to find something to brace my feet against. I pull my knees up and place the soles of my boots flat against the wall. I quickly move my left hand over to another bar and try to walk my way up the wall. It turns out to be a lot harder than I thought, but I finally get a knee on the ledge and am able to pull myself up until I can stand.

The window is taller than me. It is taller than I can reach. But the one above it is within reach if I can get to the top of this one, and if I can do the same again getting to the roof will be easy. First I have to get to the top of this window.

My fingers cramp because I am holding on to the bars too tight. The only way I can go up is to slide them up as far as I can reach and then toe myself upward. The leather soles of my boots are slick against the bars, and I slide nearly as much as I move upward. I am glad it is dark because someone would surely see me in the daylight. I feel as if I have been out here for hours, yet I know it's only been minutes. The longer I hang on to the side of the building, the better my chances of being caught.

I hike myself up an inch at a time. The hardest part is releasing my hold on the bars long enough to move my hands up and start all over again. Every muscle in my body screams for relief, but I dare not stop. I just grit my teeth and refuse to give up. I refuse to stop until, finally, my fingers grasp at the top ledge of the window and I wrap my legs around the bars.

My foot bangs against the windowpane with a sound similar to a gunshot, and I hold myself motionless for what seems like an eternity waiting for someone to discover me. There are no shouts and no lights appear. The only thing I hear is the cooing of pigeons. They must be resting on the rooftop. If only I had wings to join them.

It takes some thought to figure out my next move, and then I realize it is quite simple. I just have to reach up and grab onto the next window sill. The problem is there are no bars on this window. Why would there be? This is my father's floor.

Getting to the roof will be harder than I thought, but I've come too far to turn back. Turning back means admitting defeat and that is something I will not do. Especially to my father.

I push up as far as I can with my legs braced against the glass and grab onto the sill with the fingertips of my right hand. I hang there for a moment, paralyzed, because I am afraid my grip is not good enough to let go with my left hand. I take another stab at it and get a firmer hold before I let go with my left hand and reach up. Now it is just a matter of once more walking my legs up. The muscles in my shoulders groan in agony as I pull myself up until I am able to swing a leg onto the sill. I spread my arms and grab on to the sides as I slowly stand on trembling legs.

I am sweating. I lean my forehead against the cool glass for a moment as I try to gather myself once more. The thought that my father could be asleep on the other side of the glass does not escape me. I will survive without seeing him. I have survived my entire life without his notice, so I see no need to have it now. If he wanted to see me, he's had two weeks to do so.

I must get to the roof. I have no bars this time to help me. It is going to take all my strength to get there, and I know I have little of it left. I decide just to go for it, instead of thinking about it, because thinking about it might turn me around.

I grab on to the top of the window and walk myself up once more. My boots bang against the glass. I have no time to worry about the noise. I just keep going until I manage to get my knee up, and then I just let go with my right hand once more and grab onto the roof.

Simple. Until I try to put my left hand beside it and miss. I am so surprised when I don't grab on that my legs flail and I swing sideways, barely hanging on with one hand. My shoulder screams at the abuse as I try to bring my left arm up again. It is out of my reach. I feel my fingers slipping and I clamp down. Somehow my body twists and the strain on my arm makes me yelp out in pain. I see the buildings around me, dark and still, and the streets below me darker, beckoning . . . I am going to die. They will find my broken body on the cobblestones, and I will simply be gone. My friends will never know what happened to me.

"Pace," I say. Is it a prayer, or am I begging for forgiveness?

A hand clamps around my wrist, and I am boldly yanked upward by my arm, over the ledge and dropped onto the roof.

"Wren!" Findley exclaims. "I wasn't sure you were going to make it."

I need a moment to gather myself. To catch my breath. To realize that I am not dead. I look up at Findley, my father's man. His face is pleasant, handsome in a way that is hard to define, and his age hard to say. He could be ten years older than me or he could be twenty. His hair is dark blond and his eyes a shade of bluish gray. He's the same height as Pace but broader and harder. He wears the uniform of the enforcers, what we shiners have always called the bluecoats. I have yet to figure him out.

"Were you watching the entire time?" I finally ask when I am able to breathe again.

He pulls me to my feet. "Yes. Yes I was."

"What would you have done if I'd fallen?"

"Luckily, we will never know," he replies as he pushes me to an enclosure with an open door. I realize now that the stairs *do* go all the way to the top. If not for Findley I simply could have walked down the stairs and to my freedom.

"Where are we going?" I ask.

"Back to your room," he says.

I want to cry. But I don't. I would never give Findley or my father that satisfaction. The trip back to my room is relatively short.

Just down two flights of stairs and through the door, where Findley shoves me in the general direction of my bed. I land on it with a bounce and twist around when I hear the rattle of a chain.

"Where did that come from?" I ask.

"I picked it up while you were out," he replies. To my horror I see that it is looped through the bed frame and attached with a lock. The end of it holds a shackle and he grabs my ankle. I kick out at him but he is much bigger and very much stronger. He grabs my ankle again and twists it so hard I have to flip over to keep it from breaking. When I land on my stomach Findley presses his knee into my back and quickly closes the shackle over my ankle and locks it into place.

"This will hold you until we can do something about that window." All I can do is glare at him. "See you in the morning," he adds and walks out, closing the door behind him. I hear the turn of the key in the lock, and I am alone once more. I jump up from the bed and check where the chain is attached. There is no way I can release the chain or lift the bed to release it. It is so short that I can only move two feet away, so I have no choice but to lie down, defeated.

But only for the moment.

· 2 ·

Memories have a way of coming to you when you least expect it. The littlest things, long forgotten, suddenly sneak up on you and capture you. As I lay on the bed, seething in anger, the memory of the first time my grandfather took me above comes over me and leaves me with an ache of regret for things left unsaid.

I could not have been more than four years old the first time he took me aboveground. At first it was painful because the light was so much brighter than I was used to, underground where we lived. After my eyes finally adjusted, I stared at the dome soaring high above the rooftops, marveling that the world could be so big. My only reference was the cavern we lived in below. My grandfather lifted me onto his shoulders to sit as he walked, and I felt safe, since I was above those who milled about us as we made our way to the library for the single day of the year we were allowed in. I stretched my hands high above my head, certain that if I tried hard enough, I could touch the glass that covered us and kept us safe from the flames that raged outside.

My grandfather was a practical man and did not encourage my dreams, so I kept them to myself. I dreamed about going outside when I was old enough to go up the lift on my own and climbing up to the rooftops to watch the light come to the dome. I had no idea how to make my dreams come true, nor did I realize the price that we would all have to pay. I was younger then, and in my heart and mind I was certain that once I and everyone else was outside our lives would be perfect. I would have achieved the pinnacle of my desires and could live out the rest of my days content that I had nothing more to worry about and nothing more to strive for.

I realize now how foolish I was.

Once outside it did not take me long to find that I was wrong. Opening a door and stepping through does not solve everything. For me and for those who believed in me, it led to another set of problems, and to another set of principles, with the sure knowledge that mistakes are made by everyone. The best that you can hope for is that you learn from your mistakes and are able to move on to make things better for yourself and the ones that you love.

If only we had the ability to look at our lives in advance and know which path to take. I suppose that would take all the mystery and maybe even the joy out of life. How can we appreciate what we have if it all comes easily? Is it something worth having if it does not come with trials and tribulations? Do we take the things we are used to for granted? Things like food, water, and air? Things like freedom?

I know now that I did not really appreciate what I had, even with all the problems that came with it. I had thought myself a prisoner of the dome and its society before I escaped. That was before I knew what real freedom was. Freedom was my ability to choose. I chose to leave the dome. I also chose to come back inside, even though I knew there would be risks involved. Even though every fiber of my being cried out to me to stay outside. Perhaps in my heart I did know what the best decision was and I just ignored it.

Or maybe I just have a habit of making terrible decisions. The last one I made led to this. Are Pace and Levi locked up also? I believe Pace intended all along to stay inside, because he was worried about his mother but also because he knew I was conflicted about my feelings for both him and Levi. To Pace, choosing to stay inside meant I wouldn't have to choose between them. Pace thinks he is considerate that way, taking the decision away from me, so I wouldn't have to deal with it. Right now I hate him for it.

I don't know why Levi surrendered. Maybe he thought that because he was an outsider to our world that my father would value him as a hostage. Maybe he thought that because he was a prisoner of my father, his uncle, Lyon Hatfield, would be that much more determined to rescue all of us instead of leaving us to our fates. All the things I don't know greatly outnumber the one thing that I know for certain.

I am a prisoner in my father's house.

◆

"Got in a bit of trouble last night I see." The woman, Ellen, is the only other person I've seen since I arrived here, except for Findley. She smiles in satisfaction when she sees the chain around my ankle. I sit up and push my hair out of my eyes as she sets my breakfast tray on the table and leaves, knowing full well that I won't be able to reach it. I throw a pillow at the door as I hear the key turn in the lock and flop back down on the bed.

How long will I be stuck here? Some people might scoff at the idea that the room I inhabit is a prison, but there are locks on the door, and no matter how luxurious it is, the fact that I cannot come and go as I please makes it a prison. It does not matter that I have a wide comfortable bed piled high with exquisitely soft linens or shelves full of leather-bound books or a wardrobe full of clothes made of satin and velvet. Or even the fact that there is a water closet attached to my room for my exclusive use. It is still a prison. For the Hatfields outside the dome and the royals within, the wonderful things in my room are a part of their everyday life. Before I was invited onto Lyon Hatfield's airship, I never dreamed such things existed. Today I would gladly trade all the luxuries that surround me just to be able to leave this place.

The smell of food makes my stomach rumble in hunger. That reminds me that I need to use the water closet. How long will I be chained to the bed? The sound of the key turning in the lock gives me some hope. Findley comes in with two men behind him, both carrying boards. They glance my way and then just as quickly ignore me as Findley probably instructed them to do. Their faces are pale and gaunt and their clothes hang on their frames. They must be hungry. How many more people in the dome are hungry now? Certainly not the royals. Nor am I. While I am not given a lot, I am given enough.

One goes into the water closet and another to the tall window that overlooks the city. Findley comes to the bed and unlocks the chain around my ankles.

"What are you doing?" I ask suspiciously.

"Making sure you don't try to kill yourself again," he replies. He kicks the chain beneath the bed. I know he's leaving it to remind me what will happen should I try to escape again. He goes to the water closet and motions the man inside to come out. "Give her a moment," he says, then he turns to me. "Do I need to come in there with you?"

I shake my head. I don't need any more humiliation at the

moment. I hear the sound of pounding while I am inside and come out to find a board covering the bottom inches of the window and another one going up above it.

"Don't," I say. "Please . . ." I know I'll go mad if I can't see out. If I cannot see the light fill the dome. I hate begging, but in this case . . .

Findley sends the man back into the water closet and then looks at me for a long moment. I feel tears well in my eyes and I blink them back. I don't want to seem weak, and I definitely don't want him to know that this can be used against me. I have spent so much of my life in darkness. I don't want to go back to that feeling, ever again.

"Leave one off," Findley says to the man who works at my window. "Eye level so she can see out."

I did not realize I was holding my breath until I let it out.

"Eat," Findley instructs. "While it's hot."

Ignoring my food will only hurt me. But I feel guilty eating when the men are obviously hungry. My plate holds a piece of toast with a fried egg on it. I slice it in half and offer it to the man working on the window. He looks at Findley, tentatively, who nods his permission. He takes it and it is gone in three bites. "Thank ye," he says with a bob of his head. I take the remaining half to the man in my water closet and offer it to him with a smile. He quickly gulps it down.

I am hungry, but my feeling in my heart makes the hunger seem insignificant. Findley merely shakes his head at my foolishness. I don't care what he thinks. I sit back down at the table and watch as the room grows dimmer and dimmer with each board that goes into place. I do not need the light to see, but, still, I miss it. As long as I can see the light, I have hope.

I watch as the nails are pounded into the window frame. Long thick nails that I will not have a chance of pulling out. To make sure I know that, Findley pulls on each board to make sure it is secure, then he goes and checks the same in the water closet. He sends the men out and makes a big show of stowing the spoon I'd used as a tool into the inside pocket of his uniform. He leaves without another word, and the turning of the key in the lock echoes in my dark and lonely room.

I am trapped.

◆

My window overlooks the royal side of the dome. Through the opening left between the boards I can see the privileged of our society as they walk the promenade in clothes of velvet and satin. The women carry parasols to shelter their faces from the tiny bit of sunlight that streams through the hole. I scoff at their foolishness. The sun is nowhere near them. Instead of looking stylish, they look ridiculous, protecting themselves from something they know nothing about. I have felt the sun on my skin, and I know that it burns. It also warms and gives me a sense of hope.

The royals stop and talk to one another as if much time has passed since their last meeting, yet I know they see the same people every day because nothing ever changes for them. They die and new ones are born, but the monotony of their lives is never-ending. The royals don't know the agony of worry, and the not knowing that haunts people when someone they care about is gone from them. The royals continue to act as if their world has not changed at all, even though the fans do not run and part of their world has been destroyed.

How can they act as if nothing has happened when there is a

hole in the dome that shows the sky? Don't they wonder what is outside? Don't they want to see it? How can they believe the lies about the flames when the proof is right above them? How can they be so frivolous that they carry on as if they don't have a care in the world?

Perhaps it is because they don't have a care. They have nothing to worry about beyond what clothes they will wear tomorrow. They cannot see what is beyond their part of the dome. But I have seen it all, and I know this routine they live will soon be interrupted. The weather outside will change, the air around the dome will warm up and the inside will become hot and uncomfortable. Maybe then they will notice what is happening around them.

As long as they are comfortable, the royals have no reason to leave. Why would they, when they have at their fingertips everything they could possibly want to make their lives easy? I had no idea of the luxuries they have at hand until I experienced them for myself here in my father's quarters. But even with all this ease and comfort I would not want to be one of the royals. Their sense of complacency has to be as confining as the locks that hold me in.

There is nothing more to see outside. I am weary and I am frustrated. I want to beat on the doors or kick something or someone. Instead I go to the bookshelves and look at the titles for what feels like the hundredth time. The names have become familiar to me: Charles Dickens, Jane Austen, Emily Brontë, and a particularly scary story titled *Frankenstein*, by Mary Shelley. Reading them fills me with a sense of wonder at how the world was before the dome, along with anger that such knowledge was kept from the majority of us who lived inside. At least now I have a better understanding for the world as it was and, since I've been outside, can envision the stories actually happening. I pull a book of poems from the shelf, but they do nothing to distract me from my worries.

◆

"When are you going to change out of those clothes?" Ellen asks, when she comes back for my breakfast tray. She has not said much to me since I've been here, so her question surprises me. I still wear my shiner clothes. I take them off each night before I climb into the soft, comfortable bed and put them on again after I wash each morning. My father provided me with a wardrobe full of beautiful dresses to wear, and I refuse to put them on. Wearing them would mean compliance on my part, and as my father well knows from our brief meeting before I escaped the dome, noncompliance is a part of who I am and the reason I am here. It may be a small victory for me to refuse his gifts of clothing, but it is one I will cling to for as long as I can.

"You are only making things more difficult for yourself," Ellen advises in a condescending tone. "Your father has been most generous with you, yet you thumb your nose at him and try to escape." She gestures to the boards on the window.

"If my father is so generous, then why am I a prisoner?" I ask.

"You are here for your own safety," Ellen snaps at me. She doesn't look at me, and hasn't since the first time I saw her, when she carefully studied me and apparently decided that the sight of me disgusted her. Why, I don't know. I feel the hatred emanating off her, and it is unpleasant at the very least. Her answers never change no matter how many times I ask her. Why am I a prisoner? Where is Pace? Where is Levi? When will I talk to my father?

Today she surprises me with something she's never said before. "You should just be grateful that your father has acknowledged you as his daughter. If not for that, you'd be in the flames like the rest of the trash that litters our streets."

"What?" I look at her, and in her blue eyes I plainly see her hatred along with something else that seems hauntingly familiar. As if she knows she's revealed too much, Ellen clamps her mouth shut, picks up my breakfast tray, and practically runs from the room.

"Wait!" I call out and the door slams behind her. I hear the turning of the key. I run after her, grab the knob and twist it, knowing that it will not give. I pound on the door, just as I did the first time I was locked inside. "Let! Me! Out!" I scream in frustration. I lean against the door and hear the staccato of her footsteps as she leaves me alone until morning.

What did she mean by saying I'd be in the flames? Does that mean Pace and Levi have been burned like Alex? My stomach heaves at the thought, and I run to the water closet attached to my room as I lose my last meal.

◆

Ellen's visit has left me more restless than usual, if that is possible. I have to do something to fill my time until I am so weary that I will fall asleep. I am used to being active, and the hours of having no place to go and nothing to do try my nerves until I feel like screaming and pulling out my hair.

I go to the window. The sun is high in the sky now. I can sense it. I now know for certain that we did take shelter on the opposite side of the wall from the royals and that only a thick pane of glass divided us.

Break the glass. Lyon said that was the solution to bringing people out of the dome. As I gaze at the iron girders that soar from the ground upward to the sky, I see that it is that simple. The royals would still be protected within, but the dome could be opened to the sky and the sun and the rest of the population could go outside and prosper. But only after the rovers are dealt with.

So much to do for so simple a task. Doing it right means the difference between life and death for several people. If only I can make my father see that we all need to work together to make things better. If only I can make him realize that the decisions he makes are not the best for everyone. But before I can do that, I have to make him *care* about the rest of the lives in his care. I have to make him see that we all have something to offer for the greater good and that if everyone survives and prospers, then the royals will too.

I cannot convince anyone of anything as long as I remain locked in this room. There are too many people that I care about for me to sit and do nothing. I have to know if James and Lyon made it out safely. I am concerned about my friends Lucy, David, Jilly, and Harry, all part of the seekers who, like me, believed there was a world outside. They were all trapped inside the dome after the explosion and asked for our help by tying a message to the tiny leg of Pip, Pace's canary.

I am also worried about Jonah, my cat, and Ghost, the blind pony that depends on me. Do they miss me as much as I miss them? Is someone on the outside caring for them, or have they been pushed aside and forgotten? Are my friends outside safe? Have there been any more rover attacks? Why are the streets we walked on when we came back inside the dome so deserted? They used to be home to the scarabs, the group of people who live on the edge of our society with no other purpose than to stay alive. The streets were strangely clear of them when we came back inside, and it has me worried about the lengths my father would go to.

Being stubborn has not gotten me the answers to these questions. I need to change tactics. It is obvious that my father is not going to come to me, so it is up to me to get to my father. I leave the window and go to the wardrobe.

The clothes inside were not made for me. The fabric is fine but old, with faded lace and adjusted seams. Luckily, I learned the effects of dressing nicely after wearing the yellow dress that Zan, Lyon's daughter and Levi's cousin, loaned me to wear to dinner one night. I do not want my father to see me as a shiner, beneath his notice as we lived beneath his streets. I want him to see me as his daughter and, more important, as an equal. Maybe then he will listen to what I have to say.

I search through the frilly ruffles and flowing sleeves contained in the wardrobe until I find something simpler and refined that reminds me of a dress that Jane wore the night we all dressed up for dinner. It is the same color as the evergreens from outside and has simple lines. The sleeves are long and the bodice is much more modest than Zan's yellow dress. I go to the large mirror that adorns the dressing table in my room and hold it in front of me to judge the fit. It should work, although I am not sure about the abundance of fabric gathered up in the back.

I go to the water closet and bathe. Ellen is consistent in her routine, so I know I have a few hours before she arrives with my next meal. I want to be ready when she arrives. I hope that surprise at my appearance will catch her off guard and possibly lead her to revealing some answers.

I take a hard look in the mirror before I dress. The scratches on my face and the bruises on my body have faded, but the memories of the people I killed have not, nor will they ever, even though it was either them or me. I have a scar on my forehead from my fall on the pavement and another on my upper arm where I was creased by a bullet. I cannot hide them, nor do I want too. They were hard earned.

The first time my father saw me, he called me by my mother's name. I have been told my entire life that I look like her. I have dark brown hair that is hard to tame, and my eyes behind the shine are brown also. I do not know if I look like her or not, as she died when I was born and I never saw her. I can only hope that the next time my father looks upon me he sees her once again.

Because right now that is the only weapon I have to use against him.

· 3 ·

I was right. My appearance catches Ellen off guard. I stand at the window when she comes in with my tray. I found some pins in a drawer and used them to put my hair up but a few curls escape my best efforts. I turn at the opening of the door, and Ellen stops in her tracks when she sees me. Her eyes narrow and her body tenses even more than usual. I see her as one of the explosives that my grandfather worked with. She is primed and just needs a single spark to make her explode.

She rushes to the table, drops the tray with a loud crash and rushes from the room, slamming the door and rattling the lock as she goes. I stand there for a moment, looking at the locked door. I am not sure what it was I expected. Maybe deep inside I hoped I'd be set free. I know that wouldn't happen just because I put on a dress and fixed my hair, but something has to change eventually. I'm just hoping to expedite it.

I can't help but laugh a bit at my thoughts. I want more than to get out of this room. I want to change everything. I sit down to eat since I did not have breakfast. I know what hunger is and know we

all would have starved if the Hatfields had not arrived in their airship when they did.

I take no more than two bites when there is a rap on my door.
This is the first time anyone has bothered to knock, and I look at it
in shocked silence for a moment.

"I am to escort you to Sir Meredith," Findley says.

"Am I in trouble?" I ask with mock innocence.

"There's only one way to find out," he replies. "Go ahead and
finish your meal."

I quickly finish my meal and try not to smile as I step into the
hall before Findley. This is what I wanted. I do not consider putting
on the dress giving my father what he wants. I consider it a way to
get what I want. Meeting with my father is the first step.

Findley opens the door to the staircase. We go up a flight of
stairs. I have to carry the tail of my dress to keep from tripping
over it. While the dress fits me well, neither pair of the shoes in
the wardrobe appealed to me, especially since they had heels that
seemed dangerous and unwieldy. So I still wear my boots and each
footstep echoes loudly in the stairwell. We go through a door, and
I recognize from my first visit here the hallway that leads to my
father's office. The only thing that's changed is the number of guards
accompanying me.

The beautiful paintings along the hallway capture my attention
just as they did the first time I was here. What would Dr. Stewart,
the scientist who travels with the Hatfields, have to say about them?
Would he recognize the different artists' names? Their beauty af-
fects me strongly this time, because I know what it is like outside
now. I've seen the grandeur of the world. It's a scary place out there,
but it is also beautiful beyond words when you take the time to look
at it. I am afraid I didn't take enough time to appreciate it when I had
the chance.

Findley raps on the door and opens it immediately upon hearing my father's response. He waves me through and I hear it close behind me.

My father sits at his beautifully carved wood desk with his head down and his eyes on a paper in his hand. An oil lamp casts a soft glow around him where before he had bright light provided by the coal power of the dome. Sacrifices have been made everywhere it seems.

I know it is his intention to intimidate me. Instead of waiting for him to notice me, I walk to one of the windows. I gratefully inhale the fresh scent of the potted plants that sit on either side of the floor-to-ceiling glass. I saw nothing like these plants when I was outside, but after hearing about the world and the different regions from Dr. Stewart, I realize they must come from some place other than England. How ingenious that the creators of our world sought to preserve them also. Someone besides my father has to be responsible for keeping them alive. I cannot imagine him giving tender care to any living thing.

The window I look out holds the same view as I see from mine, so there is nothing different to look at; still I am, as always, drawn to the light and the busy people who now fill the streets, going about their business as if nothing has changed.

I see my father's reflection in the window yet I ignore him, as he ignores me. I have to admit that he is a handsome man, with his black hair and dark-as-coal eyes. I know this is a test of wills, and I can wait him out now that I am here. He will feel smug because he thinks he has broken me. He will find that I am as stubborn as he is about what I feel to be right.

I catch my reflection in the window. The lighting is much different here than it is in my room, or maybe it is the fact that I have time to study my face now where before I was rushing about. I nearly do not recognize the girl who looks back at me. The angles of my jaw are leaner, as if I've lost the softness of my youth since the night Zan fixed my hair. My neck seems longer and the bones of my clavicle more pronounced. The rosy glow of my skin from the days spent in the sun has already faded in the two weeks since I've been removed from its presence, and the pale hue of my face makes my eyes darker and larger. I look older. I feel much older now, and possibly wiser. I hope I am wise enough to have the coming battle of wits with my father.

I look past my face to my father's reflection. He looks at me, then at the clock in the tall standing case beside the door. I hear its ponderous ticktock and wonder how much more time he will allow before he speaks to me. He bends his head back to the papers on his desk as if he has all the time in the world. I imagine to him he does. When will he admit that the time inside the dome is running out?

What made my mother love him? I cannot bear to think that she did not love him. How else did I come to be if not from love? I may not know my father well, I may not know him at all, but I cannot believe my mother did not love him or think that she loved him.

An insistent voice rises in my mind. Is he any better than a filcher? He may not actually be a part of capturing young women and boys and trading them to the rovers for weapons. But he certainly is an instrument of its occurrence. Yet he would deny his role in it because he is not the sort to get his hands dirty. He sits in his office and makes decisions and hobnobs with the royals he protects because he's on their level. My mother was not, thus he discarded her. For my father, it is all about the means to an end. But I would like to think that he had some feelings for my mother, and that he regretted setting her aside.

"She wore that dress," he says. I've been so caught up in my own thoughts that I did not realize that he was watching me once more.

He sits back in his chair and stares at my back until I turn around to look at him. A wry smile crosses his face. "I find it interesting that, of all the things in that wardrobe, you chose to put on that dress."

"I find it strange that you have a wardrobe full of women's clothes," I reply as I rub my hands down the soft velvet of the dress and hope that no one else has worn it since my mother. "It was the only thing in there to my liking," I add.

He laughs silently, no more than a jerk of his head and a smile. "You probably would have liked the women the other things belonged to even less," he says.

What a strange comment. Is he one to collect tokens of the women he's had? Does that mean there's been a parade of women through the years? And what happens to them once he is done with them? Do they go back to their lives as if nothing has happened, just as my mother tried to do? There was no denying me, yet she never spoke of who my father was to anyone. The fact that I look just like her is the only reason he has to acknowledge me, and that was quite by accident, as he was shocked when he saw me for the first time.

"Just like her, you grow more lovely each time I see you." He almost sounds wistful.

I want to believe him. For some strange reason I feel the need to have his approval. I do not understand why, since he is the epitome of everything I hate about the dome, but still I cannot help seeking his favor. So I smile at his comment and blush in what I hope is a pretty manner and then immediately feel ridiculous for preening under his attention.

"Please sit," my father says pleasantly, indicating the chair before his desk. "We have much to discuss." His tone makes it sound as if we are planning a party and it instantly puts me on the defensive.

I go to the chair and gather up the excess fabric before sitting down. I wonder at the waste. The skirt of the dress I wear would easily clothe two women, possibly three if care were taken. My father looks amused as I try to find a comfortable way to sit.

"Bustles, while attractive, are not very practical," he says.

"I was just thinking the same thing," I reply, assuming that he is talking about the back of my dress. I settle into the chair and put my arms on the sides. The last time I sat here I was covered in blood from the filcher I killed when he attempted to rape me. There is more blood on my hands now, more dead by my hand, but like my father's clean façade, it does not show.

My father steeples his fingers as he sits back in his chair. "Shall we start with why you were in the dome when I graciously allowed you your freedom?"

A lot has happened to me since I last saw my father. "If you are talking about when you had your men escort me to the door, I didn't leave then."

"Why ever not? Was not that your heart's desire?" I did not think him capable of sarcasm, yet it is evident in his voice.

"It still is my heart's desire," I reply. "But not just for me. For everyone else who is tired of living under your restrictions."

"You are not responsible for all the people who may or may not want to leave the dome." He shakes his head as if I am foolish.

"But that doesn't stop me from caring about them." Perhaps I am foolish. I'd rather be foolish than heartless.

"Yours is the route to heartbreak, my dear girl," he says in a sorry attempt of fatherly advice.

"Why do you care?"

"I could ask you the same thing." He sighs with impatience, sits back in his chair, and contemplates the papers on his desk as if he is determining which task is more important at the moment, me or the never-ending monotony of his job. He pushes the stack aside and picks up a pen. He turns it in his hand, touching the point and then the top and then the point again to the surface of his desk. He repeats it several times as if the movement hypnotizes him, and he speaks as he watches it. "Why don't you bring me up to date on what you've been up to since I last saw you?"

I don't want to play these games with my father. I want to know what has happened to my friends. I think he gets some sort of perverse enjoyment out of our battle of wits. Still, I have nothing to lose and everything to gain, so I tell him my story.

"Your men had me in the glass tunnel when we heard the explosion."

"Your friends blew up the fans," my father interjects.

I ignore his comment. There is no need to give my father any evidence against my friends. James, Adam, and Alcide blew up the fans. He does not know them nor ever will, if I have my way. "Your men left us. Jon went outside. I stayed in."

"Jon?"

"The boy who was with me. The one the filchers mistook for Pace."

"Ah yes. I remember."

"I made my way back to my friends and went below. I was in our village when your men attacked us with the flamethrowers that caused an explosion in the tunnels."

"My men attacked you." He did not phrase it as a question, more as a statement of disbelief. Surely he knew what happened in the tunnels since he was the one who sent the bluecoats after us. I must be holding his interest now, as he puts the pen aside.

"Your men killed us!" My anger explodes out of me, just like the methane in the tunnels. "They came into the tunnels with flamethrowers! How could you not know the dangers such a weapon would cause?" I stop, desperate to get my emotions under control so my father cannot use them against me. "Your men are the ones who caused the destruction to the dome," I continue. "The holes, the cave-in."

Shock flares in his eyes but he quickly hides it. "Continue," he bids me.

I gather myself once again as tears threaten my eyes. "Our village was destroyed by the flood. When the gas exploded some of the tunnels collapsed and the river changed its course, taking everything in its path with it, including part of your streets." I cannot help the trembling in my voice. "My best friend, Peggy, was killed."

He arches an eyebrow, his way of expressing sympathy I suppose.

I swipe at my eyes. "After that we just followed the river until it led us out."

"Out?"

"Outside, by the sea." How can he not know what is out there? "The dome is built on a cliff that overlooks the Atlantic Ocean."

"How do you know about the ocean?" Confusion, followed by curiosity, flashes across his face. "How do you know what it is called?"

"Levi told me," I say. "But Pace knows the names of things also. He told me many things about the outside world before we escaped."

"Who is Levi?"

I look at him in confusion. "He was with me when we surrendered."

"So that's his name," he says with a sense of satisfaction.

I am still confused. "Where is Levi?"

"He's in a cell, being just as stubborn as you have been. No one seems to know who he is."

"That's because he's from America." I watch my father carefully. "No one on the inside would have reason to know him."

He hides his surprise well. His face doesn't change a bit, but I watch him carefully and see the flare of surprise in his dark-as-coal eyes.

"That's a rather outlandish claim, Wren," my father says evenly. "Do you have anything to substantiate it?"

"Go outside and look at the catwalk. There's an airship docked there." I know he would have no way of knowing what an airship is, but the name describes it well. I hope the sound of it intimidates him. This time his surprise is tangible and I press my advantage. "Levi has a family, and they have the ability to remove him by force if necessary."

"It's been two weeks and he's still here." He leans back in his chair and crosses his arms. "I think you've overestimated your friends."

"I know you've underestimated us all, actually. Levi's family will do what they must to ensure his safety." I retort. "I suggest you treat Levi kindly."

"He's been treated much the same as you, although his accommodations are not as luxurious."

I can only assume Levi is being held in the cells below, much like Jon was when we were my father's guests before. "What about Pace?" I ask.

"Pace has been reunited with his mother and is quite content." He says dismissively and then he leans forward. "Tell me more about this airship and the rumors of America."

His remark about Pace bothers me, yet I cannot let his statement about America go unchallenged. "America is not a rumor," I say. "It is a real place. You know it has to be, as it existed before the comet. It is in the history books. The ones my people were not allowed to read." I cant my head to the side as if that will allow me to see him better. "You know there have to be other places in the world that survived," I say. "We are not the only society left on earth."

"Thus the need to remain inside," my father states. "Where it is safe."

"You plan to live the rest of your life in fear?" I challenge him. "In hiding?"

"I do not consider it to be hiding. I consider it to be prudent behavior." He steeples his fingers—a habit of his, I realize—and studies me. "Be honest with me, Wren," he begins. "Life is not easy out there."

"No," I confess. "It isn't. We were ill prepared for it. If not for Levi's family, we would have had a very hard time of it." I look my father in the eye. "Even without their help, I would still do it. It is worth the risk. Anything worth having is worth the risk."

"And what do you have out there? Food? Shelter? Safety?"

"We have the right to choose for ourselves." I say with a sense of satisfaction.

"All you have chosen is a certain death at the hands of the rovers."

"They can be beaten," I say. "We have survived two attacks. They suffered more losses than we did. We can survive more."

His dark eyes move over me in assessment. What does he see when he looks at me? I still bear the remnants of the battles I fought on my face, although they have faded since I came inside. I do not flinch from his gaze, but inside my heart is pounding as I wait for his next words as if my very life depends upon them. In a way, it does. He has the power to do anything he wants, and unfortunately I am at his mercy, as is Levi. Pace, I am not so sure about. What did my father mean when he said he was content?

"It seems I have underestimated your capabilities," he finally says, and sits back in his chair. "Findley!" He raises his voice. The door opens, and I realize my guard has remained stationed right outside during our visit. Or maybe I should say interrogation. "Escort Miss

MacAvoy back to her quarters," my father instructs, and he goes back to his paperwork, dismissing me as if I am already gone from his presence.

"Wait!" I say as Findley takes my arm. "What about Levi? I want to see him. I want to see Pace."

He stops at his task and looks at me once again. "I find it interesting that you said Levi's name ahead of Pace's. And here I thought Pace was the love of your life."

I am momentarily stunned by his observation. I never told my father about my relationship with Pace. Which means it had to come from Pace, unless there is someone else I don't know about who he holds prisoner. Could it be Lucy and David? But why would they even have a need to discuss my feelings for Pace?

My father nods his head at Findley, who pulls me from the chair. I jerk my arm from his grasp and slam my hands down on my father's desk. His eyes dart upward to glance at me with impatience for a brief moment before they turn back to his papers.

"You can ignore me all you want," I say. "But that will not make me disappear, any more than it will make the world out there go away. You will have to deal with it and me, eventually, whether you want to or not."

Findley takes my arm, more firmly this time, and pulls me away from my father. I pull against him, indignant at his and my father's disregard for me, until we reach the hallway and he shuts the door behind us. He releases me, and I am tempted to kick him and make a run for it, but I know I will not get far and I will not leave Pace or Levi behind until I am certain of their safety.

"How much longer will you pretend that there is not a world out there?" I ask Findley. "The dome is dying and everyone knows it, inside and out." He doesn't answer me, just pushes me toward the staircase.

Ellen comes through the door as we approach it, and she stares at me with the same disdain as always. As I am escorted to the staircase I hear her rap on the door and my father's command to enter. I manage to glance her way before the door closes behind me and see her do something I have not seen before. She smiles as she walks into his presence.

· 4 ·

My father called me Miss MacAvoy when he dismissed me from his office. I am certain he said it to remind me of my place, which he considers to be deep beneath the ground. Possibly in a grave, if he has his way about it. Not that I think he would kill me, personally, but neither would he go out of his way to save my life, if the occasion should arise. I am nothing more to him than a constant reminder of his moment of weakness with my mother.

So much for my hope to make him see reason. That lasted about as long as our meeting. I change back into my shiner clothes and go to the window once more.

My solitude is my enemy. It leaves me with nothing to do but dwell on my many mistakes. *"What about Levi? I want to see him. I want to see Pace."* Just because I said Levi's name first does not mean I value him more than Pace, does it?

I can't forget about Pace that easily. We shared so much since we met. Without him, I never would have had the strength to do what I did. He is so kind and gentle and sweet, while Levi is . . . dangerous. I still need time to figure things out. Unfortunately, the time that I have is not helping me with that dilemma; it has just given me another one.

The knock on my door comes as a surprise to me since I just got back and it is a long while until dinner. Findley comes in and announces, "You are to come with me."

"Where are we going?" I ask. He doesn't answer as he stands in the doorway waiting on me. I study him for a moment, hoping to see some indication of what awaits me. He has that look that is hard to define. His face is easily lost in a crowd, yet his eyes see everything. They have a slight crinkling around them that makes me think he spends most of his time watching, but for what I do not have a clue, neither is he likely to tell me. My father apparently trusts him completely. I cannot help but wonder what he has done to earn that trust.

Findley motions me toward the door that holds the staircase. "Are you getting tired of using the stairs instead of the lift?" I ask.

"No," he replies, and the fact that he has even bothered to answer me catches me off guard. "It keeps me fit," he continues. He sweeps his arm at the down staircase. I'd assumed we were going up to see my father again so I am momentarily taken aback. Perhaps I am going to my execution. Or the opposite, I'm to be thrown outside again so I won't be a nuisance to my father.

I go down the stairs. Findley stays on my heels and keeps me within reach. I do not fool myself into thinking I can outrun him on the stairs. He would grab me before I took three steps. If he takes me outside, I might have a chance of escaping into the alleyways, but then I recall that the streets were eerily empty of the scarabs.

I stumble as we round the landing and start down another set of steps. Before we came inside, two of my friends went to the entrance of the dome on a scouting mission. Jon and Peter reported that there were burned bodies staked outside. Men, women, and children. And Ellen had said something to me this morning about being lucky that I wasn't burned with the rest of the trash.

The bodies Jon and Peter saw were the scarabs. That was why the streets were empty when we snuck into the dome. They were rounded up and killed to conserve the resources of the dome. I grab on to the railing as my traitorous stomach flips inside me. I shut my eyes tightly against the truth that fills me. The only one who wields enough power to do something so dastardly is my father. He would not hesitate to do the same to my friends, or to any shiners who are still alive.

Findley gently touches my shoulder. It surprises me more than the horrible realization of my father's deeds. "Are you ill?" he asks in a somewhat gentle voice.

"How many?" I ask.

"How many what?" Findley tilts his head curiously as I stare up at him. I see something in his eyes. Kindness? Or is it merely curiosity. Perhaps I am a novelty to him also, a welcome distraction from the everyday.

"How many people did my father order killed? How many scarabs were murdered?"

His eyes widen. For a brief moment I think he's going to answer me, that I've touched something inside him with my question. Instead his mouth hardens into a thin line and he takes a firm hold of my arm and starts me once again on our journey down the staircase.

There are windows on every landing. Light filters through them, but as we go down, the light dims until I begin to think I might be able to break away from Findley because of my ability to see in the dark. Then we round another landing and I catch the flare from a lantern. The air feels cooler, damper, and I realize we've gone below ground level. The stairs end at a heavy door. It has an opening in the top half and three iron bars fill it.

I shiver. Not from the damp cold that feels so very familiar. It is dread that fills me as Findley knocks on the door. I hear the heavy clanking of metal and a wizened face appears behind the bars.

"She's to see the prisoner," Findley says.

I practically sigh in relief. For a moment I thought I was trading my luxurious quarters above for a cell. The door opens with a clank and a heavy creak, and Findley puts his hand on the small of my back and urges me through. The man on the other side is much older than Findley. He reminds me of a barrel, short and stout, with thick arms that round out from his shoulders instead of hanging straight and legs that are bowed as if he's sitting on a barrel. He is bald on top with a ring of gray hair spiking out around his head like a collar. His nose looks as if it's been smashed innumerable times, and he opens his mouth in a grimace to reveal broken teeth.

"This away," he says and motions me forward, past a desk and a set of chairs. A thick book sits on the desk, along with a half-eaten meal. Across from the desk is a small water closet. Water drips loudly from a pipe. I look back at Findley, who turns to go down another corridor without a backward glance at me.

The light is dim, but that doesn't bother me as much as the smell of desperation that permeates the long hall of thick doors and barred windows, ten in all, five on each side. I know behind each door is a prisoner and can only wonder which prisoner I am to see. Levi or Pace? Even though my father said Pace was reunited with his mother and quite happy, it doesn't mean he's not in a cell. The last we heard, his mother was a prisoner of my father. For all I know, they could be sharing a cell.

We finally stop before the last door on the right and my escort rattles a ring of keys as he searches for the one he needs. He opens the door, shoves me through it, and slams it behind me with a finality that rattles my bones. I wrap my arms around my body as I look around. The cell is drab and dim. The only light comes from the barred window in the door. A narrow cot is bolted to one wall and there is a small toilet in the corner. The cell is no more than eight feet square, if that.

Levi. I have no trouble seeing the golden hue of his hair as he sits on the cot with his back against the wall and his head down on his knees. He raises his head to look at me, and a smile spreads across his face like a beacon in the darkness.

"Wren!" He comes to me and throws his arms around me. I am so relieved to see him that I crumble in relief against him, even though he reeks from his imprisonment. I don't care. He's alive and whole, although battered.

Levi turns me to the window in the door. He pushes my hair away from my face and his brown eyes are full of concern. "You are well? They haven't hurt you?"

I shake my head. It is obvious he has not fared as well as I have. His face is covered with an assortment of bruises, and his lip is scabbed from a split. I tentatively touch the bruise around his eye and he flinches.

"Funny, we call this a shiner where I come from," he says as he covers my hand with his.

"We call it a wall-eye."

The side of his mouth lifts in a half smile. "I ran into a fist, not a wall."

"They beat you?"

Levi shrugged. "I've had worse, believe me."

I know he has. He has the scars to prove it. The story he told me about his rite of passage with his grandmother's tribe made me wonder how anyone could stand it, especially someone as young as Levi. Yet he did and his courage and patience are only part of why I am drawn to him.

Levi turns my hand in his and kisses my palm. My eyes fill with tears as I look into his warm brown eyes, so full of life and determination, yet shadowed with pain. His skin is pale. The days spent in the darkness have taken his bronze glow.

"What do they want from you?" I ask.

He gives me another lopsided smile. "Answers."

"To what?"

"Everything." Levi leads me to the cot and we sit down. "What about Pace? Have you seen him? Is he safe?"

I shake my head. "I haven't seen anyone until you. Except for my father."

"Yes. Your father," he gently chides me. "You really should have mentioned that before we came inside."

"I didn't think it was important." I turn my head away with shame. "Perhaps if Lyon . . ."

Levi hastily puts his finger to my lips to stop me and turns my chin back to face him. He points to the corner of the ceiling next to the door and I see a copper pipe that opens with a flare into the cell. Someone is listening, and I have a feeling it is Findley if not my father himself.

"It doesn't matter," I say so quietly that only Levi can hear me. "My father knows everything. I told him about the *Quest* and how you came from America," I confess. "I saw no reason not to. All he has to do is walk outside to see for himself."

"And what did he say?"

"He sent me away. He doesn't want to hear it. He doesn't want to think that life could be better outside. He doesn't want to acknowledge that life is possible outside."

"He's probably given instructions to ignore any attempts my uncle makes at contact."

"Do you think they——" Levi moves his finger to my lips once more to stop me before I say something that could endanger my friends. Even though I told my father about the Hatfields and America, I did not mention the fact that Lyon and James entered the dome with us, and I certainly have not mentioned Lucy, David, Harry, and Jilly, who would be easy to find inside the dome. We have no way of knowing if Lyon and James are still inside or if they made it out. The last we knew of our friends inside was that they desperately needed help, which is why we came inside. The note they sent attached to Pip's tiny leg was the only news we had had of them since the disaster that led to our finding a way out. Pip. I haven't even considered where Pip could be. The tiny canary that became Pace's friend in the dark hours he spent in the tunnels could be anywhere. All I know is I have not seen him in my many hours of staring out the window.

The last thing I would ever want to do is be responsible for any of my friends' being hurt. I have enough lives on my conscience without being responsible for any more. I crumble against Levi as I realize what I almost did.

He wraps his arms around me and runs his hand over my hair as he whispers in my ear. "It's okay," he says. "It's all part of their plan, and you didn't fall for it. That's why they brought you to see me. To see what more they could learn."

"How are we going to get out of here?" I say quietly against his chest.

"I don't know. But just knowing you are safe is enough for me at the moment." Levi kisses the top of my head. Such a comforting kiss. Such a contrast to the wild and passionate one we shared after the battle. "Do you remember the rainbow?"

I look at him in confusion.

"The morning I shot the stag. It was over the water."

"The beautiful colors," I say. "So that's what that is."

"How sad, that you never knew what a rainbow is until now," Levi says.

"I will never forget it." How could I forget it? It was the morning after the *Quest* arrived and Levi came upon me in the forest. I was crying with relief because I realized that I had not killed a rover who was trying to steal one of our goats. Since that day, I've killed many times to stay alive. That morning Levi made me realize that when you kill and do not feel remorse, your soul is in jeopardy. That, sometimes, killing is necessary to survive, especially in the world outside the dome. The facts of that statement were made very real to me, when we came upon a beautiful scene of a family of deer in the forest next to a stream. Mist filled the air, and as the sun came through the canopy of trees a rainbow formed. I had never seen one before, but now I realize what it is from reading the story of Noah in the Bible. It was God's promise that he would never again destroy the world by water. A beautiful thing that I should have been in awe of, but the beauty of it was overshadowed by the death of a stag at Levi's hand. A necessity, to feed the lot of us. I had not thought of the rainbow again until now.

"A rainbow is like a promise," Levi says against my hair. "There's supposed to be a treasure at the end of it. I knew that day that you were the treasure."

Such sweet words made all the more sweet because of the circumstances. Yet I still cannot tell him that I choose him over Pace because I do not know which of them I truly love. All I can do is press against him and offer him some reassurance that we will come through this. That we will survive. I know in my heart this moment will not last long. Seeing Levi and knowing he is alive might help get me through another day. But it doesn't solve any of our problems.

Still, I relish the feel of him, the warmth of his body, the beat of his heart, and the way his hand drags over and over through my hair until we hear the rattle of the key in the lock and the heavy creak of the cell door.

"Let's go," Findley says.

I don't want to go. I want to stay with Levi. But my protest at leaving would only make things worse for him, so I reluctantly let go. Levi stands up, straight and tall, facing Findley, who smirks. Levi grins at him. Findley gently takes my arm and herds me through the door where the guard is waiting to slam it behind me. I wince at the sound and at the thought that Levi is once more all alone in the dark and cold cell.

"Your friend is a tough young man," Findley says as we start up the staircase. "Too bad it will probably get him killed."

I stop and turn to look at Findley. I am amazed that he is being so open with me. His words also strike terror in my heart. "What do you mean by that?"

Findley shrugs. "He doesn't serve a purpose, and you know how your father feels about those who do not serve the good of the dome."

I put my hand to my stomach, sick at the implication of his words. Does Findley enjoy torturing me like this? Is it part of my father's plan to see how scared for my friends I will become? I would do anything to keep them safe. I've lost too many to be casual with their lives. Each one is precious to me. Which makes them a weakness that my father will surely use against me.

"You can't be serious," I say. "You can't mean that. You don't know about him. You don't know the things he knows, how he can help us."

There are voices on the stairs above us. "Quiet," Findley barks. He puts his hand on my arm and guides me to the wall side of the staircase. I hear the murmur of voices as they come closer and then a high titter that could only be from a woman. They are on the landing above us, and Findley makes me stop on the landing below as they turn to come toward us.

It's Ellen. Her smile quickly disappears. She stops for a moment and stares at me in disgust before gathering her skirts a bit closer and taking the next step. Behind her is Jilly, and I open my mouth, only to clamp it firmly shut. Her green eyes flare in recognition but something in them warns me. They dart to whoever is behind her, just now coming around the bend of the landing. I will not betray her, so I keep my face passive and free from emotion, but that all crumbles in the next moment as I hear a voice, gentle and true, seconds before he turns the corner.

Pace.

· 5 ·

*P*ace.

Findley's hand clamps down on my shoulder, keeping me in place, keeping me from running up the stairs and throwing myself into Pace's arms. His beautiful blue eyes widen when he sees me, and he pauses at the top of the staircase. Jilly lays her hand on his arm, intimately, holding Pace just as surely as Findley holds me.

Ellen walks by with her head turned away and her skirts gathered to her as if I just climbed up from the sewers. She does not pause, nor does she give any indication that she knows me or even sees me, which is fine as far as I am concerned. What I do not understand is how she knows Pace and Jilly and why the three of them sounded so chummy as they came downstairs.

Why is Jilly here, and why are they together? Jilly wears a very pretty green dress with a matching jacket that makes her red hair seem brighter and eyes even more striking, yet I plainly see the stress behind them. She seems tired, but she smiles politely at me as she walks by with one hand on the stair rail and the other holding her skirts.

Pace.

I search his eyes, looking for answers to the barrage of questions that fill my mind. To my surprise, Findley's hand on my shoulder relaxes. Ellen is well past us, and Jilly rounds the landing and continues down.

Pace. Am I breathing? Does my heart still beat? I could not swear to either as time for me has stopped, yet Pace moves onward. Slowly. Steadily, with his eyes on mine, yet he does not smile as he usually does when he sees me. Findley takes his hand from my shoulder and steps away to the lower staircase. To go down? Or to stop anyone that chooses at this moment to come up?

Pace looks well. Healthy. No bruises or cuts mar his face, not even the remnants of the battle he fought before we came inside. He has not been beaten or tortured for answers like Levi. He does not seem to be imprisoned like me. If anything, he is more handsome than I have ever seen him, with his dark brown hair neatly trimmed and his muscular body once more in the uniform of a cadet. No, I think as I see the gold bands on his sleeve, a *full* enforcer. He even wears a medal pinned over his heart.

How can this be? He was a wanted criminal when we left the dome. Even though he was not guilty of the crime, there was still a price on his head, a reward bigger than anything ever offered before. So how could he be back in uniform and promoted when he was only a cadet a month ago?

A bitter taste fills my mouth and my stomach lurches as realization fills me. Pace has betrayed us. It is the only logical answer that comes to mind, yet I do not want to believe it. But what else could it be?

His eyes dart to Findley, then to me once more as he comes down the steps. I hear the beat of my heart and the sharp intake of my breath as he leans close and whispers into my ear.

"*Things are not always what they seem.*"

Thank God. It is as if he has read my mind and, as he always does, he offers me comfort. But these are also the same words he said the day we met, when he chased me after Alex died. Before I can blink Pace moves on, catching up to Jilly and placing his hand in the small of her back as if he's afraid she will fall. Jilly steals a look my way and gives me a quick shake of her head and mouths "*No.*"

What is going on?

I grab on to the rail and look over at them. I want to follow. I need to talk to Pace. Jilly too. I open my mouth to call after them, and Findley once more takes my arm, gently this time. He shakes his head also and inclines it to the top of the stairs.

I have questions. Hundreds of them. And my answers are walking down and away from me. Laughing and chatting as if nothing has happened while my entire world caves inward upon me. My feet drag as Findley urges me up the stairs.

I must find out what it all means. I falter on the stairs, trip, and pitch forward. It is a ploy to catch Findley off guard and it works. He bends to help me up and I kick backward at his knee. I have the satisfaction of hearing him grunt in pain as I connect, and I turn to dash down the steps.

Findley is behind me and Pace is in front of me. I can still hear their voices, their casual and quiet laughter. Before I catch the handrail to make the turn, Findley grabs the collar of my jacket and pulls me back against him. I strike out at him, kicking and flailing, and he wraps his arms around me, places a hand over my mouth, and traps me soundly against his chest. He is immovable, his arms like iron bands and his body as solid as a tree trunk. I cannot escape him, and I finally stop fighting him and relax within his hold.

"Ellen is his mother," he says in my ear. "It won't help to catch him because she will give you away." He takes his hand from my mouth.

"What? Who? What are you talking about?"

"The woman. Ellen. She is Pace's mother." He turns me around to face him. He keeps his hands on my upper arms and bends so he is looking me in the eye. "She hates you. You will get no help there."

"You are lying," I say.

Findley smiles at me. It is not condescending or malicious, and I realize that he, like me, has his own agenda. As to whether our agendas mesh is something I am not yet certain of. "Am I?" he asks.

I look down the quiet staircase as if I can see the trio that is now gone. An image of Ellen comes to me, of her blue eyes and her mouth, always set in a frown when she sees me. The only time I have seen her smile is when she walked into my father's office the day I was taken to see him. She is Pace's mother. I know it now, as surely as I breathe. Findley is telling the truth.

Suddenly her contempt for me makes complete sense. Because of me, Pace got into trouble. Because of me, she was taken prisoner. But if she is a prisoner, why is she free to come and go as she pleases? And it is obvious that Pace is not a prisoner either. It seems, by his uniform, that Pace is in good standing with my father. Does Jilly have anything to do with this?

Findley just shakes his head. I will get nothing more from him today. "Back to your room," he says and urges me back up the staircase.

"You could let me go," I suggest as I start up once more.

"I could," he agrees. "But you have no place to go."

These words frighten me more than anything that I have seen or heard so far today. I take the next set of stairs in silence, my mind spinning as I try to figure out everything that's happened this busy day.

My world is suddenly not what I thought, and it frightens me to the core. My feet drag on the steps as we continue upward until we enter the hall that holds my room. I don't want to go inside. I don't want to be locked away from the world again. I turn to Findley, who narrows his eyes at me.

"If I stay locked up in here much longer I'll go insane," I say.

Findley herds me through the door and blocks it with his frame as he fold his arms and looks at me. "I could move you to a cell down below," he says, and I actually see his mouth quirk into a smile. I know he's teasing me, so I test him further.

"Why don't you just forget to lock the door?" I suggest.

"Isn't running about without a plan what got you into this trouble in the first place?" he asks. "Don't forget to eat," he adds, pointing to my tray of food that sits on the table. Findley closes the door behind him as he steps out without another word, and I hear the key rattle in the lock behind him. I go to check the door.

It is locked, as I knew it would be. Silly me, always holding out for that elusive moment of hope. I know it is foolish of me, but I just can't give up. Not now. Not when we've come so far.

The irony that my estimation of *far* is a full circle does not escape me. I am back where I started, once more a prisoner in the dome and at the whim of those who make the decisions for everyone.

I look out the narrow opening in the window and try not to think about Pace. I wish I could see the hole in the dome from here. I wish I could see the sky. Even without the thick haze that covers everything I would not be able to see it. It is to the left of my location and slightly behind, I think. Closer to the library and the buildings with the orchards on top.

Do the trees feel the difference now? Do they stretch their branches to the sun in gratitude, and do their leaves flutter in the wind? I can't help but think about Max, the dome washer who was always so kind to me, even though I was a trespasser. What would Max say about the hole in the glass? I imagine he would be a lot like me and want to go out.

There are so many people inside the dome that don't have a voice. The decisions that affect their lives are made for them. It's time they all have a vote. A choice in where they will live and what they want to do. It is time they get to decide for themselves. If every faction in the dome were to rise up, just as the shiners did, then perhaps my father would realize that his way of life is done.

What if the price is too high? We shiners were nearly wiped out. And the scarabs too, as far as I can tell. My father would think nothing of taking more lives. He would bring the fire inside, if that would preserve his way of life.

What about the royals? Do they all believe as he does? Jilly didn't. Surely there are others like her, other seekers. If only there were some way to find out. Some way to bring all the dissidents in the dome together.

Like Jilly and Pace were together.

Things are not always what they seem . . .

Findley was right. My dashing about without a plan was what got all of us into trouble in the first place. For once I need to think things through and consider all the options and the consequences of my decisions.

I turn from the window and sit down at the table to eat my meal. I pick up the ham and cheese sandwich without much appetite. To my surprise, there is a piece of paper between the ham and the cheese. I pull it from my mouth and find a note.

They got out

Who got out? Lyon and James? David and Lucy? Harry? All of them? Some of them? At least I know who didn't get out, not that that helps.

Who sent the note? Surely not Ellen, yet she is the only one I know of who comes in and out of my room.

It has to be from Jilly or Pace. It is the only logical conclusion since they were with Ellen. One of them could have slipped it into my meal while the other distracted her.

Whoever it was that sent it wanted to allay some of my fears, and for that I am extremely grateful. Still, I wish I knew exactly who it was. It would make my next steps so much easier.

Once I figure out what they are.

· 6 ·

The thought that I am worse off now than I ever was before crosses my mind several times. I alternate between agonizing over what happened in the stairwell with Pace and Jilly and chastising myself because I did not realize Ellen was Pace's mother. Combine that with the uncertainty I have over the note and my worry over Levi all alone in his cell, and I chase myself full circle throughout the long and slow hours of the afternoon and evening. For the first time since my imprisonment Ellen does not arrive to collect my tray after my evening meal, and my mind starts on the many possibilities of why this occurred, the foremost being that it has something to do with the note on my tray.

Does this mean Pace and Jilly are in trouble? Their casual ways in the stairwell make me think no. Still, my mind and my heart are troubled and sleep eludes me. I finally fall asleep and wake up the next morning to find Ellen staring down at me.

"Get dressed, your father is taking you out."

"Out where?"

"You'll find out when you get there."

I am tired of her hostility, especially now that I know who she is. I see no sense in it. She should be grateful to me. I saved Pace's life. If not for me he would have been killed with his friend Tom. I fling back the blankets and stalk from my bed, not caring that she will see me in the well-worn muslin gown that I sleep in. Something else left behind by one of my father's women. The fabric is so old that it is nearly transparent, but it is serviceable and so I make use of it.

"Where is Pace?" I ask.

Her blue eyes flare and then narrow as she stares at me. Her look is so full of hatred that I am tempted to cross my arms over my breasts as if that will offer some protection. Luckily she turns away and I put on a robe that is not much better than the gown. Still, I feel somewhat less exposed as I tie it around my waist.

"I should have known Findley would not keep his mouth shut," Ellen says. "He enjoys the game too much." She turns to look at me once more. "Where Pace is is no longer your business, Miss. He's gotten his life back, no thanks to you and yours." She crosses her arms and smiles but there is no heart and soul in it, just deadly intent. "He's to be married. To Miss Jillian Pembrooke."

I know she wants to see me suffer as she must have suffered when Pace was missing. She wants to see me crumble, to see me humbled and destroyed. How could someone so wonderful, so sweet, so caring, and so full of humor come from someone like this, who is full of hatred?

Things are not always what they seem . . . Indeed they are not. But which of us has been fooled, me or Ellen? Her words scorch my heart in the same manner that the sun burned my eyes and skin, but I cannot show it. I *must* not show it.

Even though I feel as if my heart is shattered in two, I speak from it, with honesty. "I only want Pace to be happy," I say.

"You have a funny way of showing it." Ellen rounds on me. "Putting him in danger. Making him a suspect in your radical plans. Taking him away from his mother and making me a suspect too!"

I cannot do this now. I need time to think, time to absorb what she's told me about Pace and Jilly. I refuse to believe it, yet my mind fills with doubt. After all the time I've had alone, I suddenly want to be alone again, more than anything, so I can figure things out. Yet I cannot let Ellen's words go unchallenged.

"Don't you know I saved his life?" I say. Surely Pace told her what happened and why he went below. It was the only place he could hide. "If not for me, he would have died that morning with Tom." Would he? Or was it all just a lie he told me to gain my trust?

"You didn't save his life," Ellen sputters. "Miss Pembrooke did." Before I can figure out what that statement means she goes on. "You are the one who put him in that situation in the first place. All of it is your fault. If it were up to me you'd be burned on the dais for all to see. You should be executed immediately for what you've done. You are a traitor to your people."

"I would look closer to home for a traitor to your people." Our voices have risen during our argument. "The people of the dome have been lied to for years. What more do you need to see before you realize that our only hope for survival is outside? The proof is right before you, all you need to do is look up. Or are you just like the royals you serve, blinded to the truth?"

Never in my life would I have dared to speak to anyone this way, especially someone who is older than me and of a caste that I have always been told is better than mine. Perhaps I did not realize how much I had changed until now. Or maybe it took Ellen's outright hatred and lies to awaken the angry beast that dwells in all of us.

When James told lies about me and accused me of things I did not do, I kept my mouth shut. I can see the wisdom of that in hindsight. I should have done the same this day, but it is too late to take back the words now. I will not be ashamed of them, as I am certain I could not make Ellen hate me any more than she already does.

Ellen's face turns red with rage and she comes close with her index finger outstretched, ready to use it as a weapon as she waves it under my nose. "You are beneath contempt," she begins and is interrupted by a sharp rap on the door as Findley comes in, without waiting for an answer.

"The Master General Enforcer is waiting," he says. He arches an eyebrow at me, in that way that has become familiar, and a slight mocking grin flashes over his features as he looks at me.

I quickly realize my state of dress does little to hide my body. Ellen clamps her mouth shut, and I dash to the water closet and slam the door behind me. I turn on the water and splash it on my face, letting the coolness of it take away the burn of my anger and embarrassment. How can Ellen hate me so much? Surely Pace told her how he felt about me.

Or did he? After he saw me kiss Levi, Pace may consider our relationship to be over, which could explain his hasty engagement to Jilly. But there has to be more to it than this. I refuse to believe that he was lying to me all along. I know he spoke from the heart. There are so many things left unsaid between us after he saw Levi kissing me. I have been so confused about so many things and so much has happened, yet the past few weeks, when all I've had time to do is think about how I feel about Pace and Levi, haven't brought me any closer to solving that problem. Perhaps fate is seeking to solve it for me.

So why don't I feel at peace? Why do I know, even without Pace telling me, that things are not always what they seem?

My father has skewed Ellen's thoughts to suit his needs. That is the only explanation for her hatred. As a mother, she is desperate to save her son, and she will do anything she can to keep him safe, thus her treatment of me. I will treat her with patience and kindness from here on out, so she will see that with me, things are not always what they seem.

I realize that the weeks of my imprisonment have served a purpose. It has helped me to learn something about my adversary. My father likes to manipulate people. He likens himself to a god, and the dome is his world. Why else would he refer to himself as the Master General Enforcer? How many titles does one man need to suit his ego? How many more people have to die to serve his purpose?

Beyond the door, I hear Ellen and Findley. Her voice is still shrill and angry and Findley's nothing more than a low rumble. A door slams, and I realize Ellen is gone and Findley still waits for me. As my father does.

I take a long hard look in the mirror. What game does my father plan to play with me today? There is only one way to find out. I quickly dress in my usual clothes and open the door to find Findley standing at my window and staring out through the opening.

"I had a talk with your friend last night," he says, keeping his focus on the window. "He told me about America."

"And you believed him?"

"I see no reason not to. He had to come from somewhere, and the history books talk of the country across the sea. Did you know that it was one of our colonies until the late 1700s?" He glances at me over his shoulder.

"No," I say. "I only learned of how it is now. About how the entire world is now, after it recovered from the comet."

"Knowledge is power," Findley says, turning back to the window. "And that was the last thing they wanted you to have. Yet you managed quite well without it."

"I learned as I went," I say with a shrug, and Findley chuckles.

His use of the word *they* interests me. I don't trust him and I find it interesting that Levi talked with him, although he had nothing to lose now, since I told my father who he is and where he is from.

"I hope Levi is none the worse for your conversation," I add, recalling the cuts and bruises that marred his face.

"It was all quite cordial, I assure you," Findley says. "And you can thank Mr. Pruitt for any damages he might have gotten while in his care."

"Mr. Pruitt?"

"The jailer," Findley says, turning once more to look at me. "You met him yesterday? It seems that your friend, Mr. Addison, is quite clumsy. Always tripping in his cell and running into walls."

I know better, and I also know that this is not a point to argue with now. Nothing I say will make a difference to the man Pruitt. All I can hope for is a swift and safe escape from the man's tender care for Levi.

"What do you think of the things Levi told you?" I ask. "About America."

"He told me about the Indians. About a saying they have. One that applies to both you and the boy's mother." He looks at the door to the hallway and I turn that way also. Is Ellen listening outside the door? I do not believe Findley would be this open if he thought that were true. Besides, the walls and the doors are thick and strong. I have never heard anything from the hallway, until someone pounds on my door. I turn back to Findley and he continues. "It is something like this . . . 'Do not judge a man until you've walked a mile in his shoes.'"

"I can see where that would be wise." I wonder if Levi told him about his scars and the sun dance ceremony. I am doubtful that he shared that experience with Findley. I know Levi well enough to know that there is a purpose to everything he says and does. "In other words, you think I should be kinder to Ellen."

"You don't need any more enemies."

His humor reminds me of Pace's, and I can't help but grin. "Then you should be glad to know that I've already decided to treat her more kindly. She is his mother after all."

"And that, Miss MacAvoy, is what I call a plan."

"So you approve?"

He walks to the door. "Your father is waiting," he says, and, as always, he waits for me to precede him through the door.

· 7 ·

It has been over two weeks since I've been outside, not that I consider being in the dome outside, but it is much different from the close quarters of my room. The air feels different from what I am used to. It is lighter now that it is no longer encumbered with the coal smoke that was so prevalent before. I have no idea what to expect from my father, beyond the news from Ellen that he is taking me out. Findley became his usual stoic self again once we were outside my room, so the trip down the many flights of stairs was done in silence.

I did expect to be walking wherever it is my father is taking me, as that is the only way I have ever traveled around the dome, therefore I am surprised to find a steam carriage waiting for us at the curb when Findley and I exit the building. My father is already outside, and from the look on his face I can see that he is impatient with waiting. I take a petty bit of pleasure from knowing that I have once more inconvenienced him.

I've never seen the inside of a steam carriage before, as they sit too high to look into from street level. This one is painted dark blue, much like the uniforms the bluecoats wear, and the ornate trim that decorates the carriage is a bright gold. An insignia is on the middle of the door, and I imagine there is one to match it on the opposite side. It serves as notice to everyone that the Master General Enforcer is riding among the people.

Findley opens the door and I climb the five high steps that fold down from within.

There are two benches inside, one faces front and the other is opposite, facing the back. They are both covered in fine, soft leather that is dyed blue, and the seat and backs are heavily padded. A driver sits up front with a guard, and there is another guard who stands on a platform on the back. Both carry the awkward rifles that the rovers use. What will my father do when he sees the sleek, new models that Lyon's men use? I like to imagine that he would be shocked. The armed guards also trouble me. Does my father expect trouble, or is this just a show of power?

There is no roof on the carriage, nor is there a need for one, given the fact that it never rains inside the dome. But it must now, as there is a hole in the roof. A large hole that lets in rain, wind, and warm rays of sunshine, something that my father can no longer deny.

I sit down on the bench facing forward, and my father sits beside me. Findley closes the door and sits across from us. He sits back and crosses his arms, and even though his face remains remarkably impassive, I know he is relishing the thought of watching my father and me in our coming battle of wits.

"I thought it was time that you see what you have wrought," my father says as the carriage lurches forward and settles into a steady *putt-putt*.

We move down the promenade, past the center fountain and dais where the inhabitants of the dome gather for news and would assemble for my execution, if Ellen had her way. I look up, trying to find the hole. The smoke is still there, close to the top, but it is weaker and wispier, as if a stiff breeze would blow it away.

Break the glass . . . I imagine what it would be like to do so. To swing a hammer and a pick and shatter the sides of the dome and let in the fresh, clean air and let it sweep the inside clean. What a wondrous day that would be, for everyone. If only I could make my father see that.

I recognize the area we travel through. We are on the same streets that I walked with Pace weeks ago, when we were trying to figure out where Alex got out of the dome. The day we walked upon them, they were busy with workers going to their shifts to shovel coal to power the fans. Today the streets are much, much quieter. The roar of the fans is gone, along with the hustle and bustle of people going about their lives. The air close to the street is clearer than that above, which drifts and sways over us like the canvas awning Lyon's wife, Jane, erected outside to protect us from the sun.

The occasional workers that we do pass are subdued. They step away from the curb and keep their eyes downcast. They act as if they are afraid to be seen, and when we pass by they hurry onward to their destination. It is evident that they live in fear. Is this what my father wanted me to see? Is he adding this to my list of sins against the dome, another result of my rebellion? Does he want me to think that instead of freeing the people I've added another yoke around their necks?

I think not. My father does not care enough about these people to notice the burdens they bear. All he cares about are the royals, and his only goal is to ensure that their way of life does not change. He is all about preserving the past. He does not see the future or the need to change the present to make the future better for those who will come after us. Only when the royals give up their complacency will he change. And as long as he is in charge there will not be change.

The carriage turns a corner. The warehouse where Alex was murdered is gone, nothing left but a large, gaping hole and the wreckage of burnt timbers. I feared that it would fall down around me before I could escape it. The glass above and behind it is scorched black from the flames. Beyond is the door to the outside. A building sits in front of it, a miniature replacement of the former, no more than one story high where the warehouse was at least ten. It was hastily built and looks it, yet it serves its purpose, hiding the door to the outside. There is a barricade around it and bluecoats surround it. I am certain the people have been told it is to protect them from the wreckage. I know it is to keep the curious from poking around.

How many times has Lyon come and pounded on that door, looking to negotiate for Levi's release, and been turned away? Of course I wouldn't put it past my father to ignore him completely. As he does everything else that relates to the real world beyond the glass.

Next to the remnants of the warehouse is what is left of the building that housed the fans. It sits in ruins and wreckage, and the fans lay bent and blackened from their tumble from their stands. A last one leans haphazardly over the mess, daring anyone to take their life in their hands and walk below it. It will fall eventually. Above, the glass holds a long crack that splinters off in every direction. Over it I see a hole that from this distance is no bigger than my fist. A narrow beam of sunlight streams through, and it takes every bit of my willpower not to jump from the carriage and turn my face to it.

It will be a long time for repairs to be made, if they ever can be. I cannot imagine any piece of machinery inside the dome that is strong enough to put the fans back in place, although I am certain Dr. Stewart could come up with something, if given the chance.

My father says nothing. He just sits back and observes me, waiting for my reaction, or perhaps he wants an admission of guilt. I look at the destruction, caused by my fellow shiners James, Adam, and Alcide when they set the charges to blow up the fans. I know my father wants me to feel guilt, but I don't. Instead I feel a pride and a sense of power. Yes, I am very sorry for the lives that were lost. But look at what we accomplished. We put an entire society on its knees. If only there was a way to reach everyone inside and urge them to fight for their freedom. What wondrous things could we all create together?

"What happened to the workers?" I ask.

"Some died. The rest no longer have jobs." Another burden my father wishes me to bear. I am now responsible for their lives too. "Since they can no longer contribute to society, they no longer serve a purpose."

"So you are punishing them for something that is not their fault?" I say. "They had nothing to do with the destruction."

"Yet they are the ones who suffer the most."

"Have you forgotten about the shiners?" I point out. "Our entire community was wiped out and most of us are dead. Or are we beneath your notice?"

Findley suddenly coughs and turns his head to look at the street before us. I suddenly realize what I've said, but before I can react my father says something that makes me wonder for his sanity.

"So you say. There is no way to confirm the deaths. They could merely be hiding and waiting to attack us once more."

I am dumbfounded. I cannot believe he just said that. Even Findley seems shocked, if the widening of his eyes and the tightening around his mouth are any indication. My anger is so overpowering that I jump to my feet in the carriage and face my father.

"Do not dishonor my people in such a way again." I feel like screaming at him, but instead I speak quietly and with the force of my emotion. "I was there when they died. I saw the water carry them away, and then I carried their broken bodies on the beach to be placed on the pyre. I stood and watched as they burned until the sun and the heat blinded my eyes and I could see no more. I held children while they cried for their parents, and I watched my best friend's husband grieve as he said good-bye to her."

The carriage lurches to a stop at an intersection, and I pitch forward. Accidentally or intentionally I cannot tell. Findley catches me as I fall and straightens me. For a brief moment his face reveals his emotion and I see that he is as disgusted and angry as I am. He once more regains his impassive façade as I sit back in my seat. I cross my arms and look at my father.

"I wish no claim from you. Do not call me your daughter, for I am that because of my mother's foolishness. The people who died when your soldiers came into the mines with their flamethrowers were my family. They were my brothers and sisters, my aunts and uncles."

My father smiles and shakes his head. I might as well be talking to the dome for all he listens. "You have only just proven my point, Wren. Many have suffered and died because of your foolishness."

"Not because of me. It is because of you," I retort. "How many more will die because you refuse to see reason? Things will only get worse. The air outside is cool now, but the seasons will change. In a few months it will grow warmer, and soon you will be baking beneath the glass. Tell me, Master General Enforcer, Sir William Meredith, what will your precious royals have to say then?"

He seems surprised that something as insignificant as the seasons would dare to thwart him.

"I imagine they will ask you to break the glass," I say. "And that, Sir William, is something that I cannot wait to see."

· 8 ·

I would have thought that after my outburst we would have gone back to my father's building and I would be thrown in a cell like Levi. Instead we carry on, with my father wearing a bemused expression on his face. I wonder what the guards and the driver thought of my tirade. They, like Findley, remain impassive.

The carriage rolls onward into the area that houses the stock-yards. Cows, pigs, goats, sheep, and chickens all live together in an impossibly small area and their voices rise together in a cacophony of misery. The smell becomes horrendous the closer we get, until I feel as if I will gag. Without the fans the stench hangs in the air. I pull my bandana over my mouth and nose. My father, Findley, and the rest act as if they are impervious, but I know Findley's eyes are watering.

I think of Ghost and the way he buried his nose into the sweet and salty grass. The wretched livestock that live out their lives in confinement should have that opportunity also. I have to smile when I realize my rebellion should include the animals. That might be the only way to convince my father to release his hold on the dome inhabitants. Take away their resources. They have lost the fans and the coal. I imagine all the coal that is left has been commandeered by my father for his own use, such as the steam carriage we ride in. But even that will run out eventually.

I say nothing, as saying anything else would just be redundant. My father knows how I feel, and I do not understand why he thinks our tour will change my way of thinking.

Mercifully, we leave the stockyards behind and move into the area that houses the lower-class workers of the dome. These people get no more consideration than we did as shiners. The only advantage we had over them was that we lived below and therefore had some control over our lives, whereas these people are at the mercy of the internal government. They live in large tenements that have long ago lost their paint. The buildings are plain, crowded boxes with glassless windows. Lines of laundry crisscross over the streets. Noise is prevalent here also. Crying babies, screaming children, and harsh voices rise in argument. I recognize the area even though I only saw the outside for a few brief moments before I was thrown into the back of a prison cart. This is where the filchers brought me when they captured me on the street.

We move down a street that goes between two large buildings that are ten stories high. Men stand on the streets, gathered in clumps. These are the workers who no longer hold any value, according to my father, because their jobs were destroyed with the fire.

They do not move as we approach. Some who stand along the narrow sidewalk stare at us. The carriage slows and my father looks ahead at the street. Instead of moving out of the way, more men move into the center of the street, as if they want to block us. This is not good, not good at all.

"Do not stop." Findley quickly evaluates the situation and speaks into the driver's ear. The carriage chugs on and more men mill into the street. One pounds on the side of the carriage, then another. The tide slowly parts and they run alongside, yelling obscenities.

"Shiner whore!" I am shocked and sickened by the slur. How can they judge me when they know nothing about me? Yet they have been taught to hate me and blame my people for the fire that ravaged the dome. Before I have time to respond, something strikes my father in the shoulder and falls between us. More things fall, smelly and sticky things. They splash in my hair and down my side. I gag when I realize it is from a slop bucket. Someone from above tossed it out, and from the trash that follows I know it is deliberate. My father's face is incredulous with disbelief. Findley jumps to his feet and leans over us, bracing his hands on the back of the seat between us to give us shelter from the stuff that rains down around us.

"Move it!" he yells at the driver. I peer around Findley's body to see a scrum of men around the carriage, beating on it with their fists. One man dares to climb up the side. He grabs onto my hair and pulls. I scream in pain and wrap my hand in my hair to keep it from being torn out by the roots. The guard behind me smashes the butt of his rifle into my attacker's face, and I hear a sickening crunch of bones as the man falls away.

The carriage cannot move. For every inch it creeps forward, it is pushed back by the steady tide of bodies. I hear the strain of the engine as it fights against impossible odds. The men pound on the side and then suddenly they become organized and push. The carriage stands so high that we are top heavy.

"For God's sake shoot them before they tip us," Findley yells. The carriage lurches to the right so hard that the guards grab onto the sides to keep from being pitched out into the mob. The madness of the crowd lets me know that if any of us fall out or are dragged off we will be brutally killed. I slide down in my seat until I am completely sheltered by Findley, who is doing his best to protect us. The angry screams from above make me fear for his safety as larger and harder objects now shoot down from the windows. He flinches in pain when an iron kettle hits his back and crashes to the floor of the carriage.

The guards right themselves and shoot. Screams of pain rise over the angry shouts of the mob.

"Run over them if you have to," Findley yells. He decides that moving is of more importance than protecting my father and me. He opens his seat to reveal a cache of weapons. He grabs a thick club and swings it without mercy at those who are pushing on the carriage. Finally the carriage moves and moves quickly. A sickening lurch to one side informs me that we have, indeed, run over someone. More things are thrown at us as we chug hurriedly down the street.

"Send a squad to take care of that as soon as we return," my father barks out as he brushes debris from his uniform.

"Yes, sir," Findley replies as he sits down. He looks at me. "Are you hurt?"

I quickly give myself a mental inventory. I am shaken, but otherwise unharmed, except for my pride and the stench that surrounds us. "I am okay," I say. Findley looks at me in confusion. "I'm unhurt," I clarify with a half smile. I cannot help but notice that Findley is more concerned for my welfare than for my father's; his face is flushed a deep red and his jaw stretched so tight that I fear his teeth may crack. He is angry and I fear his retribution will be swift and deadly.

Even though my life was at risk, I do not fault the men who attacked us. They are frustrated with their current lot, and my father's tour was like rubbing salt in their wounds. How many more incidents like the one we just survived will have to happen before my father can be convinced that his way is no longer what is best? Will his pride keep him from doing what is right?

I think his pride will end all of us.

The carriage moves on. I feel the engine strain as the driver forces it to its limit. It doesn't move nearly as fast as the steam cycles the Hatfields use. We move into an area of the dome that I am familiar with. These are the streets that I walked every morning after my shift. Except now, there is something different about them. One of the buildings is tilted and I realize we have to be near the hole caused by the explosion.

"Stop!" I say. My father huffs impatiently but I ignore him. I jump up and climb over the side of the carriage before anyone has time to react. I hear the carriage screech to a halt as I take off at a run. I know Findley is following me, but I don't care. It is not as if I can get away. I just want to see. I need to see what is down below. A small part of me thinks that someone could still be alive down there and trying to escape.

Barriers are set around the boundaries of the large chasm. Everything around it has toppled into the hole. I approach the edge and peer down. The roaring of water fills my ears as it echoes strangely around the debris that forms a tottering tower.

"Do you think there were any people in the buildings when they collapsed?" I ask Findley as he jogs up to join me. I notice he is breathing hard and I can't help but smile in satisfaction. My lungs are clean, or at least they were when I came inside. I had no trouble running at all. The benefits of living outside are now too numerous to mention.

"There were," he says. "Some got out. Some didn't."

"Were you there?" He has to know I am talking about the bluecoats who came into the tunnels with their flamethrowers. "Were you a part of it?"

"Would it make a difference to you if I was?"

I turn to look at him. His face is as impassive as usual, but there is something in his eyes that I have never noticed before. A need? Doubt? I do not answer his question, instead I repeat. "Were you there?"

He looks down at the chasm. If there were people in the buildings, then they are still there, crushed among the brick, timber, and mortar that stand as a silent monument. How long before the river undermines it and it crumbles and falls? Will the remnants of the dome become part of the world beneath? Will it dam the water and create new tunnels? Or will it all crumble and fall in upon itself, obliterating both of our worlds?

Findley finally answers me. "I was not." I am surprised to feel that his answer does make a difference. Relief washes over me. "I was actually outside when it happened."

"Outside?" Now I am curious. "Doing what?"

He suddenly grabs my arm and jerks me about.

"What are you doing?" I try to wrench my arm away but his grip is strong.

"We wouldn't want anyone to think we are getting too chummy now, would we?" I see the carriage now. It just turned the corner and my father is standing inside it, watching us. "You need a good washing." Findley adds.

"You don't smell so good yourself," I retort as he marches me before him, none too gently, to the carriage. Right before we approach he jerks me back and whispers in my ear.

"I was outside looking for you." He shoves me forward and I stumble the last few steps to the carriage where the guards are waiting to haul me up without the benefit of the steps. I am thrown into my seat, and the carriage moves forward once again as Findley climbs aboard.

As we ride by, I look once more at the hole in the ground caused by the explosion. It could be a way out, but it would have to be a last resort attempt. The distance to the tower of debris is a great one, one I am not certain I could jump. One misstep would lead to certain death. Still, once down, I know the way out. But I am not going anywhere without Levi and Pace.

If Pace wants to go.

A flash of yellow catches my eye. I can't believe it. Pip! He dives down from the cloud that hovers at the building tops and swoops over the carriage, chirping madly, before he darts off once more, back into the cloud.

"He must be lost," the guard behind me says.

I say nothing even though I know Pip is not lost. He knows exactly where he is and what he is doing. I only wish I could say the same.

· 9 ·

I take a bath as soon as I am returned to my room by the guards, taking advantage of the time alone, as Findley has been sent out to take care of the rioters we encountered. I scrub out my clothes as best I can and hang them to dry. Luckily I still have the leather pants I was wearing beneath my clothes the night we were captured, and I put them on with an undershirt that I find in one of the drawers. When I come out of the water closet I find a box on the bed and a note that says to be ready promptly at seven, which is still hours away.

I open the box to find a lovely dress. It is pale green with a high waist and short puffed sleeves. The neckline is modest, for which I am grateful. There is also a delicately knitted shawl beneath the dress, along with the appropriate undergarments. The only thing missing is a pair of shoes. I have no idea where I am going at seven, but it requires me to look nice. I consider rebelling and wearing my regular clothes, but that might result in my not going wherever it is I have been summoned to. The only chance for escape I have is when I leave this room.

A meal has been delivered also. I sit down at the table and find an envelope beside my tray addressed to me. The writing is exquisite; done in pen and ink on thick parchment. This is no ordinary letter as paper is a valuable commodity in our society. An ornate *P* is pressed into the red wax that seals the envelope. I open it carefully because I have never seen anything like it in my lifetime.

Your presence is requested for a
Celebration of the upcoming nuptials of
Miss Jillian Pembrooke and Captain Pace Bratton.
7:00 this eve
37 Park Front

I did not want to believe it when Ellen told me. I thought it was just a ruse on her part to get to me. There is something about seeing it on paper that makes it seem much too real.

Could this engagement be real? Is it possible that Pace was sent by my father to spy on us and his crime manufactured so I would take him in? And what about Jilly? Was she at David's for the same reason? She said she wanted out because she was being forced into a marriage she did not want. Was she already engaged to Pace and part of my father's elaborate plan to trick us? Now that their job is done, they can go on with their lives.

I think back on our moments together. On the things Pace said to me and the way he treated me. His fear in the tunnels was real. Was he so desperate to please my father that he subjected himself to his biggest fear of being closed in with no escape? Am I that gullible that I was taken in by his sweet words? Is my disbelief now because I do not want to admit I was wrong about Pace or because he truly has feelings for me?

Had feelings for me.

I go to the window and manage to press my forehead against it, as if somehow the answers that are out there will find their way into my mind. Somewhere beyond the glass is Pip. I know he was looking for Pace when I saw him. But where is Pace? Is he truly one of them? Has he turned his back on all of us? I feel as if everyone has, since Levi and I are still prisoners. I had faith that Lyon could get us out when I surrendered to my father. Now I am not so sure. The only thing I am certain of is that I will go mad if I remain locked in this room for another day.

I've got to do something to get us out. Tonight may be my only chance. At least now, for better or for worse, I have a plan.

◆

Findley knocks on my door promptly at seven. He is dressed formally in the dark blue uniform of the enforcers with the addition of a white shirt with a stiff upright collar. There is also a set of ribbons and bars on his chest along with the gold bands on his arms that signify his rank. I know without seeing him that my father will have many more decorating his uniform, for all his years of faithful service.

Findley looks uncomfortable, still he raises an eyebrow in approval of me in the green dress. I can only hope that he does not notice the leather pants that I wear beneath it, or the fact that I have my shirt tied low around my hips. There can be no argument about my boots. I refuse to wear the other shoes. I wish there was some way that I could conceal my jacket. I tried several different ways and none of them passed a casual inspection. I will just have to make do without it. I do not need anything to alert anyone to the fact that I plan on escaping as soon as the opportunity presents itself. I am able to conceal my goggles in a small

beaded bag that I found in my room. I added a linen handkerchief to it, along with my own kerchief and a comb as an excuse
to carry the bag.

I am careful not to raise my skirt too high as I go down the stairs
behind Findley. The last words he spoke to me come to my mind,
and since he has been so forthcoming with me of late, I have no
qualms about asking him, "You said you were looking for me outside when the tunnels blew," I ask. "Why?"

"I was concerned for your safety," he replies.

"Why? You didn't even know me."

"But I knew the rovers. About the rovers." Findley does not turn
to look at me as we continue down the stairs. "There are very few
people I would wish them on."

"Including my friends that are outside?"

He does not answer.

"One told me that there are not enough resources for both our
worlds. Therefore they are determined to kill all of us. I overheard
them say they would just wait for us to come out the door and pick
us off one by one."

"You've been that close to them?" Findley turns to look at me. It
is obvious I have caught him off guard. "You talked to one?"

"Right before Levi killed him," I reply. If not for Levi I would
be dead many times over from the rovers.

"I knew that young man was resourceful."

"You cannot even begin to imagine how much so," I say. "All of
my friends are."

"Yet they cannot conceive of a way to get you and your resourceful friend out of the dome."

I was hoping to strike a nerve with Findley. Instead he has
struck mine. Still, I will not give up on the Hatfields. "They are

careful of our lives," I assure Findley. "They will not do anything that will put us at risk."

"Yet your lives are already at risk just by being outside," Findley points out. "And you have no way of knowing if they have fallen victim to the rovers or simply have left and given up on you."

"They would never do that."

"Are you certain of that?" Findley continues. "For all you know, the catwalk could now be deserted and your so-called airship nothing more than a memory."

"They wouldn't leave us like that. They wouldn't leave Levi behind."

"Are you certain?" This time he stops to look at me. "Is there any doubt at all in your mind?"

I am puzzled why he would say this. He's admitted that he does go outside. Does he know something? Or is he merely testing me once more because I am convinced that every time he converses with me there is an ulterior motive that I have yet to figure out.

"Is there something you are trying to tell me?" I ask.

"No." Findley continues on. "But there is something I've been meaning to ask. How did you get back into the dome?"

"Through the hole in the roof," I say, just to see his reaction. I am not about to tell him about the gliders, I would rather he think on it for a while, to see what he can come up with on his own.

"How did you get up there?" he asks.

"As I said, my friends are resourceful."

"Hmmm." I've given him something to think about, and he is silent as we make our way down the remaining stairs.

The steam carriage has been cleaned since our disastrous ride this morning. My father has chosen to make me wait on him this time, and Findley does not comment on my boots as he hands me up into the carriage. He remains by the steps to wait for my father.

"What happened to the people who attacked us?" I ask. There are no guards present this time, as we are going to the royal part of the dome and there should be no need of them. I am certain the driver cannot hear us over the steady chug of the engine.

"They have been dealt with." Findley replies.

"In the same manner everyone who crosses my father is dealt with?"

"Not everyone." His steady eyes settle on me. "There have been a few exceptions."

"If I were lucky enough to go outside, would I see more bodies burned and staked?" I ask. He grimaces and looks away. "How many more innocent people have to die before you say 'enough'?"

"How many more times are you going to ask that?"

"Until deaf ears are able to hear it."

"Maybe you need to say it in a different way." My father appears at the door and comes down the steps. "In a way that will capture his attention," Findley adds as he goes to meet my father and attend him into the carriage.

My father considers my appearance before he sits down. My hair is freshly washed after this morning, and I left it down after brushing it. It hangs in dark waves down my back. The dress fits me well enough and I keep the shawl wrapped tightly around my shoulders to help disguise the extra clothes hidden beneath. I wish there was some way I could have brought my jacket. I know I will need it when and if I get outside, especially if I have to go back into the tunnels.

My father makes no comment. He sits, and the driver takes off as if he has eyes in the back of his head. I have to admit I am excited in a curious kind of way. I have never been to the royal part of the dome. I have only seen it from a distance.

We travel down the promenade, past storefronts that hold hats, dresses, and men's suits. Another one is full of treasures that remind me of the things I saw aboard the *Quest*. I see clocks, statues, and other numerous things that are too small for me to identify from the rapidly rolling carriage.

The stores and the candlelit quarters above them give way and the street opens up to long and narrow lots surrounded by low walls. The carriage stops at a guarded gate and an attendant comes out. He salutes my father and the guards open the gate and we ride on through. Streetlamps and trees made from copper and bronze stand sentinel between the walls and the promenade. An attempt at privacy in my mind, as it seems that even the royals live on top of one another. The houses are four to five stories high and the dome curves down over them, with an abrupt ending on the street. I notice that the streetlights are lit with candles, and I feel a sense of satisfaction that we, who dug up the coal, found another way to have light without it. We used the waterwheel to generate power that lit our cavern and the tunnels, a much safer alternative than flame.

The lawns behind the walls are painted green, and the closer we get, the more I see that they are faded and chipped. Such a poor imitation of the real thing. The air around us feels old and stale, and I long to fill my lungs with the fresh scents that quickly became familiar to me on the outside.

To think that my friends are just on the other side of the dome. If only there was a way to just break the glass. The tunnel Jon found outside was a dead end, built by someone after the dome was closed. They never finished it, never made their way to safety before the comet came. To try to dig the way in to this part of the dome would be foolish. The enforcers could easily pick off whoever attempted it as they came through. As Lyon said, the best way in is to break the glass. Unfortunately that is beyond my capabilities.

We turn up a drive whose house is brighter than the rest. Every window is aglow with candlelight, and noise pours forth, a cacophony of music and voices rising together that echoes hollowly against the curve of the dome, sounding somewhat like my own familiar cavern that I used to call home.

Two men in formal suits stand at attention before the wide steps that lead up to a massive door. The steam carriage comes to a halt, and one quickly opens the door while the other unfolds the steps. My father goes first, then Findley, who waves the two men off and extends his hand to help me down the steps. I suddenly feel desperately out of place with my clunky boots. My legs are damp with sweat beneath the leather while my arms and back are chilled. I quickly look right, and then left, weighing the odds of my dashing off and getting lost in the darkness behind the houses.

There is too much openness of the lawns and too many people are around. I know Findley can outrun me, even though my lungs are in much better condition. Findley must know what I am thinking because he grabs my hand and keeps a tight grip on it as I go down the steps.

Years of being told my place consumes me. I do not belong here. Everyone will know I don't belong; all they have to do is look at my eyes. How will they treat me? Will they call me names like the workers on the street? Will they hold me personally responsible for the recent disasters? Did my father just bring me here so I would be humiliated by Pace and Jilly?

"Where is the girl who proved her father wrong?" Findley whispers in my ear as I reach the ground. "You've got a captive audience in there. Tell them what you've seen."

I look up at Findley. My father is watching us. For all he knows Findley could be reminding me of my place and how to act in such esteemed company.

"You're on my side, aren't you?" I say. "You want out as much as I do."

"Indeed I do," Findley says, and he hands me off to my father.

· 10 ·

I am in the last place I ever thought I'd be. Never in my wildest imaginings did I picture myself in a royal house and certainly never at a party. My dreams consisted only of getting out of the dome, not of moving to a higher status inside. Yet here I stand, waiting with my father in a line to greet our hosts. I can feel everyone's eyes upon me and the cloying smells of too much perfume and powder nearly overwhelm me.

The line consists of several people, including Ellen and a couple who must be Jilly's parents. Jilly's mother has the same bright red hair as Jilly. Everyone except Ellen is covered up with jewelry that glows in the candlelight.

What am I supposed to say to these people? I search the room for Pace and Jilly, but there is no sign of them. Beyond the three people I recognize is another couple wearing velvet capes and dripping with more jewels than I could ever have imagined. As the people in front of us come to them, they curtsey or bow. Dr. Stewart's comment about the crown jewels being inside the dome comes to my mind, and I realize that these two people are our king and queen and the entire reason why the dome was built. To protect the royal bloodline. I steal a look at the royal couple. The man is short and stout with a receding chin and thinning hair that is artfully arranged across his forehead to hide the fact that he is going bald. His wife is much more attractive, which isn't surprising as the king can marry anyone he chooses, or is his bride chosen for him also? Wouldn't she have to be, to keep the family lines from crossing too many times?

It comes to mind that I don't even know the king's name, nor am I impressed by what I see; still, I am frightened and it makes me angry. I know I am at risk of being humiliated, especially by Ellen. Why should I care what these people, who are the reason we have been enslaved all these years, think about me?

My father holds my hand in his. To anyone watching us it would seem nothing more than a typical father-daughter moment, or at least I think so. I feel the strength of his grip. I have no choice but to stand in this line and await my punishment. I know he will get some sort of perverse joy from it. Findley stands off to the side, calmly watching us.

"Lord Pembrooke, Lady Pembrooke. May I present my daughter, Wren." Lord Pembrooke nods at me, and Lady Pembrooke grips my hand. "My dear. We have heard your story. It is appalling that you were kept from your father all these years. I know he never stopped searching for you. How dreadful that you had to grow up under those circumstances."

My mouth drops open in shock and my father squeezes my upper arm beneath my shawl, daring me to say something to the contrary. He has told them these lies to explain my presence. Before I can think or protest I am shuffled down the line past Ellen, who barely smiles at me, and then to the king.

"Curtsey," my father whispers in my ear. Every part of me

wants to revolt. My mind screams to tell the truth and to reveal his lies, but I know that will accomplish nothing beyond having me removed from the premises. I need to find Pace and I hope to escape, so I will play my father's game for now and let him think I am as submissive to his desires as everyone else in the dome.

"Your highness," I say, and I dip down in what I hope is an appropriate manner.

"Well done, Meredith," the king says as he takes my hand into his. It is pudgy and soft, and I know he has never done a day's work in his sorry life. "She is quite lovely."

"And her eyes are most extraordinary," the queen adds. She is quite striking with her dark hair and eyes and flawless skin. She reminds me of Lucy.

I clamp my mouth tightly shut as my father murmurs his thanks and guides me away from the line, past a wide staircase, to a column that serves no other purpose than decoration. A plant similar to the ones in my father's office sits beside it, and there is a small ornamental table there as well. "Well done," he says when we are safely away. An older man dressed in a plain black suit passes by us with a tray of drinks and my father takes two and hands me one. I recognize it as wine, and it tastes bitter compared to what I had from the Hatfields. Or maybe it is just my attitude that makes it so.

"It would help if I knew what to expect," I say in return. "Or does it amuse you to see my reactions?"

"It does make things more interesting," he replies. "Since I never know what to expect from you."

"You can expect me to continue to believe as I do," I say. "Especially since I have yet to see anything to convince me otherwise." I take a good long look at him. At his fine uniform and the rows of medals. At the way the candlelight hides his eyes even though they are constantly moving and searching. Even now, when we are supposedly having a conversation he is watching the room. "It is a sad statement to your life that the only thing that holds your interest is baiting me."

"I could lock you up in a cell like your friend if it pains you so much to be with me."

"And what lie would you tell to explain that, since you've painted yourself as grieving over my disappearance all these years."

"These fools will believe whatever I tell them." As soon as the words leave his mouth he regrets them. For the first time since I've met him I can see the emotion plainly written on his face. He said it to impress me. All my life I was seeking his approval without even realizing it until the day I actually met him face-to-face. Isn't it strange that he also seeks mine? It is also so very sad that he thinks this power he holds over the dome will impress me.

His eyes, always watchful, turn from me to the people around us. I study the people in the room for the exact same reasons as my father. He is watching for signs of rebellion. People stand in small clusters all talking quietly as a quartet of musicians play stringed instruments. The music is wonderful, light and airy. It reminds me of a gentle breeze ruffling the leaves in the forest. The room glows with candlelight and everything is polished and shined, even the leaves of the plant I stand beside. The suited men move from group to group with trays full of glasses. In the room behind the receiving line a long table sits, covered with food. More than enough to feed the workers and their families who rioted against us this morning.

Yet around the edges everything seems shabby. The carpet beneath my feet is worn and the edges frayed, just like the fancy clothing everyone wears. The people seem restless, their eyes darting to and fro, just like my father's. They are all watching and waiting while they pretend that their lives have meaning.

What a waste. Life is more than just going through the everyday routine. Life should be about dreams, about moving forward, about making the world a better place. Life should be about doing, not just existing. I sit my glass down on the table and turn away from my father. I have no plan beyond walking out the front door when suddenly the music changes to a louder tone and ends with a pre-emptive note like a sharp intake of breath. Everyone turns to the staircase in anticipation.

"Ladies and gentlemen," a voice intones loudly. " Captain Pace Bratton and Lady Jillian Pembrooke." They appear at the top of the staircase as a round of applause starts around the room. Pace wears a uniform much like Findley's. One medal hangs over his heart. Jillian wears a dress of pale blue, and jewels glitter around her neck and wrists and in her hair, which is piled high upon her head. Jilly takes Pace's arm, and they slowly make their way down the stair-case. The king and queen meet them at the bottom, and the four of them turn to the room and bow as one. Pace and Jilly have received the king's blessing.

They move into the large room where we are all gathered. The applause dies down, and people, including my father, move past me to greet the couple. I hear the bits and pieces of gossip as the royals pass by me.

"He was sent down as a spy."

"If not for him the entire dome could have been destroyed."

"Single-handedly put a stop to the shiner rebellion."

"Found Sir Meredith's missing daughter."

"A brilliant plan conceived by Sir Meredith and the king."

I stand in the middle of the room with the crowd eddying around me, like a rock in the stream. I feel as if time, for me, has stopped as bits and pieces of the story come together in a tale that I refuse to believe. Either I am the biggest fool that has ever lived, or my father has concocted such a lie that is believable because it is impossible to think otherwise. I keep my eyes on Pace.

Things are not always what they seem. Is this what he was trying to tell me in the stairwell? That this . . . engagement is not what it seems, or that our time together was a lie? Which is it?

Pace and Jilly smile and talk to their well-wishers, but like the rest of the royals their eyes are constantly searching.

I feel his gaze before I see it. Just like the first day, when Alex died, Pace looks at me and his so very blue eyes implore me. He does not ask for forgiveness. He asks me to believe in him.

I do. Pace has been steady and sure since the day we met. It is me that doubts both myself and us together. There is a reason for this charade. I allow myself a slight and tremulous smile, and I can see relief flooding his eyes. Jilly must feel it also, because she looks at Pace and then at me and smiles.

"I don't think anyone would mind if you had a private word with your savior." It is Findley, behind me. "And no one should think anything inappropriate, as long as his fiancée is present."

I do not turn to look at him. I keep my eyes on Pace. "What do you know of this?" I ask.

"I know that sometimes it is best to wait for your moment instead of charging straight ahead. It is hard to fight a good battle when your best soldiers are dead."

"I know Pace was forced into this," I say. "I just cannot imagine why."

"It speaks volumes that you still believe in him," Findley says. "For both of you." He leans in closer. "You seem overwrought. If you go upstairs and to the last room on the left, you can take a moment to gather yourself."

I make my way around the groups of gathered people. I keep my head down so no one will notice me. Let them think I am shy and afraid. After all, I was held a captive by the shiners my entire life, I do not know how to act in such esteemed company. I make it to the staircase and glance around the room. The only one who is watching me is Findley. My father is deep in conversation with the king, and Ellen hangs on her son's arm as Pace talks to a group of young women. Jilly is with her parents. I make my escape up the stairs.

The hallway is long, running from the front of the house to the back. Another staircase is on the other end. It could be a way to escape. I am not going anywhere until I talk to Pace.

I cautiously turn the knob of the door and peer in. The room is dark except for one candle on a table. After one last look around the hallway to make sure I am alone, I go in. I hear a familiar chirp, and Pip flutters to my shoulder. I drop my bag and shawl on the bed and take the tiny canary in my hands. I hold him up to my cheek.

"Oh, Pip, how I have missed you," I say. "I wish you could talk and tell me how it fares outside. I miss Jonah and Ghost, and I am so worried about our friends."

The window is open, left that way by Pace no doubt, so Pip may come and go as he pleases. He only puts him in his cage to protect him, not to keep him prisoner. I realize now, he was the same with me. Yes, he asked me to tell him where I was going so he would not worry. He never put limits on me, except when he was afraid of losing me.

I go to the window. It looks out over the back lawn that stretches all the way to the dome. While the workers live on top of one another in tenements, the royals have all this room. What do they do with it? Use it for fun and games as near as I can tell.

Close to the house there are small squares filled with blooming plants. From here I can smell their sweet aroma. It is quite lovely. Benches and statues are scattered about and a plant-covered archway leads to the painted lawn beyond. From there I see a boxed-off area with a net stretched across it and rows of benches that rise up, one behind the other. Beyond that are a few small buildings tucked up beneath the curve of the dome. Probably housing for servants. The area is so open that anyone walking around would easily be seen. Or maybe it is just my shiner eyes that make it seem so. Perhaps I could escape that way and make my way to David and Lucy's place. From there it is just a matter of going down into the tunnels.

I hear a noise at the door. I sit Pip down on the sill and turn.

"Jilly."

She comes to me in a rush and grabs my hands. "It's a charade, Wren. You've got to know it's all for show." Her green eyes implore me. "Pace loves you and only you."

I nod, too overcome with relief to speak. I believed it, but hearing the words is such a relief. Jilly hugs me. "We are all in grave danger. So many things have happened."

"What has happened?" I ask. "I've been kept in a room. I don't know anything beyond what my father has let me know."

Jilly leads me to the bed, and we sit down on the edge with my hands gripped in hers. "First of all, James, Mr. Hatfield, David, Lucy, and Harry all got out as far as we know."

"Through the tunnels?"

"Yes, they sent a message back in by Pip. It just said 'all out.'"

Another sense of relief sweeps through me. "You sent me the first note." Jilly nods. "Why didn't you go with them?"

"We were all at David's when James showed up. Filchers followed them. Someone had to delay them to keep everyone from being followed into the tunnels."

"And since you are a royal it was up to you."

"Yes. I just started screaming like they were attacking me and raised such a ruckus that everyone couldn't help but watch. From there the enforcers showed up. I don't think the filchers found the tunnel, but they are watching the house. They know they went in and have yet to come out."

"Do you think if we went that way they would see us?"

"Yes, they would," Jilly says. "And not only that, your father has stationed an enforcer on the premises."

"So there is no hope of escape that way."

"Or a way for anyone to get in to help us. Pace sent a note out saying that way was compromised."

"So why the false engagement?"

"Yes, that." Jilly drops my hands and rises from the bed. "Sir Meredith knew I had to be involved with the seekers. In addition, when you, Pace, and your other friend . . ."

"Levi."

"Yes, Levi. When you arrived on the scene it was quite embarrassing for your father because there were royals present. Very high-ranking royals, one of which is my father. He had to come up with an explanation for why his daughter was being chased by filchers and surrendering on the steps of our government building.

"So he came up with Pace being sent down below as a spy and my being held captive my entire life."

Jilly smiles. "You've heard the gossip."

"Just since I arrived here."

"He manufactured the lie and made Pace and me a part of it. Our lives in exchange for our cooperation. Pace refused at first, he felt it was a betrayal to you, but between his mother and me, we brought him round."

"Stay alive to fight another day," I say, recalling Findley's words. "Ellen hates me."

"Yes, she does," Jilly says. "Sir Meredith has told so many lies she doesn't know what to believe. She was never held prisoner, you know. Your father told her he brought her in for her safety. She actually thought the shiners were using Pace. She still thinks he's under some sort of spell you cast on him. Pace is pretending compliance because he is afraid for you."

"My father has spun so many lies and manipulated so many people that it is a wonder he can keep up with it all."

"It may catch up with him soon," Jilly says. "He has downplayed the recent events. More people are grumbling now. They are worried because the fans are gone."

"They don't honestly believe that it is still burning out there?" I ask.

"They are questioning. They know it is not safe. They just don't know why."

"It could be, if we all worked together."

"So Pace has told me," Jilly says. She comes back to the bed and sits down once again. "I want to go outside so bad I can taste it."

I take her hands in mine. "It is so beautiful, Jilly. But it is also scary. We shall have to fight to stay alive."

"Isn't anything worth having worth fighting over?"

I admire her spirit. "Yes, it is," I say. "But, Jilly, I've had to kill people. It is not something I would wish on you."

"You did what you had to, to survive." She stands again. "I must get back. This party is in our honor and we will be missed."

I stand with her. "Pace?"

"He will come as soon as he can escape downstairs." She hugs me once more. "Be patient, Wren. Don't do anything rash. There are other seekers now. We are trying." She goes to the door.

"Wait," I say. "Is Findley a seeker?"

"Your keeper?" Jilly smiles. "Yes. He is." She blows me a kiss. "Wait for Pace. He misses you so much."

• 11 •

How much longer can I wait before I will be missed? If Pace and I are caught together, what will be the consequences? Jilly and Pace are walking a narrow line with their pretense, but I understand why they did it. They would be of no help to anyone if they were imprisoned like Levi and I. I wonder how far they will take it. Surely they are expected to be married soon, especially if Ellen has her way.

Pip chirps from the windowsill. I run to the door, even though my mind tells me to use caution. It has to be Pace. The door opens, and I am in his arms before he steps through. He hurries us inside and closes the door with his foot as he wraps his arms tightly around me.

"It's not real, you've got to believe me. We're just pretending . . ."

"I know. Jilly told me. I didn't believe it." We speak at the same time, in a rush because we are both afraid that we will run out of time. Pace moves his hands to my face and cradles my cheeks within his palms. He searches my eyes and a tear brims and slides down my cheek. He catches it with his thumb.

"You are the one I love," Pace says. "This was the only choice we had to stay alive. It was the only way to get to see you."

Once more he is so strong, so steady. How can I admit to him that I had doubts, and that I still have them? I will not hurt him again, not when he has sacrificed so much for a cause that I am responsible for.

He kisses me. Such a sweet kiss, so tender and gentle as if he is afraid I will shatter. He doesn't know that I might, just because I would rather die than see the hurt on his face again. I cling to him because I am so very afraid of losing him and I don't know what to do about it. And even now, he does not push me for an answer.

He smiles as he pulls away. "Levi?" he asks.

I lay my head on his shoulder. It feels like crawling into my bed after a long hard night on my shift. I remember the peace I felt when I was with him in our cave by the river. Even though our very lives were at risk, the moments we had together were worth it. "He's in the cells. They beat on him a bit."

"He can take it," Pace says, and I cannot help but notice that he's not really feeling sorry for Levi getting a beating. "They don't want to acknowledge him, because to do so would mean admitting you were right and they are wrong."

"They can't just make the outside go away."

"Yet that is exactly what your father is doing."

"Jilly said a lot of the royals are asking questions. I know a lot of the workers are frustrated. We were attacked this morning while touring the dome."

"And they were severely punished," Pace says. "There were executions."

I touch the medal pinned to his chest. "I forgot that you're a bluecoat again. Did you have to be a part of it?"

"I had the party as an excuse." Pace pulls away from me. He

looks out the window and runs his hand through his hair before he turns back to me. "But, yes, they expect me to follow their orders, even if it means murdering innocents."

"How long can you keep this up? Have they scheduled a date for the wedding?"

"Next Sunday. My mother doesn't want to wait that long."

"She's afraid for you."

Pace gives me a lopsided smile. "Thank you for being kind. I know she hasn't treated you well. I've tried to explain about us, but she refuses to listen. She doesn't even think she was a prisoner. She keeps insisting it was for her own safety."

"My father knows how to manipulate people. I could not believe the tale he's spun about all of this. He even said the royals were fools because they believe anything he tells them."

"Maybe he is the bigger fool for believing that is true."

"What are we going to do, Pace? I can't believe Lyon hasn't done something to get Levi out."

"I haven't heard anything except the one message from Pip. It has been too long. I think something has happened to them."

"They wouldn't leave. Not without Levi."

"No. But the rovers could have taken them."

"Don't say it. Don't even think it. I can't stand to think that we got out just to die at their hands."

"You know how dangerous they are."

I think back to the battle we fought, to the rovers I killed, and to the kiss that Levi and I shared and Pace witnessed. "Lyon is too smart and too well prepared for that."

"I hope so. But I'm beginning to run out of hope where Lyon is concerned."

"At least Lucy and David got out. And Harry. There was some good to come of this."

Pace puts his hands on my shoulders, and his spirit shines out from behind his beautiful blue eyes. "I hope the price we pay for that is not too high." He smoothes my hair back from my face. "I've hardly ever seen you with your hair down. You are so beautiful."

I blush. "I don't even know where the dress came from."

"Jilly."

I raise my skirt so he can see my boots, and he grins. "You can take the girl out of the mines . . ." he begins.

"I'll always be a shiner," I finish and raise the skirt higher so he can see the pants. "I think we should just go. Get out and find Lyon and tell him where Levi is. Then we can come back in with weapons and just take over. I know other people will fight. Fi—" Pace puts a finger to my lips as Pip lets out a warning chirp and flits from the sill into the dome.

We have not strayed far from the door. We stand just inside it, carried away by our reunion. Anyone passing by could hear us talking. We were too wrapped up in each other to use caution, and the creak of the floor outside the door lets me know we have been discovered. The silence outside the door is maddening. Beyond, we can still hear the music from the party below.

Pace has been absent from the party too long. I motion to the window. Whoever is outside the door will hear us move. We will have to be fast, and our escape will not be without its dangers. He takes my hand in his, and we creep silently to the window. Three bluecoats stand below. The door swings open, violently, and my father, Findley, and another bluecoat come in. I can see Jilly in the hallway. A bluecoat has a firm hold on her and her eyes are red from crying. Her cheek is red as if she's been slapped and her hair is loose from the upswept style she wears.

We are caught in Pace and Jilly's lie.

"Take them down the back way," My father says as Findley grabs Pace and the other bluecoat grabs me. Our hands are tied behind our backs, none to gently.

"Do you think no one will notice Pace and Jilly are gone?" I say to my father. "Or do you already have a lie handy to explain it?"

"It was all me," Pace says as Findley twists him around after binding his wrists. "Wren and Jilly have nothing to do with it."

My father sighs loudly. "Don't be a fool. Wren has everything to do with it. You two are just the fools who follow her."

"How much longer are you going to pretend that there is nothing wrong?" I implore him. "How many more people have to die before someone says 'enough'?"

My father looks at me. "Perhaps you three will be the end of it," he says. "One thing for certain. You will never know the answer to that question."

A chill runs down my spine. Does this mean he is sending us to our deaths? Findley refuses to look at me. He keeps his eyes straight ahead as he pushes Pace along. Our guards move Jilly and me behind Findley and Pace. Jilly cries as they bind her hands. I wish I could offer her some words of comfort, but nothing helpful comes to mind. Besides, I am so very angry with my father. I would not put it past him to have brought me here just to trap Pace and Jilly.

We head to the back staircase. More bluecoats come up. There are so many about that I am certain he planned this. My anger turns on myself for not realizing it sooner. For letting my emotions carry me away.

"What are you doing?" A voice cries out. "Where are you taking them?"

It is Ellen. She gathers her skirts and runs down the hall. Jilly's parents are behind her, concern plainly written on their faces.

"Meredith!" Jilly's father shouts. "What are you doing with my daughter?"

"Your daughter is under arrest for treason." My father says.

"No," Pace says. "She's just an innocent victim. I was using her to get information. She doesn't know a thing."

"See?" Jilly's father says. "Release her."

"No," Jilly lifts her head. Her glorious red hair tumbles from its pins and she shakes it free. "I am a seeker." Her voice is shaky, but she gains strength as she talks. "I helped blow up the fans, and I helped the people your filchers were chasing escape from the dome."

"Jillian, no," her mother says.

"I would rather die believing in something than live a life with no purpose," Jilly says. "The outside is there for us," she continues. "Wren and Pace have seen it. I want to see it too."

"But it isn't safe," her father says.

"But it is worth fighting for," Jilly finishes for him. "Isn't that why we are here? Because someone in the past thought that our lives were worth fighting for? Isn't it sad that we have all forgotten that?"

"Take them," my father snaps at Findley. I know he is angry that he allowed Jilly to speak. "To the cells. Your time of privilege is over," he says to me. We are marched down the staircase. Above us voices raise in argument. Has my father finally overstepped his power? Surely Jilly's father will not allow his daughter to be executed. As for Pace and me . . . I fear our time is up.

It is hard to go downstairs in a long dress, especially when your hands are tied behind your back and you have no way to hold it up. More so for Jilly, who wears a dainty shoe with a heel. We both trip and nearly fall several times until Findley sighs in frustration. "Help them, you fools," he barks.

Findley will help us. He has to. He is one of us. I try to be ready, but the odds are ever so much against us. We trod past the kitchen, and the staff watches us with fear-filled eyes as we are marched out the back door and past the beautiful garden that I admired from above.

The dome soars from the ground to the sky around us. Our friends are just on the other side of the glass. I wish I could see the light of their fires, but there is nothing beyond but darkness. The three of us are herded to the drive between the house and the wall, where the same steam wagon that I was tossed into when I first met my father waits. The bluecoats actually pick Jilly and me up and deposit us in the back, where we stagger and trip until we are able to sit down on the benches. Pace is pushed in behind us and the door slammed and bolted into place.

Pace sits down next to me. I glance out the small window as the wagon jerks. I see my father talking to a bluecoat, who nods and jumps on the back as we jerk once more before it rolls into motion. This will more than likely be the last trip the wagon will make. I know from the sound of the engine that the dome is down to the last bits of coal. I see Findley now, growing smaller as we roll away. My father says something to him, and he nods before following him back into the house. Shouldn't he have done something?

"Wren," Pace says. "Turn your back to me and see if you can untie my hands."

I do as he asks and our fingers fumble against each other's. "There's too much," I say. "It's too tight. I can't find the ends."

"Hold still and let me try," Pace says. I comply, sitting still while his fingers move over my bonds. I look at Jilly, who appears terrified. I do not blame her. I am terrified also. I cannot help but think of Alex and how he died. Are we bound for the fires? But then I remember, there are no fires now and no furnaces left. Still, that will not stop my father. They still have the flamethrowers, and that was what they used to kill Alex and to kill many more of us shiners.

"What you said was very brave," I say.

"I don't feel so brave now," Jilly says. "I really didn't think he would dare . . ."

"Because you are a royal?" I finish for her.

She nods. "I'm so sorry. It is my fault. Sir Meredith caught me coming down and . . ."

"It is not your fault, Jilly," I say. "I think it was his plan all along to trap us. Why else would he bring me here tonight?"

"What will become of us?" she asks

"We are going to get out of here," Pace says. He gives up on trying to untie my hands and shifts around to face Jilly. I sit back and lean my head on his shoulder.

"How?" Jilly asks. I know she is just hanging on by a thread. "Our hands are tied and we are bound for the cells. You heard Sir Meredith. He's going to execute us."

I sit up and move to sit next to Jilly. It is all the comfort I can give her. "There are others. We have friends outside, and, if you are right, we have friends within."

"Your friends outside have forgotten about you," Jilly says. "And if the rest within are cowards like me, then we are all doomed."

"I refuse to believe that he will execute us," I say. And not because he's my father. But because of Jilly and Pace.

"But he can lock us in a cell and forget about us," Jilly says.

"As long as we are alive we have hope," Pace says. "Which is why we agreed to our charade in the first place. You remember, Jilly. Live and fight another day."

"I am afraid my little speech was all the fight I have in me."

"Have faith, Jilly," I say. I look at Pace and he smiles, but it doesn't reach his eyes. I am afraid for all of us that we do not have enough faith to get through this latest predicament. The people and the things that I believed in are no longer there.

All too soon we reach the government building. We pull around to the side and, just like before, into a covered area with a door so those on the street will not see who is brought into custody. I look for Findley, and he is nowhere to be found. The three of us are herded into the building and down the stairs to the cells. Pruitt gives Jilly and me an evil leer as he picks up his keys.

"Should I put them with the other chickie?" he asks.

"No," our guard says. "Sir Meredith instructed to put the two girls in one cell and put Bratton with the prisoner that came in with them. We are to move the other female prisoner up to this one's room."

So I am being replaced. I can only wonder who else has had the misfortune of crossing my father.

"Bring them on, then," Pruitt says. We are led into the long hall. Jilly and I are shoved into the first cell on the left. A guard quickly unties our hands and then steps out, slamming the door behind him. I run to the small window in the door and look out. I can barely see anything that isn't directly in front of me, but I can tell by the noise that they are putting Pace in with Levi, in a cell that is as far away from ours as it can be.

I turn to Jilly, who stands in the middle of the cell with her arms wrapped around herself. Her party dress will give her little protection against the cold dark walls. The cell is remarkably like Levi's in its simplicity. One cot bolted to the wall with a ratty blanket and a toilet in the corner. I lead Jilly to the cot and we sit. I wrap my arms around her. As Pruitt comes back down the corridor he slams the door shut on our little cell window. We are in the dark. For once I wish I could not see in the dark. Then I would not know how dire our situation is.

"At least when we die we will be warm again," Jilly says.

I fear we will be too warm before we are allowed to die. I fear we will burn.

· 12 ·

It is so very ironic that I have just now realized something," Jilly
says. We lay side by side on the cot. Jilly uses the blanket because she is so very cold. I am more used to the damp darkness,
plus I have on the leather pants and boots. I put my shirt on as soon
as Pruitt closed our tiny window, and it helps to keep me warm.

"What's that?" I ask.

"We live in a bubble. I don't mean the people of the dome so
much as us . . . the royals." She smiles briefly, nothing more than a
flash of her teeth and a flex of her mouth. "You are the only ones
who call us that. We say titled or the gentry. It's just another way
of saying privileged, really. But what we really are is sheltered.
Oblivious. It is really so very sad when you think about it. All those
generations just pretending that all was right with the world, when
in reality we were trapped in a bubble inside a bigger bubble."

"At least you are trying to do something about it," I say. "You
saved lives. James, Lyon, Lucy, David, and Harry would surely
have died if you hadn't stepped up when you did."

"Do you think they will know what has happened to us?"

"I would rather think about seeing them soon."

"Oh, Wren, do you always see the best in everything?"

"I don't know," I confide. "I'd rather think it's just hoping for the best." I do not add that I never seem to see the best in myself. That all I see is the mistakes I've made and the things I should have done differently.

"I think you do," Jilly goes on, and I let her because it is so much better than laying quietly in the dark and letting our fears consume us. "I think you bring out the best in people. You make them want to be better than they are. You inspire people."

"I don't know how," I reply. "I know I certainly could do better myself. I had a golden opportunity tonight to tell everyone about the outside world, and I didn't take it."

"They would not have listened," Jilly says with a quiet laugh. "The minute you opened your mouth you would have been carried out and locked away. You would have been declared insane and no one would ever see you again."

"Has that ever happened?" I ask.

"I've heard of it happening. Our lives are so small that any incident, even if it happened a hundred years ago, is gossiped about for an eternity, it seems."

"It would be a simple way to get rid of your enemies," I conclude.

"Indeed," Jilly agrees. "The offenders could have simply been put outside to fend for themselves."

"They more than likely wound up with the rovers as their captives," I conclude. Which reminded me of what we were originally discussing. "Findley said I had a captive audience. I should have found a way to make them listen. I was selfish, though. I wanted to see Pace."

"He loves you so much," Jilly says. "You are all he would talk about. Yes, he told me about the world out there, but so much of it was centered on you."

"I am surprised," I confess. "Things were not going too well between us."

"Because of the American boy?"

"Levi."

"Yes, he told me of that also."

"I hurt him. I didn't mean to. It just happened."

"He must be very special to have turned your head."

"That is one way to put it," I say."

"You are very lucky, Wren. "To have two such wonderful young men in love with you."

"I don't deserve it," I say.

"But you do," Jilly replies. "And not because you are special, even though you are. Because everyone should have someone who loves them and someone to love. Otherwise, why even bother to exist? Because, without love, that is all life would be—just existence."

"Is that what you are fighting for Jilly?" I ask. "A chance to love?" When we met, she said she joined the seekers because she did not want to marry the man the matchmakers had chosen for her. The royals may have riches and comfort, but they also had to observe strict guidelines of who they could marry in order to keep their bloodlines from crossing too many times.

"Isn't that worth fighting for? You wanted the freedom to choose your path. So do I." She yawns. "I can only hope that this path does not lead to a dead end for both of us." She yawns again. "I can't believe that I am actually considering falling asleep. I thought I would be too frightened."

"Sleep if you can," I say.

"I'll just close my eyes for a minute," she says.

I stay quiet until I hear the steady breathing that lets me know Jilly has fallen asleep, finally. I am glad she is sleeping. I don't know what tomorrow will bring, but I do know it will be easier to face with rest. If death can ever be easy to face.

Jilly said that Pace still loved me, and he declared his love once more this night. When we came back into the dome I was not so certain of Pace's love. I know I hurt him when he saw Levi and me kissing after the battle. It is not that I meant to kiss Levi; it was more a result of the battle. We were both overcome with emotion after nearly dying.

With Pace, everything between us happened so fast. We only had each other to count on. I want to be sure my feelings for him are true, not just the result of the fact that we could have easily died and we did not know what moment would be our last.

Here we are, in the same situation once more. I do not know what the morning will hold for any of us. I know I do not want to go to my death with this uncertainty, nor would I wish it on Pace or Levi.

Pace has always remained true. No matter what. He could have very easily put me and his problems behind him. He was welcomed back as a hero, even though it was one of my father's lies. He had everything he could ever want right before him. I suppose knowing there was more than the dome changed his perspective.

Pace could never live a lie. No more than I could. And we shouldn't have to. No one should. I refuse to believe that this is the end of us. That we have come so far only to be beaten now. Yet I knew coming back into the dome was a mistake.

Now that Jilly is quiet I hear the background noises that fill this prison beneath the streets. Somewhere a pipe drips water. The prisoner in the cell next to us has a deep cough, one that makes me think he will not survive much longer. I hear the creak of a door

and then the hard sound of boots against the stone floor in the corridor. Another door creaks and I can hear the rumble of a man's
voice and the higher one of a response. Whoever she is she must
have been in the cell right across from ours. The walls are too thick
to catch the words, but I hear a woman's voice going on and on. It
must be the one they are moving to my room. A door slams again,
and quiet once more fills my ears, except for the steady drip drip of
water from a broken pipe. My eyes burn with exhaustion, yet I
resist the urge to sleep. I have to be ready in case Findley decides to
make a move to help us. The sound of Jilly's steady breathing finally
lulls me, and, in spite of my determination to fight off sleep, I close
my eyes.

◆

I dream about fire. It surrounds me yet it does not burn me. That
does not take the fear away. I know it is just a matter of time before
I am consumed, just like Alex. The flames lick higher than my head.
Beyond them, I hear voices calling out to me. It seems as if everyone
I know is searching for me in the flames. I turn from one way, to the
other, calling out to Pace, Levi, and Jilly. Finally I see faces through
the flames, and there are so many of them that I cannot count them
all. All of my friends from the outside. Those that we lost, including
Peggy and the man Stone, who saved my life when I was almost
killed by the rover woman. They spin around me and play hide-and-
seek with the flames until the only remaining face I can see is my
own. For some reason, I think it is a mirror, but I soon realize that
it is my mother, Maggie.

"I only wanted out," she cries out, desperately, and reaches for
me as if she is imploring me to understand. But I don't. Did she
want out of the dome, or merely an escape from her life as a shiner?
Did she feel trapped by me when she realized she was pregnant? I

realize that I will never have a chance to know, unless for some miraculous reason she can tell me now.

I try to go to her, but the flames are too high and too hot. They soar upward, twining around me and blocking me from everyone I know, until the only way I can look is up. A burnt skull hovers in the circle above the flames, and as it opens its mouth to speak, I realize it is all that is left of Alex.

I awaken with a start, thinking, as I look up at the dark and dirty ceiling above me, that I am back home in my bed, in the cave house I shared with my grandfather. I am slow to realize that it was the closing of the cell door that interrupted the nightmare. I hold my breath, wondering if someone is in the cell with us, sent to kill us in our sleep. After a long, long moment I know that we are alone, that whoever was here is now gone.

Jilly is still asleep next to me. I ease myself up and she rolls over into the space I occupied, already missing the warmth I offered. A bundle lies on the floor just inside the door. My jacket and pants, along with the shawl and the small handbag I carried to the party.

If we are all to die, then why did someone bother to return my stuff to me? I quickly remove the pretty green dress and change into my regular clothes. As I pick up my jacket something falls out and lands with a clatter on the floor. I freeze in place, afraid that Pruitt heard the noise beyond my cell, but all is quiet, except for the coughing in the next cell. I look down.

It is a knife. I pick it up. It is not much longer than my hand. I prick my finger on the end and see a drop of blood ooze out. I stick my finger in my mouth and slide the blade into my boot. It has to be from Findley. There is no one else to help us.

I shake out the shawl, as it is the only thing left in hopes that there is a note or something that will inform me of Findley's plan. There is nothing. I search inside the handbag, and it holds nothing beyond the things I put inside it. I slide my goggles down on my neck and cover Jilly with the green dress and shawl. My inner clock tells me that it is a few hours still until dawn. I sit on the end of the cot and wait.

◆

Waiting is the hardest part, especially when you do not know what you are waiting for. Morning comes and with it a bowl of something I could not identify and Jilly could not even eat. The day drags by, slowly, with no noise coming from the corridor and only the coughing in the next cell to let us know we've not been abandoned to die.

"I feel the worst for my parents," Jilly says when we can no longer tolerate the silence and the waiting. "Because of my brother."

"I didn't know you have a brother." We sit side by side on the narrow cot. "Was he at the party?" I try to remember if I saw a boy with bright red hair like Jilly's.

Jilly shakes her head. "He died when he was six. Just a few months past the date of replacement."

"Replacement?"

"Not only are we told who to marry," she explains. "We are also limited to how many children we can have. Two is the limit. If one dies before his or her sixth birthday you can apply for another. Since most couples don't really love each other, it keeps it simple as far as birth control is concerned. They simply stop sleeping together after they have replaced themselves with the next generation."

I nod my understanding. I always thought the royals had nothing to complain about, as they had nothing to worry about and all the privileges of life in the dome. But having your husbands and wives chosen for you, without any thought given to love or even compatibility would be horrible. And then knowing you had to sleep with them to keep the dynasty going. We shiners might not have had much, but we did have the right to choose.

"What happened to your brother?" I ask.

"A silly accident," Jilly says. "He was playing with his toys at the top of the staircase and took a tumble down. It broke his neck. I was only three at the time. I barely remember it. But I do remember my parent's devastation when they were told they could not have another child. Not that they wanted to replace Robbie. But because they were . . . are very much in love and could have experienced that joy again. But another child, especially a boy, would have upset the balance of the continuing population. And now they've lost their daughter. Not that I was that special, but still, my father's name and our line will expire with me. It's rather sad when you think of all the trouble they went to to preserve it." She grins ruefully in the darkness.

"It is so very personal for you," I say. "You've seen your parents suffering and you want to change it."

"I'm not that unselfish, Wren," Jilly says with a laugh. I am glad she can laugh and not get caught up in our desperate circumstances. "I just want to spare myself the same sort of suffering, especially with the lout the matchmaker wanted to put me with. He is quite insufferable, and that's his good point."

"I think you are terribly brave," I say. I need her to be brave for what is to come, whatever that may be. "And who says you, or your father's line is going to die?"

"You are not that good of a liar," Jilly says with a jab of her elbow to my ribs. "You've had a peek into my world. Why don't you tell me about yours?"

"It's very different," I say. "Or it was. It is gone now. All destroyed in the flood."

"I am so sorry," Jilly says. "You lost your family?"

"I didn't have one to lose," I say. "My grandfather was all I had, and he died a few days earlier."

"I'm so sorry. Pace said Peggy died also. I know her and Adam were very much in love. She went to the library with me that day we all met. She was quite nice. And very pretty."

"She was my best friend," I say. "I miss her."

Jilly squeezes my hand. "I would very much like to be your friend," she says.

"You already are." I squeeze her hand in return.

"So tell me about a day in the life of a shiner."

"We all lived in a big cavern underground," I say. "It is kind of like the dome, only smaller and darker. A stream ran through it and we had a waterwheel on it that gave us power for our lights."

"For some reason, I thought you lived totally in the dark."

"No, we had lights strung all through the tunnels. It made it less lonesome down there," I explain. "My job was to carry the coal. I had a team of ponies that pulled the carts, and we went from tunnel to tunnel to collect the coal that was dug each night."

"How old were you when you started working?"

"Thirteen. We go to school when we are four and into the mines at thirteen. Most of us die before forty of black lung. That's when the coal dust builds up in your lungs."

"I'm sorry," Jilly says as if it is her fault.

"It doesn't sound like much, but at least we had some freedom," I explain. "We could choose who we wanted to marry, and could marry for love, like Adam and Peggy."

"I envied them that," Jilly says. "I would like to be in love like that."

We keep talking throughout the day. We share stories from our lives until our voices are hoarse. I am not surprised at how different our lives are, even though we come from the same world. When we have exhausted the world inside the dome, I tell her about the things I saw outside, including the things the Hatfields shared with us about the world.

Evening finally comes, with a repeat of the meal we were served at breakfast. I worry for Levi. If this is all he's had for the weeks he's been prisoner, then his strength surely will not last. We finally fall asleep again, not knowing anything more about what awaits us than we did when we were placed in the cell.

I wake the next morning to Pruitt standing over us. "It's time," he says. Two more bluecoats are with him. Neither is Findley, and I am beginning to worry that he does not have a plan to save us.

"Time for what?" I ask.

He doesn't answer. Instead he steps back. I wake Jilly. We both stand, and the bluecoats tie our hands before us and lead us out of the cell. Every cell door is open, except for the one across from ours. A bluecoat stands at each one, except for the one Pace and Levi share, where there are two. A prisoner is led out of a cell down the row, and I am astonished to see it is Rosalyn's husband, Colm.

"Wren!" he starts, and the bluecoat who has him jabs him in the stomach with a thick club.

"Quiet!" the bluecoat yells. Colm grimaces and doubles over as his captor shoves him against the wall.

"Rosalyn and Stella are alive," I say, and the bluecoat who has me jerks me around. "They are outside," I call out only to be rewarded with a slap across my cheek that turns my head. My cheek burns and my eyes blur, still I can see Levi and Pace as they are led out of their cells with their hands bound.

"Both of you stay quiet!" Pruitt yells at Colm and me.

"Leave her be!" Pace says.

"All of you!" Pruitt yells again.

"Why?" I say. "Are you afraid to hear the truth?" Pruitt rewards me this time with a hard strike from his fist to my jaw. I stagger back from the blow and land against the wall. My vision is blurred with white lights of pain. I hear cries from everyone. Jilly, Pace, Levi, even Colm. I blink, trying to see the madness that erupts around me, but I cannot seem to find the will to breathe, much less stand straight and speak.

I am somehow on my feet. I hear Jilly crying, and my eyes finally swim into focus. Pace, Levi, and Colm are on their knees, breathing hard, with blood on their hands and faces. The bluecoats, more than I can count, do not look much better. I think they won only because there were more of them. If Levi and Pace had not had their hands bound, I think perhaps they would have had a chance.

"Wren!" Both Pace and Levi say.

"I'm here," I say. My jaw pains me and I wince. "I'm okay." I realize Pace and Jilly do not understand what *okay* means, but Levi smiles and nods and I can see the tension leaving their shoulders.

I decide it is best to stay quiet for now. More prisoners are led from the cells, all shiners, seven in all, men that we presumed were killed in the flood. The one who was in the cell next to me I recognize as one of my grandfather's friends, Bill. He can't seem to stop coughing, as if every move he makes rattles his lungs.

"Where are you taking us?" Jilly asks Pruitt. He doesn't answer. We are propelled along by shoves and poked with thick sticks to the staircase. We go up two flights to the ground floor and then down the hall that leads to the closed shed where the carriage is kept. I wonder if it has enough steam left to get us where we are supposed to go. I fear that if our destination is our execution then, yes, we should make it there.

We are shoved into the back of the carriage and the door locked. There are so many of us that three sit on the floor with four on each bench. Pace, Jilly, Levi, and I all sit on one side. We feel the weight of the guards as they climb on board. I wonder if the carriage can roll with all the weight it carries, but it does as the doors are opened and we roll into the dim light of dawn.

"They are alive?" Colm asks as soon as we take off. "Outside?"

"What do you mean, outside?" a shiner asks. I think his name is Tobias.

"We made it outside," I say to Tobias, and then to Colm, "They were safe the last time I saw them."

"Thank God," Colm replies, and all the shiners are looking at me. "How?"

"The flood opened up new tunnels," I explain. "We just followed the river and it led us outside."

"Who made it?" Tobias asks.

"George, Rosalyn, Sally. James, Adam, Alcide, and Peter and his sister Nancy. The children from the school. I don't know all their names."

"Peter is my nephew," Tobias says.

"If the children survived, then my Sarah should be among them," one of the shiners says.

"Yes, Sarah is there."

"And my Robbie," another says. He describes a little boy, and I smile and nod.

"I know him." They all have hope now. They are all that is left of my people, and I am not sure of all their names. But we all know, no matter what happens, some of us will survive. We will not be forgotten.

"Anyone else?" Tobias asks. I shake my head. There is no need to tell them about Eddie and his son and how he died falling over the cliff. I look at Pace. I know he is thinking of them also.

"I am so sorry," Levi says to the shiners and then looks at me. "Pace told me what happened. Do—"

"Who are you?" Colm interrupts.

"A friend from across the sea," I say. "Rosalyn is with his family. They are helping us. This is Levi, and Jilly is a royal who—"

"Who angered the powers that be or she wouldn't be here," Tobias finishes for me. "What is to become of us?"

"We're not heading to the dais," Pace says. He sits closest to the door with the window. I look up and see that we are indeed heading away from it. It looks as if we are on the same route as the morning my father took me out.

"Thank God," Jilly says. I do not feel her sense of relief. I know my father has burned people outside the dome entrance as a warning. Just because we are not going to the dais does not mean we are not going to our deaths.

"It could just mean they don't want it to be public," I say. I don't want to give anyone false hope, for anyone to think we are going to be free. I know my father well enough to know there will be a price to be paid for our rebellion.

"We are to be executed?" Colm asks.

"We don't know what is going to happen," I say.

"Anything is better than wasting away in that cell," Bill says.

"I can die happy, knowing Rosalyn and Stella are free," Colm agrees.

I fear that Bill's time is short, especially if we are going outside. At least he will be spared the agony of the fires, if that is our final destination.

"Wren," Levi says quietly after all the interruptions. "Do you think our friend has a plan to help us?" He doesn't mention Findley's name, a wise move on his part. But he does make me remember something. Something that I had forgotten after being punched and having the realization that Colm and the others were alive.

"No plan, but maybe some hope," I say. I reach down with my bound hands and pull the knife from my boot. In a matter of seconds Levi, Pace, and I have cut our bindings and the knife is quietly passed around. Levi keeps it when we are done, sliding it into his boot as Pace keeps watch through the window.

"We don't know how many are on the carriage," he says. "Or what we will face when we get out. It will be hard to surprise them," he continues. "They can easily pin us inside."

"We'll need a distraction," Levi says.

"I am certain I can work up a good cry and faint," Jilly says. "Just let the ladies out first."

I peer over Pace's shoulder out the window. Of all of us, we are the only two who know the streets of the dome. I recognize the street we are on and Pace nods in agreement. We are headed toward the building that has replaced the burnt warehouse. We are going outside the dome.

The only question that remains is are we going to our freedom or to our deaths?

· 13 ·

I am suddenly so cold that I shiver. I know it is fear and apprehension that has a hold on me. Pace puts his arms around me,
and I am grateful for his warmth. Levi has his head together with
the shiners, telling them what to do when we stop. I marvel at the
trust they show him. I know it is because leadership comes naturally to Levi. If we had known someone like him inside, someone
who could really lead us, instead of me and my many mistakes,
then perhaps we would not be in this predicament now.

I also wonder again what has happened to Lyon and why he hasn't
rescued us. What if we escape the dome and find that everything we
fought for is gone? I do not think I could stand to see the look on
Colm's face if we fight to get away, only to find that Rosalyn and
Stella are not there. Or the look on Levi's face if his family has deserted him. Surely they haven't, but I am beginning to run out of
excuses as to why Lyon has not helped us.

I look out the window. We are on the street where I was first
taken by the filchers. It is deserted, as there is no reason for anyone
to be in this part of the dome now that the fans are gone. Light fills

the dome now and I can actually see a slight shadow of the carriage, along with shadows on the side. The air above must be clearing, at last.

"There are more guards than we thought," I say to Levi. "Some are walking beside us."

He leans over me to peer out the window. "They are carrying rifles," he adds. I look and see the long silhouettes of guns. The odds are definitely not in our favor.

"Wren, you go first," Levi instructs. "Jilly, give her time to evaluate the situation before you react. It could be that we will be setting ourselves up for useless violence."

"Do you think they could simply be letting us go?" Jilly asks.

"I always hope for the best," Levi replies with a very sweet smile. He looks past Jilly, and I know his message is intended for me.

We keep going and I can see the empty ruin where the warehouse was. The only place we could be going is outside. The carriage pulls up, then backs up to the hastily constructed building that covers the exit to the outside, and finally rolls to a stop. We all still have our bindings around our wrists and disguise them by holding the cut ends in our palms. When the door is opened I wait for one of the bluecoats to help me down. I have no place to go but ahead into the building, as the way is lined with bluecoats with guns. To try anything now would be suicide. I like our chances better when we are outside. I turn to look at Jilly before I go inside. She nods quickly in understanding. She is to do nothing.

The building is full of scarabs. They are shoved into what looks like stalls, men, women, and children all locked behind a fence made of wire. There are so many of them in such a small space, and the smell of their bodies and their fear sends me staggering in shock. They stare at me, some with hatred and others with pity. A few stick their hands out as I go by, pushed on by my guard, silently imploring me to help. I can tell by their gaunt faces that they are starving and hope has long since left them. I hear Jilly's gasp of shock behind me. No royal, not even our so-called king, is worth the cost of this suffering. I am hurried along until we come to the steps that lead down to the tunnel that leads outside, where my father and Findley are waiting.

"How you can look at yourself in the mirror each morning is a mystery to me," I say to my father.

"Such hateful words, and after I've come to see you off," he replies.

"Hopefully for the last time," I grind out from between clenched teeth. Just when I thought I could not get any angrier or hate him any more, I discover something else happening that astounds me. The innocent are suffering and he is the cause and he feels no guilt about it. All because of his precious royals. But maybe now, since Jilly is with us, it will be the thing that makes them step up and say "enough."

I can only pray that it happens in time to save all of us. My father jerks his head forward to the tunnel. Findley precedes me and my father falls in behind me. Jilly comes behind him with another bluecoat behind her. They are not taking any chances with our causing a problem in front of the scarabs. If only there was something we could do, some way to free them and us, but I know any move we make in here will result in more senseless deaths. I follow Findley into the tunnel. I hear the footsteps of my friends behind me and the heavy coughing of Bill. He won't survive the transition. I know he won't, but there is nothing I can do about it. He will die, whatever happens, and I cannot sacrifice the rest of us for him. I concentrate on keeping my hands together as if they are still tied. I do not want to jeopardize this escape any more than my father wants me to stay inside the dome. We will both be well rid of each other as far as I am concerned.

There are guards at the tunnel door and they quickly salute as one opens the door. I turn my face to the warm stale air that greets me. If I am to die today, at least it will be in the fresh air of outside. I can tell by the brightness of the light that it will be a sunny day. Poor Jilly and the shiners will have a time of it with the sun, if we last that long. I hear Jilly's gasp of wonder as she enters the tunnel behind my father.

Findley reaches the door. The bar across it is thick and strong so no one could break through from the outside. I notice it is on some type of hinge so Findley can lift it easily. Poor Alex. He was so close to being free. Perhaps he would have been if he had not decided to come back in for Lucy, who is now outside.

I can only pray that Alex's fate does not await us. The door opens and with it comes the rush of fresh air from outside. My ears pop with the change in pressure, and Findley steps to the side as I walk gratefully into the morning light and find Ellen gagged and tied to a post. Several more posts form a line across from the entrance. Three of them hold blackened and rotting bodies. They have been there long enough that it is impossible to tell who they were, or even if they were men, women, or a mixture of both. Two bluecoats stand guard with rifles. Behind the posts is a stand of young trees that carry down a slope. The distant sea glints between them.

The sight of Ellen startles me and I stop in my tracks. All the hope I felt as I walked through the tunnels slides into my stomach, and I choke back the bile that threatens to rise in my throat. This is not good, this it not good at all. My father puts a hand on my back and nudges me forward and to the side so the rest of us can file out.

Jilly looks around in disbelief and gasps at the sight of the bodies. "Don't look at the sun," I warn her. I should have warned everyone. Another bluecoat comes behind Jilly, then Levi, then another bluecoat, and then Pace.

"What are you doing to her?" Pace snarls at my father as soon as he sees his mother. In his anger, he forgets that his hands are supposed to be tied. Levi reacts as soon as Pace drops his hands to run to his mother, and I am close behind him. I jump on the back of the bluecoat who follows Pace while Levi tackles one of the bluecoats with the rifles. Colm is quick to react also. He turns to attack the bluecoat who follows him.

I wrap my arm tightly around the bluecoat's neck and press hard while he tries to shake me off. I chance a look at Findley and see that he is frowning, yet he makes no move to help either side. Meanwhile Pace and Levi are grappling with two more bluecoats. Findley moves to my father, and I pray that he is going to help us. I hear yelling in the tunnel and the sharp bark of a gunshot. Jilly shrieks, and out of the corner of my eye I catch the swirl of her skirts and the bright flare of her hair.

The bluecoat I am fighting tries to throw me off. I wrap my legs around his waist and he backs into the tunnel, hard, knocking the breath from me. I do not let go and he staggers forward. He has to be running out of air. His momentum carries him forward and we crash into a post. The post breaks and he flies forward, off balance, and we tumble into the stand of trees. He falls headfirst and the momentum of his fall pitches me off his back so that I fly off and land in front of him. I put out my hands to break my fall and he careens into me and we roll together, down the hill. The way he flops around makes me realize that he is unconscious, finally, from my strangling him. That does not help with stopping either one of us, as I am tangled up in his limbs. I manage to push him away as we roll over and over and he slams into a tree. I twist around so I am feet first and manage to stop myself. I hear a crunch of bones and know that the bluecoat will wake up to find something broken. If he wakes up at all.

I lay still for a moment, to catch my breath and take a mental inventory of my injuries. Aside from some bumps and bruises, I feel fine. Still, my heart is pounding as if it is trying to beat its way out of my chest. I stare up at the treetops and at the way they sway in the breeze. After the weeks in the dome I was beginning to wonder if I had imagined the outside. My heart finally slows down and my breathing levels out and the scent of fresh dirt and evergreens fill my senses.

That is when I realize I don't hear anything up above me. I flip over on my stomach and crawl back up the incline. Levi, Pace, Colm, Jilly, and Tobias sit with their hands behind their heads and guns aimed at them. Ellen is still tied to the post. Bill and the other four shiners are in their death throes. One is on his hands and knees gagging up a thick black substance before he collapses, face down. My father stands over him and nudges him with the toe of his boot.

Something jabs me in my back and I look over my shoulder to see Findley poking me with a rifle. "Really?" I say.

"He'd never believe that you'd take off without your friends." He jerks his head, signifying I should get up. "Who has the knife?"

"I do," I lie, because right now I am not sure if I can trust him. "I lost it down there."

He pulls one from his pocket. I immediately see it is not the same one that Levi slid into his boot. "Oh look. I just found it," he says. "Let's go."

"Are you going to burn us?" I stand and put my hands on top of my head like the others.

"No," Findley says. "He has other plans for you. He wants you to disappear, so he's telling everyone you escaped." He grimaces and then looks at me. "His way of saying he loves you, I guess."

I shake my head. I am certain my father does not know how to love anyone or anything, except for his position. "Someday his lies will catch up with him."

"For your sake, I hope it is sooner than later."

I have no idea what to make of that comment, so I continue on until we join the rest and Findley gives me an encouraging shove so that I fall in line between Levi and Jilly. He then goes and unties Ellen from the post and forces her to kneel beside Pace.

"What are you doing to us?" Ellen says as soon as Findley removes her gag. "You have no right."

"I have every right," my father says.

"You lied to me!" Ellen exclaims. "You said if we cooperated everything would be fine."

"Your son chose not to cooperate."

Ellen opens her mouth to protest but stops suddenly when Pace simply says, "Stop." I cannot see his face when he looks at her, but hers shows her devastation and disbelief at the hand fate has dealt her.

Findley hands my father the knife he showed me. "She had this on her."

My father walks up to me. "Where did you get this?" he asks. "Did someone give it to you?"

"I've had it ever since I came in," I lie. "Your man missed it when he searched me." I am not about to give up Findley. Not when I think he can still help us. Actually helping us now would be wonderful. My father gives Findley a look and he shrugs. "What are you going to do with us?" I ask.

"Believe it or not, I do have some use for you." He waves at two of the bluecoats who stand off to the side. They kneel and one lights a fuse. A small tube shoots up in the air, much like the flare I used the night we were attacked. Who could they be signaling?

Levi looks at me and grins. I don't know where we are bound, but I do know that Lyon will surely check on the flare. Or perhaps it is Lyon that is being signaled. Still, I cannot forget Findley's parting words to me. I do not think our escape will be so easy.

The bluecoats who are not guarding us pick up the bodies of the shiners who died and pile them off to the side behind us. Bill and the other four, whose names I cannot recall since they were not of my generation. There were just faces to me, some I passed in my work, others I saw in the village. They saw me as Elias's girl and that's what they called me. I was never Wren to them; I was more an extension of my grandfather. And that was fine with me. But now I feel bad because I have nothing to call them as I pray for their departed souls. So many of us are lost that it is easier to count the survivors.

I look at Colm and Tobias. Their faces are grim and pale, and I know they are wondering why they lived while the others died. I should have warned them. My life is so full of *should of*s that it is impossible to count the mistakes I've made. Warning them would not have changed the outcome, no matter what.

The sun is just now reaching the treetops. Jilly looks around in wonder. "Don't look at the sun," I warn her again. "Colm, Tobias, it will blind you if you look at it. Jilly, keep your skin covered as much as you can." She is still in her pretty party dress, but she has the use of my shawl that she tied over her shoulders before we left the prison. It droops to one side now after her tussle.

"I never dreamed it was real," Colm says.

"Quiet," Findley growls.

My hands, like everyone else's, are still placed on the back my head. "May I put my goggles on?" I ask. "To protect my eyes?"

Findley nods. "You can keep your hands down," he says to me. "You too," to Jilly.

Jilly gratefully puts her arms down and immediately rubs her upper arms before rearranging the shawl over her shoulders. I wonder how much physical stress she will be able to handle. Her skin is very fair and I know the sun will fry her. Hopefully that will not be such an issue once Lyon arrives. "What about my parents?" Jilly asks my father, who is growing impatient with the wait. "Are they prisoners also?"

"Nothing will happen to them," my father says. "They have done nothing to cause any problems."

"Because you wouldn't dare touch the gentry," Ellen spouts angrily. "What about me? I've done nothing wrong."

"I thought it was your wish to be with your son," my father intones, as if he is now bored with all of us.

"He dares too much," Pace says to his mother. "If Jilly's parents protest too much they will be the next ones to fall victim to his lies." Pace looks at my father and says the words I've repeated to him over and over again. "When will it be enough? How many more good people are going to die to protect your lies?" Pace turns his head at an angle as if to see my father better. "Is it all about power for you? Because, in all honesty, you cannot continue to believe that staying locked up inside is for the best."

This is the first time I've ever seen Pace speak up like this. Before I was the one doing the talking and he was supporting me. Of course most of the talking was done in my world and to my people. Pace looks at Findley and the rest of the bluecoats who guard us. "Look at this beautiful world." Everyone except my father, Levi, and I turn their heads to gaze in wonder at the things around us. I realize they cannot help themselves. Yet I keep my eyes on Pace and my father to see what will happen next.

I have already noticed that in the few weeks that I've been inside things have changed greatly. The green of the trees seems greener. Some are covered with pink and white blossoms similar to the ones on the apple trees that grew on the rooftop of the building I always went to each morning. The sky is bluer and the clouds fluffier and the breeze holds a hint of warmth that it did not have before. Birds flit from branch to branch, chirping loudly. The earth has come alive to welcome us back.

"Why do you turn your back on it?" Pace continues. "Why do you continue to live in fear? Isn't something worth having worth fighting for?" I can tell the bluecoats don't like Pace's mention of living in fear. They shift uncomfortably and look away. I am certain it is because it struck too close to home for them to ignore. How many of them knew Pace before all the trouble started? Or knew his father, who died before he was born? How many of them believe as Findley does and are too scared to say anything to one another for fear of reprisal?

My father approaches Pace. "You know nothing," he says quietly enough so that only Pace and the few of us around will hear. The fact that he feels the need to defend himself to Pace makes me realize that Pace has struck a nerve with my father also. "All the responsibility is mine. Their lives are in my hands."

"Are you so afraid of failing?" Pace asks. "Are not we proof that you have already failed?"

My father strikes Pace across the face with the back of his hand. The strike is so hard that it knocks Pace, who still has his hands clamped behind his head, off balance and he almost crashes into his mother. He catches himself in time and rights himself. He never takes his eyes from my father. Levi and I both jerk in protest at the offense. A rifle barrel poked at the back of his head quickly stops Levi.

"It isn't too late," I quickly say, hoping to stop any more violence directed at Pace or Levi. "If we all work together . . ." My voice trails off as a group of rovers come into view. They come from the same direction as the catwalk, where the *Quest* was docked. Their appearance makes me wonder if it is still. There are at least twenty of them and they are all wearing weapons. Long rifles, axes, knives, and one has a sword strapped to his hip. Their clothing is a mixture of castoffs and hide, and the smell of unwashed bodies taints the air. I see only one woman in this group, and she looks just as fierce as the one I killed.

"What have you done?" I stand up and step between my father and Pace. "Surely you are not turning us over to them."

"It's a better fate than being burnt alive, wouldn't you say?" He turns on his heel and goes to meet the leader of the rovers. Four bluecoats join my father with their weapons readied.

I look at Findley. He shrugs. There is nothing more he can do for us. If he makes a move he will share our fate.

"This isn't good?" Colm asks as a bluecoat nudges him to his feet.

"It isn't," I reply.

Jilly looks at the rovers and then at Pace. He must have told her the stories of their viciousness. Panic fills her and she begins breathing hard. Levi looks momentarily confused, and then he shakes his head. He still believes Lyon will help us. But it doesn't make sense. How could the rovers have passed right by Lyon's location without notice? And if they did, will we go unnoticed also?

"What's to become of us?" Ellen's voice rises in panic as seven rovers come forward with rope in their hands. Each one takes one of us and ties our hands and then loops the rope around our necks. The one who claims Jilly sneaks in a few pinches and she shrieks and jumps, which only makes all of them laugh.

I stare at the one who has claimed me, daring him to do the same. He doesn't look much older than me. His blond beard is weak and scraggly, and his face smeared with dirt, but his teeth, at least, are decent. As I stare at him he looks away first.

He must feel some shame at what they are doing. I may be

desperately grasping for some sort of humanity. I do not know how anyone can retain it if they live with the rovers. I know their survival has not been as easy as ours, but at what cost?

The rope burns my neck as my captor pulls on it. I put my bound hands on it to keep him from choking me as I am led along with the rest of my friends to the trail. The rest of the rovers surround us and the smell makes me want to gag. Jilly does gag, as does Ellen, who is weeping, "What have they done, oh, what have they done?" How many tales did my father tell her to get her cooperation, and the poor soul believed all of them.

We go into the forest as a group, each of us led and cut off from the other by the rovers. I realize as the trees close around us that my father did not give me a parting word.

· 14 ·

Sunlight dapples through the trees as we march through the forest. Jilly is having problems. She keeps tripping over her dress in her dainty shoes. Colm and Tobias struggle also. I know they need rest after the purge of their lungs. There is no need to ask for help for either of them; the rovers are not known for their charity or compassion.

Finally the one who leads Jilly grows frustrated with her and pulls her off to the side of the trail. She shrieks in fear as he shoves her to the ground and pulls out his knife. All four men struggle against their bonds, but the effort serves only to tighten the ropes around their necks and choke them. Jilly tries to back away, but her captor keeps a tight hold on the rope. With the other hand he slices off her skirt to just below her knees and pitches her shoes into the dense undergrowth beside the trial. Then he hauls her up by the rope and shoves her back into the line.

My heart aches for her and the beating I know her feet will take. I am equipped to deal with this, as much as anyone can be, but Jilly is used to being pampered and has never had to do anything beyond lift a fork or spoon.

Lyon will help us. He has to.

I turn my head to look at Levi, who follows me with Pace and Ellen behind him. I am rewarded with a jerk on the rope, so I trudge onward. I listen to the sound of our troop moving through the forest and strain to hear the whistle that will tell me our rescue is imminent.

I hear nothing. Through the trees I can see the sun glinting off the water, and by its location I know we've been walking for two hours, maybe more. We have to be near the catwalk. Surely they don't plan to march us right by the *Quest*.

Something is not right. I know in my heart that the *Quest* is not there. Our troop is halted. I look ahead and see that we are near a clearing. It has to be the catwalk.

"Not a sound," my captor warns me. As if I'll be silent if screaming will save my life. We move onward, slower this time. I see Jilly limping ahead of me and look down and see blood on the track.

The trees open up and the sea gleams before us on the left. The breeze whips up from below, cleansing the horrid smell of the rovers from my nose. My hair flutters around my face. I should have tied it back when I had a chance. My kerchief is not doing me any good stuffed into my pants pocket.

I see Colm, Tobias, and Jilly ahead of me looking in wonder at the sea. There is no sign of the *Quest*. Maybe I'm wrong. Maybe we were farther away than I thought. Maybe there's another clearing along the trail. But then I hear the creak of metal, and we walk silently by the catwalk. I look to the left and see the trampled ground and the shorn grass from our campsite.

There is nothing except for the lonely sound of a gull soaring over the water. My heart sinks. We are doomed. Despite the pain from the rope around my neck, I twist around to look at Levi. He looks at me with eyes full of remorse and confusion. How could Lyon abandon his own nephew? And where are our friends? Have the rovers captured them? If so, then we are going to them. If so, then some of them are surely dead. And what about the children? The ponies? And my dear friend Jonah the cat?

I feel as if I'll be sick. And still we march onward. I know how far it is to the rovers' settlement. It will take us most of the day to get there.

Our guards seem much more relaxed once we enter the forest again. Why shouldn't they be? There is no one to stop them. I recognize the area as we move on. We pass the place where Levi and I first hid from the rovers with the deer, and then the place where we fought against them.

Jilly is limping badly. Colm and Tobias don't seem to be doing much better. They are so weak. The rovers press on. I hear Ellen crying behind me. The sun is directly overhead now. I can feel the heat of it on my shoulders. I am warm in my jacket. Jilly stumbles and falls forward, reaching out with her bound hands to catch herself. Her escort jerks roughly on her rope.

"Stop!" I say. The rovers ignore me as they laugh at Jilly, who struggles to rise. I crouch down in the middle of the trail.

"Get up." I am ready for his jerk. I already have my hands on the rope and when my escort moves to tug on it I pull back. He trips over his feet and I help him along by rolling beneath his legs as he falls toward me. He crashes into the underbrush along the trail. I jump to my feet, my heart pounding. Should I run? The thought of all the guns aimed at my back keeps me still. And right now there are several aimed at me. Everyone is silent, except for Jilly, who sobs softly. Levi gives me a half smile and Pace's eyes show their gratitude. I know he is worried over his mother.

"We need rest," I say. "What good will it do you if some of us drop dead before we get to wherever it is we are going?" I don't want them to know that I know anything about where we are going. I've killed some of them, and I am afraid if they know that they will seek retribution. I know they have a purpose for us, or they would not have come. Whatever it is, I am certain it's not good, but that doesn't mean they want us to die yet.

The rover who met with my father and the woman walk back to where I stand by the trail. He must be the leader of this expedition. I see the intelligence in his eyes, and he's somewhat cleaner than the rest. His hair is dark blond, and he wears it tied back with a piece of leather. He wears a beard, but it is trimmed, not wild and unkempt like the rest of them. The woman wears a hide vest that bares her muscular arms. Her hair is arranged in a series of braids that lead back to a thick tail of hair that sits high on her head and falls halfway down her back. The weight of it on her head must be heavy to bear. She wears hide pants and several gold chains around her neck that remind me of the delicate locket Zan loaned to me the night I dressed up for dinner. She is pretty in a wild and primitive way, yet her hold on her rifle is sure and the knives in her belt are lethal.

He goes to where my captor is still picking himself up and kicks him in the gut. He falls with a grunt, clutching his belly. The one who kicked him turns and speaks to me. "What's your ah-name?"

"Wren," I reply.

"The sir back there said not to ah-listen to your ah-nonsense."

"When I speak nonsense, I'll let you know," I reply. "But this isn't it. This is the truth. You want us alive, then you have got to let us rest."

He looks at the woman. She nods in agreement. "Let them ah-rest," he says to the rovers. "Set ah-guards forward and back," he instructs the woman, and she goes to assign the tasks. Then he walks over to where my guard is still trying to catch his breath and helps him up. I suddenly see a resemblance. They have to be brothers. He probably would have shot him if they weren't.

We are all guided rather roughly to the side of the trail. Colm and Tobias sink gratefully to the ground. I go to Jilly, and Levi joins me. Before I kneel next to Jilly I look over my shoulder at Pace. He is tending to his mother, but he senses my look and flashes me a grateful smile.

"Let me see your foot," Levi says. Jilly winces as he picks it up. Her feet are dark with dirt and there is a gash in her arch. "You must have stepped on a broken root," he says.

"I felt it," Jilly says. "I didn't know what it was."

"There are some splinters still inside," Levi explains. "I need to get them out. We can't risk infection." I hand him my kerchief. We still have miles to go, and I don't know how Jilly is going to make it.

"Do what you must," Jilly says bravely. She winces as Levi dabs at her injury with my kerchief. It is amazing that he can do as much with his hands bound. "Do you know where they are taking us?" Jilly asks me.

"I think to their settlement," I say. I look over my shoulder to see if anyone is listening. The rovers are all gathered on the other side of the trail while a few stand guard on the trail in both directions.

"What about your friends?" Jilly asks quietly. "Won't they help us? I thought they were close by."

"They were," I say.

"They are," Levi corrects me. His warm brown eyes are sad, and I see the doubt behind them. Is he trying to convince Jilly and me or just himself? He rips a strip of Jilly's dress off and ties it around her foot and she tries not to wince.

"If I had known we were going on a trek I would have dressed properly," Jilly says as she inspects the bandage. I smile, admiring her spunk. "Don't worry, Wren," she says. "This is still better than marrying that yob they picked for me."

"Now I'm sorry I didn't get a chance to meet him." I stuff my kerchief back in my pocket.

"Hopefully before this is all over with you will." Jilly smoothes her tattered skirt over her knees and adjusts her shawl. I'm glad for the trees so she doesn't burn and most glad for her spirit, but I am afraid that we are yet to see the worst of it. "I don't suppose we can get some water, do you think?"

I look at the rovers. They are drinking from hide bags that they wear strapped across their chests. The thought of drinking after any of them disgusts me, but I am thirsty, and I know Colm and Tobias have to be after their struggles. I look at Ellen. She leans against Pace and weeps quietly. If it were just the three of us, Pace, Levi, and I, I'd take my chances and run. But with Ellen and Jilly, I know we can't leave them. They would never make it on their own.

Where are Lyon and all of our friends?

"Could we have some water, please?" Levi asks the rover in charge. He frowns, but he does hand Levi his hide. I am surprised at this kindness. Levi gives it to Jilly to drink, and she does so gratefully. Then he hands it to me. There is plenty in the hide but there are those of us in more need. I take it to Ellen.

Pace rises to stand next to me as she drinks. "I can't believe they are gone," he says. "I never dreamed they would abandon us."

"Levi thinks they haven't," I say.

Pace takes my fingers into his, the closest he can come to a hand-clasp with our bonds. "I guess things didn't turn out how we planned."

"It has been pointed out to me that my lack of planning is what gets us into these predicaments."

He grins. "I'm not giving up. How about you?"

"That's about the only plan I have at the moment." I look into his beautiful blue eyes and I know he wants to kiss me. It would be so wonderful just to do so. To lean into Pace and have him wrap his arms around me and have him tell me that things will be fine, as long as we are together. Instead I have to settle for a quick squeeze of fingers before Ellen speaks.

"Stay away from my son."

"Mother," Pace says patiently. "What more has to happen before you realize that Wren is not the enemy?"

"Don't," I say. "There's no need."

"No," he replies. "There is." Pace kneels next to his mother. "Without Wren I would be dead. She saved my life. I love her. Not because she saved my life, but because she is strong and courageous and she believes and feels things deeply. Because she is beautiful and she sees the best in everyone." Pace looks up at me and smiles, and I cannot help but wistfully smile back even though I feel shame at how I've treated him. At how I've hurt him.

"The world as you knew it is ending," Pace says. "Whether you want it to or not. I have plans to fight for this beautiful new world because I believe in it. I would hope that you would join us."

"Do I have a choice?" she asks. "How are we to fight?" Her blue eyes are earnest, and without the hatred she felt for me shadowing them I see a stronger resemblance. Pace must be the image of his father, but he has his mother's eyes.

"As long as we keep hope, we are fighting," Pace says. "Are you finished?" he asks about the water.

She takes another drink and hands it to Pace who then hands it to me. "Drink," he says. I do, because I know he won't until he knows I am taken care of. The water is warm and tepid but it is also necessary so I swallow it gratefully. Pace drinks and hands it back to me. "You should see to your friends."

"Colm is Rosalyn's husband."

"Good," he smiles. "Here's hoping we have a reunion soon." I hurry to Colm and Tobias.

"What is happening?" Colm asks while Tobias drinks. "Where are Rosalyn and Stella?"

"I don't know where they are," I confess. "The last time we saw them they were at the catwalk."

"The contraption by the sea?" Colm asks.

"That's something I thought I would never see," Tobias comments.

"I'm sure they are safe. As long as they are with Levi's uncle."

"Is there a chance these bastards have them?" Colm asks.

"I don't know," I say. I don't add that I hope not.

"What happened to us? What killed Bill and the others?" Tobias asks.

"The clean air purged your lungs of the coal dust," I explain. "We all went through it, some more than others."

"Get up," the lead rover barks.

"Be ready for anything," I advise them before I rush back to Levi. He is yet to drink. "Do you still have the knife?" I ask. He nods and then he drinks deeply from the skin as I help Jilly to her feet. I'm not sure the rest has done her much good. She is much more unsteady on her feet, and she limps badly when her guard takes her rope once more.

I take the skin back to the leader. He studies me for a moment as he takes it. "I am Ragnor," he says. He jerks his head at the woman. "My wife, Janna."

I don't know what to do. Saying I am happy to meet them would be strange, and introducing them to my friends stranger still. Still, the fact that he told me his name and introduced the woman as his wife gives me an odd sense of comfort to think that they do have some civility. And they did give us water, even if it was nothing more than to protect their investment, whatever that is.

"Thank you for the water," is all I can come up with to say as my captor jerks me back into line.

We walk on. It seems like it is taking forever to walk the distance Levi and I rode on the steam cycle in less than an hour when we went to rescue Lyon, Pace, and Dr. Stewart. My neck and wrists burn from the constant rubbing of the rope. I am exhausted, I am hungry, and my nerves are on edge because every sound I hear in the forest makes me think Lyon is coming to rescue us and when he doesn't it just adds to my fear that he is never coming.

We should be coming to a field soon. A large open area with one lonely tree and the ruins of a castle in the distance. Perhaps he will make his move there.

We go off the trail. When I think we will continue on straight, we are led off to the left on a path that is only wide enough for one. My captor puts the rope over his shoulder and leads me. It is more awkward because it holds my hands at a strange angle for walking and the way is treacherous with tree roots and rocks while the path meanders up and down. Jilly is limping badly and the distance between the prisoners spreads. Colm and Tobias keep pace with the leader. Jilly has slowed her guards down. Levi and I come behind her and Pace and his mother are behind me. Ellen is having trouble keeping up, and Pace slows to stay with her.

Our guards become frustrated, especially Jilly's. She falls again and he does not stop, instead he drags her by the rope. Levi and I both stop in our tracks and yell as Jilly cries out in pain.

"I'll carry her," Levi yells. "Just stop." The rope tightening around his neck cuts off his yell. I try to pry my fingers beneath mine because of the pressure. I see my guard grin. He's happy to get his revenge on me; still he backs off on the rope so I can breathe.

Pace's group has caught up with us, and Ragnor walks back to us. "Ye're all ah-daft," he says to the rovers. "Their'n no good to us ah-dead." He looks at Levi. "Ye want to ah-carry her, then do it. Take the rope off his ah-hands but leave it on his ah-neck."

The rovers do his bidding. All I can do is watch as Levi gathers Jilly into his arms. "I'm going to put you on my back," he explains. "You'll have to hang on." Jilly nods. Her foot is bleeding again, along with her wrists and neck. They leave her rope on. It would be too generous of them to take if off and give her tender skin some relief. Levi stands her up and then turns and bends. Jilly climbs on his back, and he wraps her legs around his waist as she puts her arm around his neck. He adjusts her weight and then nods, and we take off again.

The sun is behind us now. My weeks of inactivity in my room have weakened me. I used to walk for twelve hours at a time when I worked my shift in the mines. Now I feel as if we have walked forever and this trip will never end. The trail is much harder than the flat road we left. We go up only to come down again. We have to be getting close. The area reminds me of the place where Lyon and Pace were ambushed. They weren't that far from the rovers' camp when it happened. It seems like a lifetime ago.

I trip and stumble forward. The jerk of the rope on my neck twists me around. I feel as if I'd fallen asleep on my feet, and it takes me a moment to recognize where I am. I see Pace's face. The worry and anger twisted together.

"I'm okay," I say, using Levi's word. I concentrate on putting one foot in front of the other so I don't drift off again. I focus on Levi's back and on Jilly, who clings to him. Her cheek lies against his shoulder and her eyes are closed. How does he hang on? He has to be weak after his days in the cell. I know that he has more strength than he shows. He has the scars from the sun dance ceremony to show it. He survived it. I can survive this. I have to. We all do, or everything we've done and the people we lost were for nothing.

Would that be a tragedy to the world we left? Would we all fade from memory, nothing more than a minor event in the history of the dome? There was an uprising, and they all died or disappeared, and we don't even recall their names.

Someone has to stay alive to remember the names and to tell our story.

I smell fire. The trail we are on winds up a hillside. I realize this one is wider and well used. The rovers seem more relaxed, and they pick up the pace a bit. The sun is well behind us now. If there is one thing to be grateful for, it is that we were not out in the sun all day. We would not have survived it.

· 15 ·

We crest the hill and before us in a wide and shallow valley is the rover settlement. It is bigger than I imagined, more primitive than I could have guessed, yet it reminds me of the city within the dome. There is a center area, marked with a tall wooden platform. A large fire burns close by, and the smell of roasting meat carries on the evening breeze, causing my mouth to water with hunger. From the center point of the settlement several huts spiral out in a circular pattern. The huts look like they are made from sticks and grass. Next to them are lean-tos, some with cows and some with goats. Chickens scratch in the dirt, dogs bark, and children cry. Surrounding the village are gardens with tiny buds of new growth. There are too many huts for me to count, and the number of people below scares me. There has to be at least five hundred people in this settlement. How will we ever escape them?

We start down the path that leads to the village. I realize, in my weariness, that there are guard towers stationed around the rise that circles the village. The valley is also strangely barren of trees.

As we get closer I see that a stream runs through the middle of it. A ways off to one side is a trench, and the sight of a woman squatting over it makes my weak stomach squirm. Two hundred years of survival, and they live more primitively than their forefathers? Why?

Ellen is praying. I hear her say the Lord's Prayer, over and over again in a weepy voice. I would join her if I had the energy. We move down to the valley floor and children run out to greet us.

Except their greetings are taunts. They are grubby and dirty and they throw rocks and clumps of grass at us. Ragnor ignores them, as does Janna. The rest of the rovers shove them out of the way when they get too close or hit them, knocking them to the ground. If this is their life, then it is no wonder there is no forward progress. This kind of abuse can only result in an endless cycle of nothingness, just as we had. At least we had some civility in our world. We treated our own with kindness.

We are led to a hut on the edge of the settlement. Levi lowers Jilly to the ground, and she blinks with bleary eyes as she looks around. Our ropes are removed and we are all shoved inside. The door is latched shut with a piece of wood stretching across the door. We can see the shadows of two guards through the openings in the sticks. Ellen, Colm, and Tobias all sit while Pace and Levi walk around the hut that is only ten by ten, if that much. I go to Jilly, who just stands on one foot and looks around numbly.

"You should sit down," I say and help her down to the ground. I sit beside her and put my arm around her. She leans her head on my shoulder and sighs heavily. At least she isn't crying, although I am not certain that is a good thing.

Levi and Pace crouch before me. "Even though it looks like a stiff wind will blow it over, it's pretty solid," Pace says.

"So there's no way to escape?" I ask.

"Not at the moment," Levi says. "There are guards all around. We need to just wait and see at this point."

"What do you think will happen next?"

"It depends on what they want with us," Levi says. "I can't imagine any of it's good."

While I appreciate his candor, I'm not certain it is good for Ellen and Jilly to hear how dire our circumstances are. I look at Pace and he nods in agreement with Levi.

"I wish we could see the center of town," Levi adds. "It might give us an idea of what to expect."

"Right now I'm more concerned with relieving myself," I say.

"I'm afraid all the privacy we can give you is turning our backs," Pace says.

"I'll take it," I say. "Jilly, do you need to go?" She nods wearily, as does Ellen, and Pace and Levi help them both up. Levi digs a trench with the heel of his boot that leads under the wall of the hut. I prop Jilly up, and with my help she hobbles to the trench. Colm and Tobias climb to their feet, and all four men turn their backs and look through the gaps in the sticks. I help Jilly as much as I can, and when Ellen is done she takes her so I can squat and go. As soon as I'm done I shuck off my boots and take off the pants I wear over the leather ones Zan gave me. I also take off my socks and put my boots back on. Jilly needs them more than I do.

When we are done I help Jilly into my pants and put the socks on her feet. She is taller than me so her ankles show, but she is grateful. They will help keep her warm, along with my jacket.

"Try to rest," I urge her. She leans against Ellen, and they both close their eyes. The men have taken advantage of our distraction to go also. While they finish up, I stand and look between the openings in the sticks.

Dusk has settled over us. Fond memories of our evenings with the Hatfields fill my mind. Will we ever see them again? And what about our other friends? I cannot imagine what has happened to them, I can only pray they are not in this village. I can only pray that they are still alive and well.

The smell of the roasting meat is stronger now, and my stomach roars at the abuse it has suffered this day. I see people moving about. They all seem to be going to the center of the village. Do they all eat together, or is tonight cause for special celebration? Whatever it is, I hope it does not center on us or any of our missing friends.

Colm and Tobias join Ellen and Jilly while Levi and Pace join me. "It's funny how much this reminds me of the Indian villages back home," Levi says. "Although if it was up to me, I would have settled on higher ground. That way you can see your enemy coming."

"They do have the guard towers," I point out.

"Yes, but they are surrounded by forest. It would be very easy to coordinate an attack against them if you had enough men."

"Do you think they've been here that long?" Pace asks

"I'd say so," Levi says. "Several years at least. I noticed gardens. They live rather primitively. It is surprising after all this time they have not advanced more. They certainly could have made use of some of the castle ruins that are about and made a settlement there."

"It's the leadership that has held them back," I say.

"What do you mean?" Levi asks.

"Did you see how they treated the children?" I say. "They shoved them and hit them. The one who I knocked down got kicked by his brother."

"His brother?" Pace asks. "The leader?" Of course he would not have noticed since he was so worried about his mother.

"Ragnor. They have to be brothers because they look alike," I explain. "It seems to me like they live in fear and subjectivity. They are probably ruled by the strongest one, who oppresses all of them to keep his power. Anyone who challenges him, or suggests something better, is probably beaten or killed so he can stay in power."

"And it's a never-ending cycle." Levi smiles as he reaches the same conclusion as I do. "They were abused growing up and therefore they continue the abuse, since that is all they know. The current leader weakens or is killed, and someone stronger takes over. There is no growth because it is stifled."

"So how do we fight this?" Pace asks. "How do we show them that there is a better way?"

"I think if we convince Ragnor and his wife that they do not have to live like this, that we can show them a better way, we might find an ally," I suggest.

"It won't be easy," Levi admits. "How would we even begin?"

"We just have to watch for an opening," I say. "And pray." I look over at Colm and Tobias. "I need to talk to them."

"Can you tell us what's happening, Wren?" Colm asks when I kneel before them. I know he is anxious to hear about Rosalyn and Stella, as Tobias is to know about Peter and Nancy. I sit down across from them on the cold earthen floor and tell them about our escape from the village when the flood came and everything that happened to us since that time.

"Are you sure they are safe?" Colm asks again.

"Colm, all I know to tell you is that if they are with Levi's people, then they are safe. I have no way of knowing what happened to them since they weren't where we left them. I cannot imagine where they are."

"They could be prisoners here, like us," Tobias says.

"If they are, then hopefully we will find out soon," I reply. "How did you get out?"

"We had come around behind the bluecoats to shut down the lift to cut them off from reinforcements," Tobias explains. "When the gas blew, the only place we had to go was up. It knocked the lift askew so we climbed the cable."

"You climbed all that way?" I ask in disbelief.

"We had no choice," Colm explains. "The water was chasing our arses. It was that or drown. When we got to the top, they were waiting to arrest us. Threw us in the cells, and we've been there since."

"Without any idea of what was going on below," Tobias adds. "We imagined the worst, of course, and we were right."

"At least some survived," Colm says. "If I die tonight I can go happy that Rosalyn and Stella will go on. I hope."

I squeeze his hand. "We're not finished yet," I say.

"Just let us know what needs to be done," Tobias replies. "I'm not going out without a fight."

"They are coming." Levi and Pace are still watching through the cracks. Colm and Tobias quickly rise to their feet while Jilly and Ellen, startled from their naps, look about in confusion. The bar on the door is raised, and Ragnor opens the door.

"Come," he instructs. Levi and Pace help Jilly and Ellen to their feet. Levi moves to pick Jilly up and he's stopped. "She must walk," the rover says.

"I'll be fine," Jilly says haughtily, and she manages to limp after Levi as we file out of the hut. Several guards fall around us, cutting off any chance of an escape to our sides or behind us, so the only direction we can move is forward, toward the center of the settlement.

The entire population is gathered there. Men, women, and children. They part as we approach, and we are herded to the platform next to the fire, where several deer are roasting on spits. We stop far enough out that we can see what is on the platform. Men stand around it as if to protect it. The platform stands nearly as tall as me with steps leading to it. Upon it are two posts and a man is tied between them so tightly that his arms look as if they will pull out of the sockets and he has to stand on his toes. His back is bared to us. I am afraid to think of what this might mean. Three more men are on the platform. Two stand and another sits in a large and ornate chair that would be more at home in my father's office than here in this village. The one who sits looks the same age as my father and Lyon. He wears a long coat and pants but no shirt. His chest is massive and muscular, wider than anyone I've ever seen. He has some of the strange markings on his face that I've seen on some of the other rovers. The other two flank him, standing with their arms crossed and huge knives in their belts. This has to be the leader of the rovers.

Beneath the platform are baskets full of rocks. I don't want to know what they are for either. The crowd presses at our backs, and our male friends move instinctively behind us to protect us. Levi, on the opposite side of Jilly, is on my left, Pace on my right, with Ellen beyond him. Colm and Tobias stand behind me. Jilly leans heavily on Levi, and Ellen clings to Pace. As soon as the crowd behind us quiets and stops jostling for position, the man in the chair inclines his head to someone standing off to the side.

A man strides to the platform and climbs the steps. He is tall with large arms. He wears pants and a vest and his hair in a long braid down his back. Leather bands cover his wrists and his face also bears markings. When he gets to the platform, he uncoils a long thick rope made of braided leather. The ends are not part of the braid, and I see shiny flecks of metal tied to them.

"This is not good," Levi says quietly. "Be strong, all of you. Try not to show any emotion or they will take it as a sign of weakness."

I barely nod. Jilly takes a deep breath. I already know that for Ellen it will be impossible. And when the first lash hits the back of the man tied to the posts, she cries out and buries her head in Pace's shoulder. Ragnor frowns and Janna goes to Ellen and with her hands twists Ellen's face around so that she has to watch as the next lash falls.

I always knew death by fire was painful. Accidentally burning my hand at one point in my life gave me an idea of the agony one would experience, and seeing it firsthand for myself with Alex gave me a healthy fear of it, especially because I knew if I was captured it would be my sentence.

Having the flesh stripped from your back one agonizing stroke at a time has to be a close second.

Why are they doing this? A sentence was not pronounced. A crime was not mentioned. Why is this man being punished? And there is no doubt this is punishment. I cannot help but flinch with every strike of the lash and wince as the one holding the whip pulls his arm up and back and coils it for the next strike. How many more will fall? I remember reading in the Bible that Jesus was lashed thirty-nine times because forty would be enough to kill him. I have not kept up a count. Will they beat him until he is dead? The man's head hangs limply, yet he still cries out with pain. He looks to be strong, or he was before this. Being strong now is nothing more than a hindrance.

Levi said it took four days to pull the wood through his skin during his sun dance ceremony. How much pain can the body take before it gives in? Alex managed to speak to me before he died, even though his pain had to be unbearable. Is the mind stronger than the body or is it the soul that drives one to act beyond the point of pain?

I want to know why they are doing this. Surely this is not just for our benefit. Is this simply a show of strength or an example of what will befall us? I wish I could see the faces of the people behind me. They are silent. Is it because this punishment could have fallen on any of them?

I know my father traded people for weapons. With us there was no trade, the rovers simply took us away. I know there are other people from the dome in this crowd, but how will I know who they are? They could be dead now, used as fodder for the perverse needs of this leader.

All these thoughts run through my mind as the lash whistles and falls. I clench my hand and realize that I am holding tightly to Pace's fingers. I don't even recall taking his hand, yet I cling to him now, channeling the fear that I dare not show on my face into our connection.

Finally, the lashes stop and the man in the chair stands and walks to the edge of the platform, directly in front of us. "Let ah-this be ah-lesson," he says in their peculiar accent as he stares down at us. "Stealing will not be ah-tolerated."

The crowd yells out behind us in agreement and they carry on for a bit, until the leader raises his hands to quiet them. "We have new ah-slaves," he says. "We will ah-test them tonight so you ah-may decide on whether they ah-will be worth the ah-price tomorrow."

Test us? Like the man who was whipped was tested? Panic fills me, and my stomach, as usual, threatens to rebel. This is not the time for it. They plan to sell us as slaves. For what purpose? Fear fills me. I know what that means for me and Jilly, but what about the men? What about Ellen?

"What does he mean test us?" Ellen asks in a panicked voice. "What are they going to do?"

The crowd jostles around us and the band that brought us in surrounds us and herds us to the edge of the platform while two long lines form. Men pick up the baskets of rocks and begin to pass them out.

Jilly stumbles as we are pushed into an awkward line. The sun is gone now, lost behind the trees to the west, and the large fire casts an eerie glow along the endless line of rovers.

"Ye must ah-run," Ragnor says. "Or ye will ah-die."

I look down the long line of people, most with rocks in their hands. Some hold stout branches. I recall the ride I took with my father in the city through the workers' quarters and the things that were lobbed at us. Findley protected me from the worst of it with his body. Jilly will never make it, and I have serious doubts about Ellen too. Her skin is deathly pale and she is visibly trembling. I can only imagine that I look the same.

"Jilly can't do it," I protest over the calls from the crowd.

"I will run the gauntlet for her," Levi says to Ragnor as the noise grows louder. Rovers of every age, man and woman alike, call out for our blood.

"I'll run for both of them," Pace has to shout. "My mother and Wren."

"Ye can't ah-run for a woman," Ragnor replies. "Only she can," he says and points to me. "A woman for a woman. A man for a man."

I have no choice. Jilly and Ellen will surely die. "I'll do it," I say, even though fear holds me in its grip. "I'll run for Ellen too." I shiver as if I am cold, but it is merely fear, a constant companion.

"That's three times," Pace puts his hands on my shoulders. "Wren, you can't."

I look into his beautiful blue eyes. "Which one would you choose to die?" Ellen stands beside him with her knuckle in her mouth as if it will stop her sobs. To my side I see Jilly, shaking her head in denial. Whether it is to me or to the situation, it does not matter. Pace knows there is no choice. I am the only one who can do it. I can save their lives by doing this, and it is not lost to me that I may lose mine by doing so.

"Wren," he says, saying all the unspoken things, the unresolved between us in my name.

I have no reply. I can't. If I say what is on my mind, I might not have the courage to do what needs to be done. I take my kerchief from my pocket and tie my hair back. "Let's do this," I say to Ragnor.

He studies me, and as he does I notice his eyes. They are pale blue, like the sky. I see the intelligence in them and know that if we can convince him to help us, he would be a strong ally. But first we have to convince him. He will not risk his life, or his wife's. "If ye fail the ah-first time, then they have to ah-run," he informs me. "If ye fail the second time, then ye choose one to ah-die. The third time, ye are the only one to ah-die."

I nod. I understand. Ellen and Jilly do also. I can tell by their frightened faces.

He puts his hands up in the air, and the crowd quiets. "This girl will ah-run for the others," he shouts and the people roar in approval or anticipation, I cannot tell which. The leader on the platform dips his head in acknowledgment.

"Keep your head down," Levi says into my ear. "If you fall, you must get up or they will beat you to death. Whatever happens, you just keep on running until you reach the end." Levi pauses for less than a second. "You can do this, Wren. I believe in you."

I look at the long row of people. The line curves away from me so I cannot see the end of it. How will I do this three times? I have no choice. I have to do this. I take a deep breath and start off.

They scream at me, long and loud. They beat at me with their branches, whacking them across my back as others throw them at my feet in an attempt to trip me. The rocks are the worst. They sling them at me and they land on my arms as I hold them up to protect my head. My side and back take a beating, and I can feel the bruises blossoming as they thud against my body. All I can do is concentrate on putting one foot in front of the other, staying on my feet and making it to the end. I do not even know I have until Janna grabs my arm and spins me around to keep me from running out of the village.

"Ye did well," she says, as if she is congratulating me. I can only nod as I try to catch my breath. She leads me around behind the line, and the crowd roars to life once more. I see a flash of gold and know that Levi is running, much faster than I did. So fast that the blows barely catch him and he is through before I make it back up to the start of the line. My heart is still pounding in my chest and my breathing is ragged. The noise starts again and I see Pace fly by, as strong and as fast as Levi, and I have no doubts both will survive this.

I still have two turns left.

"Oh, Wren," Jilly sobs as I come round again. She leans on Ellen, who has her eyes on her son with her lips moving in a silent prayer. "To say thank you isn't enough." All I can do is nod. I haven't survived yet, which means their lives are still in the balance. The crowd seems angrier now. They want blood and neither Levi nor I gave it to them. I pray Pace didn't either.

I take off again, before the crowd has gathered itself after Pace's run. It was my hope to take them by surprise, and I did. I run almost a quarter of the way before they realize it. But when they do, I pay for it dearly. Rocks come at my face as the people down the line see me coming and aim at me. I run awkwardly and slowly with my hands before my face and my head bent. One blow with a rock hits my kidneys and staggers me sideways. I stumble into the line and am pushed back. Whoever pushed me, saved me, I am certain, because it was the only way I stayed on my feet. But I also lost momentum and the blows land with more frequency. A rock hits my temple, where I was hit in the past, and stars shoot across my vision. I taste blood. The impact made me bite my tongue. I don't know how I stay on my feet, but I do and nearly run into Janna, who is once more waiting for me.

"Keep yourn ah-head up," she says, as if she wants me to succeed. Does she? Does my success mean more profit for her when I am sold as a slave? Will this be my father's ultimate revenge on me? That I am once more a slave? Only he would think of this. Giving me what I asked for while taking it away. It is a shame he will never see it to fruition. But I am sure he will think on it and smile.

Either Colm or Tobias is running now. My vision is too blurry to make out which, and I have to concentrate just to stay upright as Janna hustles me back to the front of the line. I put my hand to my temple and come away with blood on my fingers. My head hurts so bad that I feel like throwing up. The crowd shrieks in excitement, and I know whoever it is has fallen.

How will I ever make it through again? At least this time, the only life I risk is my own.

"Wren!" Levi and Pace both call out my name as Janna and I arrive at the front of the line. Neither of them have a mark on them, a benefit of being so fast. I stand between them as they alternate between looking at my temple, smoothing my hair, and desperately looking for a way to stop the madness. I can only look at them and blink, because their faces seem strange to me, distorted, as if they are floating in a heavy cloud.

"She must ah-go now," Ragnor says from far, far away.

Levi has his hands on my shoulders and is talking to me, but I can't quite make out the words. I see Pace over his shoulder, shaking his head, his beautiful blue eyes brimming. I just want to lie down. I want to close my eyes and my ears to the spinning and the noise that feels like a pickax pounding in my brain.

"You can do this, you can do this, you can do this." The words are forefront, but the cacophony of screams and yells behind them are meaningless, except that they fill me with fear.

"You must," Pace says, and I only know what he is saying because his mouth forms the words. Janna pulls at me, propelling me forward.

Pace shoves her away and wraps his arms around me. "I love you, Wren. Now stay alive."

I want to stay alive. But only if I can stay wrapped in his embrace and have the rest of the world go away. I want to crawl back in our cave where it was just me and Pace with Pip and Jonah. I want the water that wiped out our village to have carried us away that day too, because I am so tired of fighting, so tired of the confusion, so tired of being responsible for lives other than my own.

Wouldn't it be easier to just die, because I am certain I cannot do this thing again?

But I must.

Ragnor and Janna pull us apart. I would think Ragnor would be violent with Pace because he dared to push his wife, but he isn't. I can see compassion in both their eyes. They stand on either side of me as they guide me to the front of the line. I stare down the length of it. At the flames that shoot up behind the one side of people and the dark and distorted faces that scream and yell for me to come on so they can kill me.

I will not let them win. I will not let my father win. And just like that, the world goes silent so all I can hear is the sound of my heart beating in my chest. I take off.

· 16 ·

I do not remember running the third time. All I remember was after, when it was over and someone carried me to the hut. Either Levi or Pace, I don't know which, all I know is that I thought I was floating as I looked up at the endless sky and the innumerable stars, thinking the world is spinning like a top and I could feel it move. When I opened my eyes later I realized we were all, for the moment, safe.

The hut has no light except for the torches outside that shine through the openings in the walls. My head lies on something soft, and I realize it is Jilly's lap. She smiles at me as I stare up at her, trying to get my bearings. "We're all here," she says. "Thanks to you."

My head hurts and I automatically raise my hand to touch my temple. I can feel the dried blood on my skin and the jagged cut. Another scar for my collection. At this rate there will be nothing left of me by the time I am twenty, if I survive that long. Somewhere along the line I lost my kerchief. It's been a part of me for so long that I feel naked without it being somewhere on my person.

Pace and Levi rush to me and kneel next to me, one on one side, one on the other. Beyond them I see Colm and Tobias turn from their posts of watching outside to glance my way with their shiner eyes.

"What happened?" I ask.

"You were amazing," Levi says. Pace takes my hand into his and smiles his sweet smile.

I move and groan as my body protests. "I don't feel amazing," I say. "I feel like I got caught in a cave-in."

"You're going to be covered with bruises by tomorrow," Levi says. He sits back on his heels while Pace settles next to me, still holding my hand. I move to sit up and he helps me, but every place he touches screams in agony.

"What did you call that?" I asked. "You seemed familiar with it."

"A gauntlet. It is something used by the Indian tribes in America as a test of courage, so I was surprised to see the rovers use it also, especially since their level of education is so primitive. But it was well known before the comet, so I suppose some American history could have been remembered along with your own throughout the years."

"What happens next?" I ask.

"We are to be auctioned off as slaves," Levi informs me. "Which means we will likely be separated, so we have got to come up with a plan tonight."

"They're coming," Colm says. "Looks like with food and blankets." Colm and Tobias leave their positions and sit on the ground. Ellen perks up from where she sits beside Jilly. It is only a few quick moments before the sound of the door being unlocked is heard and Ragnor and Janna come in, along with Ragnor's brother. They carry a basket of food and what looks like loosely woven rugs. Janna and the brother set everything down right inside the door.

"Wren," Ragnor says. "Ye are to ah-come with me."

"Why?" "For what reason?" "Can't you see she's hurt?" Levi and Pace both rise in protest. Ragnor holds his hand up to stop the discussion. "She will not be ah-harmed, I promise ye."

I hold up my hand to Pace because I know I do not have the strength to climb to my feet on my own. He helps me up and my muscles scream at the abuse. Still he does not let go of my arm. Levi steps in front of both of us. "When will she be back?" I cannot see his face, but I can tell by his posture that he is ready to fight if he feels the need.

Ragnor pins Levi with a stare. "I cannot answer ah-that," he says.

"Please don't take her," Jilly implores.

"No," I say. "I'll go." I look at Ragnor. "Can I have a moment with my friends? In case I don't come back?" Ragnor looks at Janna who jerks her head in agreement. They step out of the hut and shut the door, but the shadows of their backs are still there.

"This might be my chance to convince him to help us," I whisper to Pace and Levi as Colm and Tobias help Jilly up and they, along with Ellen, join our tight circle.

"You have no idea where he is taking you," Levi says.

"I think I know," Pace says. "He's taking her to the man on the platform. The leader. I saw him watching Wren. He wants to meet her, to see what she's like."

"Examining his purchase before he buys it?" Jilly offers. "The pig."

"It's a chance to learn about them," I say. "And maybe see a way out for all of us."

"You will see more than the rest of us," Levi admits. "But Wren . . . if you don't come back, how will we find you?"

"You'll think of something," I say. "And it's not really as if we have a choice. Ragnor has just decided to be nice to us. He doesn't have to be. If we make too much of it, the rovers might take it as a sign of weakness on his part and we will lose what little we have."

Regretfully, Levi and Pace nod their agreement. Jilly grabs on to me and hugs me tight, then Pace does the same and I try not to groan in pain. The urge to stay sheltered in his arms is great, but I know by the impatient shifting we hear beyond the walls of the hut that our time is over. Levi walks me to the door.

"You think like a leader, Wren," he whispers in my ear. "Do not doubt yourself now. Follow your instincts."

All I can do is nod as Ragnor opens the door. As long as they believe in me . . . I must succeed at finding something that will help us.

"It would have been nice to eat first," I say to Ragnor. Every inch of my body feels bruised and battered and each movement is painful. I am afraid to see what I will look like come morning.

"You will be fed," he assures me. Pace was right. I am going to see the leader. That notion somehow is a lot more frightening now than it was when I was inside with my friends.

The settlement is quiet now. I hear the murmurs of voices within the huts and that, along with the running water of the stream, reminds me of home. Funny thought, that. The cavern was my home, now I am without one. Instead of a place, the people I love are my home. Wherever they are is where I want to be. But I want it to be everyone, including Pip, Jonah, and Ghost.

Where are they? There was no sign of any of our friends during the gauntlet, but that doesn't mean anything. They could simply be imprisoned elsewhere.

Or dead.

I am not paying attention to my purpose. I let myself get caught up in my own thoughts.

"Do you like your life?" I ask Ragnor. Janna walks on the other side of me, and she jerks her head in my direction after my comment.

Ragnor doesn't answer, but I clearly see the tightening in his jaw. I have struck a nerve, and unfortunately I don't know what else to say. We walk by the platform, and I am glad to see that the man who was beaten is gone. Either to his death, or to be cared for. Which would he prefer at this point?

The fire has burned down to embers, and a few men stand around it. They watch us as we pass and one utters something so gutturally filthy that I nearly stumble. Janna rushes from my side, draws a knife and has it at the rover's throat before I can regain my footing. Ragnor takes my arm and we turn to watch.

"She is ah-worthy of yer respect," she says, and the man nods and his eyes are wide as he holds out his hands in surrender. Janna holds her knife there for another moment and then backs away with a look of pure contempt on her face.

This is how they live, and we are to be their slaves. God help us.

We continue on over a narrow bridge that is nothing more than a plank and through the village until we come to a hut that is much better made than what I've seen so far. It sits apart from the rest, and a ring of stones circles round it as a boundary. The hut is much larger than the others and almost perfectly round. The holes are chinked with mud and thatch and a cylinder piece of metal rises out of the middle of it, scavenged from someplace. Smoke rises from the pipe and buckets of water are lined up around the hut, in case the roof catches on fire, would be my guess.

If they can find pipes for chimneys and buckets for water, then why can't they build a better house? Or is this just another way for their leader to control them? Hopefully, I will soon find out.

Ragnor stops me at the rock boundary, and the three of us stand and wait until one of the guards from the platform sticks his head out of the door and waves us in. We walk through a line of torches. Janna stops at the door and Ragnor follows me in.

I am surprised. Thick rugs cover the ground, and I look again to make sure they are not the same ones I saw on the *Quest*. They are drab and dirty, old and frayed, and I almost sigh in relief. The rugs aboard the *Quest* could not have aged that much in a few weeks. There are rugs hanging on the walls, also frayed and old. Off to my right is a table with six chairs. It is covered with plates and mugs made of heavy pewter and more food than I've seen in a long time. My stomach actually growls as I look at it, so I turn away. To my right is a low sofa covered with pillows. One of the legs is broken off the sofa and it is propped up with a thick chunk of wood. Two women lounge on it and they are wearing . . . or perhaps it is they are not wearing, not much more than a piece of fabric as big as the shawl Jilly loaned me. Their legs are exposed and the top dips dangerously low over their breasts. One has the marks on her arms and more around her eyes. She stares at me lazily and licks her lips in a way that makes me think she is considering me as a meal. I wonder about the marks I've seen. About how they are made as they seem to be permanent. I don't understand why anyone would want to do that to their skin.

Before me is a fire pit, and the pipe hovers four feet above it, capturing the smoke. Behind that is a large bed surrounded by heavy drapes. The two men who stood guard on the platform are there, along with two more. As Ragnor and I stand there, the leader rises from the bed and opens the curtain. A woman lies in plain view, naked, with her legs spread wide, and the leader smirks as he looks at me before slowly closing the curtain.

He sent me a message with that look and the display on the bed, and I know that I am in way over my head. Just like with my father.

He walks to me and puts his large hand on my jaw. He is bigger than any man I have ever seen. He is so close I can see the details of the marks on his face. They resemble the *s*'s I'd seen in the Bible. They always used fancier letters to start a new book or chapter. These are more ornate, with elaborate curlicues on the ends. They start on his forehead and curve around his eyes and then onto his cheeks before flaring out again as if to loop around his ears. His beard is trimmed differently than anything I've ever seen. Shaved on the sides, just hair on his chin where it is braided to a length of four or five inches. His eyes are a greenish gold, like Jonah's, and there is something in them that makes me want to turn away, but I don't. I know he wants to intimidate me. He wears his pants and a pair of boots made of hide and nothing else. There is so much skin, stretched tight over muscle, yet he is thick through the middle instead of having the lean torsos of Ragnor, Levi, and Pace.

He turns my head one way, and then the other, none too gently, studying my eyes and the wound on my temple. He puts two fingers in the strap of my goggles, pulls them up to look at them and then drops them back into place around my neck. Then he walks to the table and picks up a mug and drains it before turning back to me.

"Why did you ah-run for the others?"

I must not show my fear, but the scene on the bed makes me realize how vulnerable I am. I swallow deeply. "Because they would have died if they were made to run."

"What is it to you if they ah-die?"

"I care for them," I say. "I care for all of them that are with me," I add with a bit more force to my voice.

He studies me again and then sits down at the head of the table. He motions to the chair at his right. I hesitate. "Eat," Ragnor urges me in a quiet voice. It does not go unnoticed by the leader. I go to the table and take a seat. I am so hungry that I feel sick, and, combined with my head wound and the bruises covering my body, I know I am barely holding on. I do not make a move lest I do something to offend. The leader serves me after he serves himself. A large piece of venison, boiled potatoes and carrots, and something dark green and limp that looks like it came out of the water is placed on my plate.

"Ragnor," the leader says after he takes a bite of meat. "Bring in your ah-wife and join us. Ah-give me the word from the ah-tower."

I realize he wants to know what is going on inside the dome. I desperately need to know what has happened to our friends on the outside. But I dare not mention them, lest I give away the fact that I was with them and was part of the attacks. I do not want to end up beaten like the man we saw earlier, and I certainly don't want it to happen to Levi or Pace, which I am certain it will if the rovers find out we killed some of them. I must tread carefully. But first I must eat, or I will not have the strength to keep my wits about me.

Ragnor fetches Janna and they both sit down at the table. I have no idea what to expect since all I've seen from the rovers is brutality. While they don't have the manners of the Hatfields, they do have some civility in that they don't act like barbarians at the table.

The leader punches his thumb into his chest while he holds a huge fork with the other. "I am Wulf," he growls.

I bob my head. "Wren."

"Why do yer ah-eyes shine?"

I almost cry in relief. I am the first shiner he has ever met. Which means he hasn't been around my friends, or he is a very good liar. The curiosity that shows on his face makes me believe it is the former. "I lived underground," I explain. "I gathered the coal for the dome . . . the tower."

"Ah," he nods his head in understanding. "Tell me ah-boot the battle."

I shake my head in confusion. I will not admit to the fight with the rovers because I am certain it will lead to all our deaths.

"We seen the ah-smoke," Ragnor explains. "And the ah-boat from the sky. They ah-tacked the tower?"

My mind spins as I try to decide what I should say and shouldn't. As long as they don't know I've been outside before, then I see no reason to tell them. I have no qualms about telling them what happened inside. "I do not know about a boat from the sky," I lie. "There was an explosion below ground," I say. "It damaged the tower. We call it the dome," I explain. "It made the ground cave in and destroyed my home. It also cracked the glass, and that's how the smoke got out."

"There are ah-more like ye?" Wulf asks. "With the ah-eyes?"

"Just the two men who are with me," I lie once more. "We are all that survived."

"Why were ye sent ah-out?"

I shrug. "Does it matter? The leaders inside wanted to get rid of us."

Wulf sits back in his chair where before he'd been leaning forward, gleaning every bit of information he could from our conversation. He looks at me for a moment and then he laughs. "There was not even a trade fer ye," he says. "They must hate ye inside. So why did he not ah kill ye like he has with the ah-others?"

I shake my head. "I was in a cell. Then I was brought outside to a place I was told did not exist except for flames. I do not know what they think or why they do the things they do. I just know my home was destroyed, and now I am here."

He smiles and it does not reach his eyes. Then, before I can blink, he slams his fists on the table in front of me, rattling my plate. "Ye lie." He sweeps my plate down the table as I shrink back from his anger.

"Out," he spits at Ragnor and Janna, who have remained quiet throughout the meal. Ragnor opens his mouth to protest and Janna touches his arm. They exchange a look and then they both rise and go.

The guards leave also, and the women leave the room, moving back behind the bed. I can only assume there is a door there. I cannot see, and I am too scared to move.

The thought that I may not get to go back to my friends fills me as Wulf takes another long draught from his cup. I smell the same bitter smell that surrounded my grandfather when he drank. Alcohol and anger are a bad mix, and I fear I may bear the brunt of it.

I know that is the least of my worries. Wulf's earlier friendliness is gone. Why I thought I could handle this situation I will never know. He wraps his large hand in my hair and drags me from the table. Chairs fall over and he ignores them. I have no choice but to go, even though I would willingly let him pull every hair from my head to escape him. My hair just will not let go and neither does he. I am swung around as if I am nothing more than a rag doll and thrown through the curtains onto the bed.

I am so scared that I tremble violently as I try to escape him but it is useless. He grabs my ankles and twists them. I scream out in pain as he drags me back to him.

Why is it that men use the fear of rape to dominate women? It isn't fair that they hold this over us. This has happened to me twice before, and I escaped it. Once by my own measures, once by Levi's. Both resulted in the death of my attacker.

I know there is no escape for me now. I am battered and bruised, and my head is still woozy from the blow to my temple. I am tired and I am weak and I am so frightened that I can't think. All I can do is react, and I do, screaming and kicking and fighting, but it is like battering the dome. There is no give in the glass or in this man who holds me down. I exhaust myself waiting for the inevitable.

Yet it does not happen. He stares down at me as he holds me in place with his hands. "If I ah-take ye now Ragnor will protest as ye are his until the morrow. But ye ah-will be mine. I ah-have yet to decide if ye are ah-worth killing over."

It takes a moment for my mind to comprehend what he says. He releases his hold on me, but I am still afraid to move. He goes back to the table, picks up his mug and fills it from the pitcher that miraculously still sits on the table, then he goes to the fire and sticks the poker into the flames.

"Garth!" he yells, and one of the guards comes through the door. "Hold her."

I knew my escape was too good to be true. Before I can make my sore and trembling body scramble from the bed, Garth has ahold of me and drags me to my feet as Wulf removes the poker from the fire. He blows on the end, making it glow even redder, and then brings it perilously close to my face.

"If ye came from ah-below ground, and have been in ah-cell since the smoke ah-came, then why do ye care so much ah-boot the others?" He leans the poker in closer, not close enough to touch me, but close enough that the heat singes my cheek.

"I shared a cell with Jilly," I say. "The other woman is older and weaker than the rest of us. I knew she would not survive it. Jilly is crippled from the walk. I don't want anyone to die when I can save them." I speak the truth yet I continue to hide much. At this point I know that whatever I say will not make any difference. Wulf will do what he wants to do. Still I cannot help but think of Alex. Of how he burned.

"The boy knows ye." I know he is talking about Pace. He had to have seen us together and have known there was something there.

"I knew him before," I say. "He is from above. It was forbidden for us to be together. The woman is his mother. The other one is his friend." Once more I have told a version of the truth. I dare not lie. I know Wulf will see it.

The heat from the poker is less intense, yet I know it will still burn me. Wulf looks at it for a moment, then at the fire. Then he tosses the poker aside as if he has decided it is not worth the effort to heat it up again.

Please don't ask about the Quest . . .

"Take her," he says to Garth, who promptly propels me through the door and shoves me at Ragnor and Janna. Janna, surprisingly, puts her arms around me.

"It was your ah-courage that captured his ah-tention," Ragnor says with approval.

"I wish I'd have known that beforehand," I say as I try to make my trembling subside. Janna releases me as quickly as she grabbed me, as if she is embarrassed by her show of emotion.

"He will ah-give a good price for ye," Ragnor says.

"Why? Why are we yours to sell? What gives you the right?"

"We ah-answered the call," Ragnor says simply.

I don't know what to say. And I am finding it very difficult to put one foot in front of the other. Too much has happened in too little a time, and my body and mind are reeling. I cannot keep up with it all. I still don't believe I have escaped, and I realize that I haven't. Not really. Come morning, I will belong to Wulf and my friends will be sold as well. We will be separated and have no way to escape our fates. We can't let that happen. We have to find a way out of here tonight.

"You can't do this," I say. We are walking across the bridge now, and I know there is not much time. "There is a better way. A better way to live than this. You are better than this, both of you. I've seen it in you."

"Quiet!" Ragnor barks, and Janna looks around to see if anyone is listening.

"You must help us escape. You must." I plead.

"No more," Ragnor says. "Ye will not ah-speak again, or I will gag ye."

I open my mouth and clamp it shut just as quickly. If only I had time to make them see. I can understand their fear, and I have nothing better to offer them. If only we knew where the *Quest* was. Even if we escape, where can we go? Where can we hide?

For the first time since this all began, I am truly helpless. My fate is not my own. Were we not all better off before we began this crusade? Certainly there were things we did not like about our lives, but we had homes, food, security, and choices.

All the deaths, all the losses we suffered were for naught if this is where we end our days, as slaves to the rovers. It would also give my father the satisfaction of knowing he was right all along. Despair fills me. I have accomplished nothing. I left my friends hoping I could fill them with hope. Now I am going back to them to tell them there is no hope, there is no future, and there is no hope of rescue.

What have I done? Especially to Levi, who of everyone is innocent in all this. He got caught up in our battles, and now he will likely lose his life because I know he will fight with everything he has against being a slave. If not for me and my misguided dreams that life outside would be better, he would be sailing across the sky and exploring the world, far, far away from my petty problems.

I've ruined lives. It was never my intent. I wanted to make life better for everyone. Instead I've killed everyone and everything I love.

I am ashamed to go back and face everyone. But like everything else in my life, I no longer have a choice. Still, it is hard to make my bruised and battered body cooperate, and I stagger and stumble until Ragnor is forced to take my arm just to hold me upright. There is one thing I can do for Levi. I can hopefully find some news about the *Quest*.

"What is the airboat?" I ask, hoping that this, at least, will not make Ragnor mad. "I don't understand why Wulf thought we were at war with someone else."

"Ah-big boat that ah-floated in the sky. It came ah-with livestock and weapons to settle," Ragnor explains. "We ah-passed where they were. The ah-shelf on the ah-rock." I know he is talking about the catwalk.

"If they come to settle what happened to them?"

"We ah-beat them in battle," Janna says. "We ah-scared them off."

"You killed them?" I asked. "What did you do with the airboat?"

Janna shrugs. "It was ah-gone. Since the ah-full moon."

"This is our ah-land," Ragnor says. "We ah-do not mean to ah-share."

The moon was full when we last saw Lyon and the rest. Dr. Stewart had told us of the cycles and what to expect. If what Janna says is true, then they had to have left shortly after we went into the dome. But why? How could they give up on us so easily? And did they take everyone with them? What about Ghost and the rest of the ponies? I've seen no sign of them here. They certainly could have some of our goats. The thought that Ghost could have wound up eaten does not escape me. Nor does the thought that there was another battle and a lot of people could have died. But surely we would have seen some sign of it. When we walked through the area where our camp was, we could see where the grass was cut back, but even that was nearly grown over again. It is as if they never existed. If not for Levi, I would think that they hadn't.

We reach the hut. There are two guards by the door, and I see four more close by, all with guns. Torches are set around it so that there is no shelter of darkness for us to escape under. All we have is a knife and two people who definitely would not survive if we made a run for it. I know Pace will not leave his mother, and I refuse to leave Jilly, yet with them we are handicapped.

I have no idea what to do or what to say. Levi was wrong about me. I do not think or act the way a leader should. All I have done is lead my friends to their deaths. But at least with death the suffering would mercifully be over. Death will be preferable to this future that looms before us.

· 17 ·

I knew Pace and Levi would be waiting for my return. I wish they weren't. I wish they were asleep so I could slip inside and curl up in a corner and go to sleep and pretend like tomorrow would never come. Mercifully, everyone else is asleep. Colm and Tobias stretched out on their backs and Ellen and Jilly curled together, on a blanket and under one. After what just happened to me with Wulf I really do not want their attention. Especially since I know the memory of their care will soon be replaced by something more horrible.

But I can't hurt them. I've hurt them enough. Both of them.

As soon as I enter the hut Pace takes me into his arms for a bone-crushing hug that makes me grunt in pain. "I'm sorry," he says. "I just didn't think you would be back."

All I can do is nod. My emotions are such a jumble, and my mind still does not want to accept the fact that I barely escaped being brutally raped, again. Meanwhile I have the realization that my reprieve will be over soon. "I've got to get out of here," I say and realize that I am babbling. But I can't help it. I cover my mouth with my fingers to keep anything else that sounds crazy from slipping out.

"What did he do to you?" Pace demands. He has his hands on my upper arms and he is just short of shaking me.

I have reached the point where I have had enough. I shrink away, pulling myself free of Pace's touch and go to a corner of the hut, as far away from everyone else as I can get. I sink to the ground, put my hands to my head, and drop my head to my knees, wishing with all my might that I could remain unseen and unnoticed. That everyone would just leave me alone. Funny, was it just a few days ago that I was so lonely in my room and consumed with worry for everyone?

Even though I have shut my eyes to block them out I can still hear Pace and Levi talking quietly. I can't make out the words, and I don't want to. I know they are talking about me. I keep my head down and try to think of something, anything, other than where I am and what is going to happen. I concentrate on my bed in the cavern, on the weight of a cat on my legs, on the way the water sounded as it went on its course, and on the steady creak of the waterwheel.

Someone touches my hand. Levi. I recognize the rough feel of his fingertips. He does nothing more than squeeze my fingers, and I regretfully open my eyes to find him crouched down in front of me.

"Wren," he asks quietly. "We have to know. Did he touch you? Did he hurt you?"

I look up and see Pace standing away and to the side. He is trying not to crowd me, but the anguish is there on his face, waiting for my answer, as if this is the determining factor in our moving forward. He doesn't understand yet that there will be no moving forward, that this is the last best moment we will ever have. That this will be the last night we will remember, when we were sort of free. That we dared much and accomplished nothing except for long years ahead of us full of regret. Or death, which would be much more preferable to me.

"Tonight or tomorrow, what does it matter?" I say.

"Wren." Levi moves his thumb over my cheek. To wipe a tear I didn't even know was there, I realize, still I wince when he touches the place where I was burned from the proximity of the poker. I did not even know I was hurt, so great was my fear. "We are concerned for you," Levi says.

"I am concerned for all of us," I reply. I shake my head. "Don't you realize it is over for all of us? That tomorrow we will be auctioned off to the highest bidder? We are to be their slaves. All of us." I try to keep my voice down, but fear makes it rise. Ellen stirs, and I realize what I've done. I don't want to frighten them any more than they are. I want them to have this one last night of peace, if it is possible for them to feel it. Pace lays a hand on her arm and offers her a word of comfort to settle her.

"You can't give up," Levi says. "We are not sold yet. The night is still young. There is hope."

"Lyon is gone," I say. "Who is going to save us?"

"How do you know he's gone?"

"Ragnor told me. They've been gone since right after we went into the dome."

"He's not gone," Levi says.

"Then where is he? Why didn't he rescue us? Where is the *Quest*? Where are our friends?"

"Did you see any sign of them?" Pace asks. "Anything from the ship?"

"No. I was looking. There was nothing there. The things he had were old and well used. Rugs, a sofa, a bed. But nothing from the *Quest*."

"Good," Levi says. "You were paying attention. I knew you would be."

"Did you see anything else?" Pace asks.

I think back on my trip through the village. "Wulf's hut is on the other side of the village, away from everything else. There were four men inside and two out. And three women." I feel the heat rise in my cheeks at the thought of the women. "More men by the fire. The one they whipped was gone. I really didn't see anyone else. Most everyone was in their huts."

"Any luck talking with Ragnor?" Levi asks.

I suddenly realize what they've done. They have distracted me from my feeling sorry for myself and got me thinking about a possibility of escape again.

"He wouldn't hear of it," I say. "I had nothing to offer him that was better than this."

"We will," Levi says confidently. I wonder if Ragnor knows something that I don't. He couldn't. There is no way he could know anything about Lyon.

"What are we going to do?" I ask Levi.

"Wait for our opportunity." The answer is vague, and I know he's just saying it to keep my spirits up.

"We should try to get some rest," Pace says.

"All I've done for the past few weeks is rest," Levi says. "You two sleep. I'll keep watch."

"Wake me in a bit?" Pace asks.

"I will." Levi goes back to the other side of the hut, where he can see through the slats.

Pace looks at me for a moment. "May I sit?" he asks.

I nod. "Of course." Pace kneels next to me, and then sits tentatively, as if he is afraid he will scare me. "Nothing happened," I say.

Pace's beautiful blue eyes study my face in the dim light that leaks through from the torches outside the hut. He smoothes my hair back from my face and touches his finger to my chin with a crooked smile. "You have a burn on your cheek."

"It could have been much worse," I keep my voice pitched low. No one else needs to hear us. "He was trying to scare me." I shake my head. "He did scare me."

"I'm sorry," Pace says. He slides his arm around my shoulder, and without thought, I lean my head against him, settling into the place that is so familiar to me.

"You can't be sorry," I say. "It's not your fault, it's just our fate now. We have to deal with it."

"You can't give up, Wren," he says.

I reach up and wind my fingers through the hand that strokes my arm. "Pace," I say. "I wish . . . I wish we had been together . . . before . . ." I drop my head and swallow. "I wish we'd made love that night in our cave." I look up at him. "I don't want my first time to be . . ." I choke the words off. I shouldn't do this to him. He has his mother to care for, and himself. He doesn't need to add me to his worries too.

Pace closes his eyes. I feel the tension in his body. I know he is full of anger, regret, and frustration, the exact same things that I feel. My chin trembles because I want to cry but I can't. Not here. Not now, possibly not ever again. I will not make this harder on us, but I also will not leave things unsaid between us. Not now.

"I'm sorry I hurt you," I say. "I'm sorry I betrayed your trust."

He opens his eyes and looks down at me. He brings his free hand up to my cheek and cups it, gently. "I'm sorry I pushed you so hard. I'm sorry I didn't give you the space you needed." He dips his head and kisses me, so very tenderly. "If this is our last night, then I want to spend it just holding you."

"I would like that very much," I say. Pace wraps his arms around me, and I lean into him, winding my arms around his waist and placing my cheek against his chest so that I can hear the steady *thump-thump* of his heartbeat. He kisses the top of my head and leans his cheek against it. I close my eyes and give in, finally, to the exhaustion and pain that fills my body.

I do not know how long we stayed that way. Sometime during the night we shifted positions and I lay stretched out on the ground and covered with a blanket. Through the haze of my sleep, I hear Pace and Levi talking.

"You should have wakened me," Pace says.

"She needed you," Levi replies.

"Get some sleep," Pace says. "She needs both of us now." I hear movement, yet I am too tired to open my eyes. "Keep her warm," Pace adds.

How does he know I am cold? *Because he is Pace.* Because I am cold, because the ground is damp and I've become spoiled the past weeks, sleeping in a bed. My body aches too, and I am afraid to even shiver or move because I feel like one big bruise. I feel a body stretch out beside me, an arm slip under my cheek, and another one over my waist and the blanket, and I know it is Levi.

It should be Pace. My mind protests but my body settles up against him and into his warmth and once more I drift off to sleep but hopefully not to dream. I am afraid of what I might see in my dreams. The reality we have to face tomorrow is bad enough.

· 18 ·

Morning is always inevitable. There is no stopping it no matter how badly you want to deny it so that you don't have to face the horror. As always, my body feels the coming dawn and yearns for it. I awaken to the shocking awareness that on this day my choices will be taken from me.

I open my eyes. I lay on my side facing the back of the hut. Levi's arm is still around my waist. My body feels like a thousand tons of rock has fallen on it, and I wince in pain as I carefully slide out from under Levi, causing him to flop over on his back and cover his eyes with his arm. Pace, who stands at watch, hears me stir and comes to me.

"You kept watch?" I ask quietly.

"Levi needed sleep too," he says. "Although we probably could have both slept since there was no way to escape. The rovers took different shifts too. Changed three times that I saw."

I can't help myself. I lean into him, and he hugs me tightly. It aches where my bruises are, but I do not complain because the hug warms my soul. "What are we going to do?" I ask.

"Watch for an opportunity. Take it when it presents itself."

"In other words, nothing," I say, and I can feel Pace grinning against my head. This is the moment I will remember. This moment where we are together in mind and in spirit and his lovely sense of humor comes through. I will try to keep this moment foremost in my mind as the day consumes us.

Colm and Tobias stir, as does Ellen. Jilly murmurs in protest as Ellen sits up. Levi climbs to his feet and stretches. He puts his hand on Pace's shoulder as he walks by.

"Nothing has changed," Pace tells him.

"A bit of privacy, ladies," Levi announces. The men line up along the wall that has the trench, and I go to Jilly, who sits up and blinks sleepily.

"I was hoping it was all a nightmare," she says as she sweeps the tangled mass of her hair away from her face. "But I'm glad to see you made it back to us."

"Are they really going to sell us as slaves?" Ellen asks.

"I'm afraid so." I kneel down and take Jilly's hand and give her a reassuring squeeze. "But as long as we are alive, there is hope." Funny how the morning gives one a different perspective on things. Or perhaps it is distance. All I know is I will be close to my enemy soon enough. While I am with my friends I will try to soak up what happiness I can.

"Wren," Ellen says. I turn to her and see the earnestness that Pace carries in her blue eyes. It is strange how hatred can mask the true visage of a person. Now I see more of a resemblance between them. "I just want to say I'm sorry for how I treated you," Ellen says. "Pace and I had a long discussion last night while you were gone." My heart swells at the thought of what he'd done. With everything else that is going on with us, he still made sure that his mother knew the truth about me. Ellen continues. "It turns out I was led to believe some things about you that I now realize were not true."

"My father is a master of manipulation," I explain. "I don't blame you for anything you said or did, especially since you were driven by your love for your son."

Her smile lights her face. It's the first time it has ever been directed at me. "Thank you for forgiving me. I see now how special you are, and why Pace loves you so." She looks over my shoulder at Levi, who has finished and gone back to the watching place, and then turns back to me. "Since I am his mother I cannot help but say this. Please don't hurt him."

"That is the last thing I would ever want to do," I say it, knowing that I already have hurt Pace. But it is true; it is the last thing I wanted to do.

"You do resemble your mother," Ellen remarks. "You have her face, and her brave heart."

I rock back on my heels in surprise. "You knew my mother?"

"When Pace was a year old I worked as a governess to Sir Meredith's brother's family. Maggie worked for them as a maid. Once she caught William's eye she didn't stand a chance."

"What do you mean?" This is the first time I've ever heard anyone talk about my mother and I am overwhelmed with curiosity, despite our circumstances.

"As you said, your father is a master of manipulation. I'm actually furious with myself for not remembering how he was with Maggie because I watched them quite a bit when it was happening. I hate to admit it, but I was attracted to him. Pace's father died before he was born so I had been alone for a while. Your father still is a fine man, but when he was twenty he was so very dashing and quite charming."

I listen to Ellen, caught up in her story, and try to imagine my father at twenty years of age.

She continues. "As I said, I was attracted to him, but he only had eyes for Maggie—the girl with the diamonds in her eyes, is what he called her. Because of the shine, like yours. And he was determined to have her."

Ellen takes my hand. "Don't blame her for giving in," she says. "I'm certain he promised her marriage and everything that went with it. But his career was much more important to him than a woman ever would be. There was no way he could advance with a shiner for a wife. Your mother stayed until it was impossible to hide her condition, and I know she always thought he would marry her. She even confided in me, after she was dismissed for her immoral behavior, which wasn't fair in my mind. She told me leaving might be what it took to bring him around, so certain was she of his feelings for her." Ellen drops my hand and rubs her arms as if she was cold. "But he didn't. I overheard him tell his brother that it was relief that she was gone, because he wouldn't have to deal with . . . you." She rolls her eyes. "I can't believe I let him manipulate me, even after knowing all this."

"She died in childbirth," I say. "She never mentioned him to my grandfather once."

"He broke her heart," Ellen replies. "I'm sorry you never knew her. I know you would have made her proud."

"Thank you." I look at Ellen and smile. I am so very grateful for her memories. "You've told me more about my mother than anyone ever has. All I ever knew was that I look like her." I have much to digest now and no time to do it. But I am very grateful for this brief glimpse of my mother's life.

"She must have been very special," Jilly says.

Levi crouches down next to us. "Should we have a look at your foot?" he asks Jilly.

"I think it is better," she says. "I'd actually forgotten about it until you mentioned it."

I stand up to give Levi room to look at Jilly's foot. Ellen stands also. She smiles at me and extends her arms, and we hug, somewhat awkwardly, but still it feels good. We have made our peace. As I look over her shoulder I see Pace smiling. For the moment, everything is well with the world.

Regretfully, the moment does not last. In a matter of minutes, Ragnor comes for us. One by one we are called to the door, our hands are tied before us, and we are led to the platform. I am the first one out, and I watch my friends as they come forth, Jilly limping, Ellen and Tobias pale and nervous, Colm resolved yet steady, and Pace and Levi alert and watchful. I keep my eyes on them, in case they see something I don't.

Once more the entire village is assembled. It is easier to see them in the early morning light. Men, women, and children, babes in arms and old . . . older than I have ever seen, with bowed bodies and wrinkled faces and toothless mouths. How old are they? Much older than the forties that are the limit of a shiner's life. Sixty? Seventy? They are quieter this morning, chatting among themselves, some of them studying us, as we are paraded by their ranks.

We stop before the platform, which is empty except for Wulf's chair. The sky opens before us, clear and so very blue. The air smells fresh, even with the press of bodies behind us. Dew covers the hilltops of green in the distance, and birds flit overhead, busily seeking out their morning meal. This world could be so beautiful, for every one of us. Why do tyrants seek to ruin it? Why is one person's power more important than the good of the whole? When you come down to it, my father and Wulf are not that different. And even though the rovers live outside, they are just as trapped as the people in the dome. All of us are victims of self-serving, power-hungry mad men.

We wait for Wulf to make his appearance. And he does, striding up in his cape, with his men trailing behind. Two stop at the steps, and the other two follow him up on the platform, where his chair awaits him.

The crowd presses closer. Wulf nods his head; Janna points to Ellen, and two of Ragnor's men take her arms.

"No," she protests. "No." She twists in their arms and tries to reach for Pace. She does not have a chance against their raw strength, and they haul her up the steps. The crowd grows louder as Ellen tries to shake off her escorts. The crowd laughs and jeers, yelling insults at Ellen and the guards. Pace bristles beside me and looks over my head at Levi, who shakes his head. Ragnor's men stand around us, their guns ready. We can't do anything to help ourselves now. We would not stand a chance.

Wulf lets the crowd work themselves up before he rises from his chair and silences them by lifting his large hands. When he is satisfied that he has everyone's attention he speaks. "Who ah-bids on this woman?"

"What's she ah-fit for?" Someone yells out.

"Ah she's too old to warm a bed!" someone else yells.

Ellen cringes with humiliation. She lowers her head and bites her lip.

"Damn them!" Pace yells out and is promptly punched in the gut with the butt of a rifle. He bends over in reflex and curses again before he rises up with such a look of hatred on his face that I barely recognize him. I want such to help him, but I can't. Ragnor's man keeps a tight hold on me so that I can barely move, much less comfort Pace.

Ellen starts to cry, and I hear Jilly crying also. "Jilly, don't give them the satisfaction," I say. I don't know if she can hear me over the crowd.

"I'll ah-give a goat for the goat," someone yells.

"Buying ah-wife to replace the one ye lost?" someone says, and the crowd laughs.

They aren't much different from us, I realize. People are people no matter where they are. But we would never use people as slaves. We would never buy or sell them, even though we were given no more consideration than slaves. We, along with the rest of the workers in the dome, were slaves to the royalty of the dome, just as the rovers are slave to the whims of Wulf. And now we are to be slaves to those who are enslaved. And I have no doubt that Wulf will make sure this auction ends up the way he wants it to.

Wulf looks at Ragnor, who nods in agreement. Ellen is sold for a goat. The man who bought her walks up to Ragnor and hands him a token, which is nothing more than a round and smooth piece of wood, no bigger than my palm, with an insignia of some sort carved in it. The man is one of the older ones, definitely older than Ellen. He has only a few wisps of hair on his head and one of his front teeth is gone. His clothing, like everyone else's, is a hodgepodge of hide and cloth, yet his looks a bit more ragged than the rest. Ellen is brought off the platform and the rope around her wrists given to the man. She tries to jerk away and is promptly slapped.

Pace explodes beside me, driving through the guards and trying to reach his mother. One of Ragnor's men drives the butt of his rifle into the back of Pace's head and he falls forward.

"No!" I cry out. I try to get to him, to shelter him from their blows as the rest circle around him and kick him and jab him with their guns. Janna shoves me aside. "Stop them!" I cry out. Ragnor wades into the melee and pushes them off while Janna grabs their ears and turns them around. I try to keep my eyes on Pace, who I am afraid will be beaten to death before Ragnor can save him.

Ellen cries as she is led away, and I hear Jilly choking back sobs. Someone jostles me, one of the men who was beating on Pace, and

I stumble. As I try to right myself I catch Levi out of the corner of my eye. He stands behind Colm and Tobias, and I catch the glint of the knife in his hand. Was this their plan? Surely not. It is too much of a risk, especially for Pace.

Ragnor finally hauls Pace to his feet and both their faces are livid. Pace's already shows the bruises from his beating and blood drips from the side of his mouth.

"Where is she?" Pace yells. "Where did he take her?"

I shake my head. "I couldn't see." I reach out to touch the blood on his lip, and he pushes my hand away, searching the crowd for signs of Ellen. Meanwhile Ragnor thumps his men in the chest and shoves them into place.

"Ye fools," he yells. "He is ah-profit for all of us."

"Is that how you see us?" I ask, and he turns his head in surprise. "Nothing more than profit? We are people, just like you and Janna. How would you feel if your mother was sold? Or your wife?"

Ragnor comes perilously close to me, so close that I can see the gold flecks in his pale blue eyes. "Ye are not to ah-speak." Within his eyes I see doubt. I do not back down, and it is Ragnor who is the first to turn away.

I finally look up at Wulf. His eyes are on me, and he smiles evilly. There is no doubt in my mind he is enjoying this. Every bit of it. Wulf points to Tobias.

Tobias's sale, followed by Colm's, goes through fairly quietly. I do not understand some of the things that are bid for them, but the process goes on. Ragnor is given markers by the bidders, and Colm and Tobias are led away.

I steal a look at Levi. What has he done with the knife? As far as I can tell his hands are still bound.

Wulf points to Jilly, and Ragnor carries her up the platform and leaves her standing with her weight on one foot. Jilly is still dressed in my pants, socks, and the remnants of her dress with the shawl wrapped around her bare shoulders.

"Whuts she ah-waring?" someone yells out.

"We need to ah see whut we're ah-buying," someone else yells.

Wulf stands and raises his hands over the crowd to quiet them. Then he goes to Jilly and the crowd seems to take a collective breath.

"No," I say. I look at Levi, who shakes his head. "No!" I yell again, looking at Janna. She shrugs.

Wulf rips the shawl from Jilly's shoulders with a flourish, and the crowd cheers. Jilly flinches. I am afraid that she will crumble, but she stays strong.

"Oh God." We need a miracle, and there is no place for it to come from. Still I pray, because there is nothing else I can do.

Wulf grabs the tail of her dress and teasingly lifts it to more yells and screams. Jilly crosses her arms and Wulf smirks. A breeze teases her hair and lifts it so that is streams across Wulf's face and the crowd laughs.

He doesn't like that. Not at all. He whips a knife from his belt and Jilly shrieks in fear. He lifts her skirt and with his knife quickly cuts my pants away from her body and flings them into the crowd, who fight over the pieces as if they are the last morsels of food and they are dying of hunger.

Animals. And to think I thought we were alike. They are nothing more than animals.

Wulf grabs Jilly's dress at the nape and holds his knife to it. I thought the screams from the crowd were loud before. Now they are deafening. All because they want to shame a young girl. I look to the sky, because I cannot stand to watch what will happen next.

I see a flash of yellow. To my utter amazement, Pip swoops down over our heads, chirping madly. He quickly circles us and then soars upward, landing on the post where they tied the man who was beaten.

A shadow covers us, surprising because there was not a cloud in the sky when we came out. Wulf stops what he is doing and looks to the east. Explosions suddenly fill the air. The crowd screams and yells. Some fall to the ground with their hands over their heads. Others run, shoving weaker and smaller ones out of their way. Before I have time to react, Levi has my hands and has sliced through the ropes. Pace is next and we scoot under the platform.

"I've got to get my mother," Pace says.

"Is it Lyon?" I ask.

"It is," Levi says with a wide grin.

I can't believe it. Lyon. I can't help but grin back at Levi. It is a miracle, and I send up a quick thank-you like shooting an arrow into the sky. He's here. Lyon is here to save us.

The encampment is in chaos. Levi pops up, grabs one of Ragnor's guards, who is looking at the sky, and slits his throat before anyone sees what is happening. He drags him beneath the platform and gives Pace his rifle. The ground shakes beneath our feet and shakes again. It is rhythmic, like a thousand people or more marching in time or like the hammering in the tunnels.

"What is that?" I ask Levi.

"More than likely something Dr. Stewart has put together." Levi replies.

Shots ring out and people scream and run in confusion. I can hear Wulf shouting on the platform and the stomping of feet.

"We've got to get Jilly down from there," I say.

"I'm working on it," Levi says. He nods to Pace. They both reach out at the same time and grab two men by the ankles. They drag them under. Levi stabs the knife into the base of his victim's neck and then takes out Pace's man with a quick slice of his throat.

We now have three guns. I quickly look at the victims. I am not averse to killing rovers, but I don't want Ragnor to be one of the dead. For some reason I think he can still be of help to us.

The pounding is louder now, heavier, so much so that the ground shakes beneath us. People scream in terror as shots continue to come from the *Quest*. I see it now, floating above, well out of range of the rovers' guns. The sun's rays wink off of it, almost blinding me, so I slide my goggles over my eyes. I can see two of Lyon's men on the deck around the cabin, picking off the rovers who are trying to shoot back.

"Go find your mother and see if you can find the rest," Levi says. "Wren and I will go after Jilly."

"Wren?" Pace looks at me, his lovely blue eyes torn with indecision.

"Go," I say. He nods, takes up his gun and slides from beneath the platform before he disappears into the crowd.

Levi darts his head out and back under before I can blink. "He's using her as a shield," he says.

"Bastard."

"You got that right."

"What do we do?"

"Do you think you can take him from behind if I distract him?"

I have to, to give Jilly a chance, but I cannot help but remember my meeting with Wulf. I have never felt such terror, not even when I thought I would be burned alive. He is evil incarnate. I want to stay as far away from him as possible.

I look around the platform. Every place is clear except for where we originally were standing. Rovers are still milling about in confusion. I see a child, five or six years old, crouching under the platform behind us with his eyes screwed shut.

"I can do it," I say.

"That's my girl," Levi says with a grin. He's actually enjoying this. He cups my cheek and drops a quick kiss on my lips before he slips out from beneath the platform. Once again I am caught up in his golden glory. I can't go through this again. This is not the time to think about him, or Pace. I must concentrate on what I have to do. I go to the back of the platform, which borders the stream, see that I am clear, except for the child, and come out. Now I just have to figure out a way to get on the platform while carrying one of the awkwardly long rifles.

Luckily there is a huge boulder right off one of the platform's supports. I climb on it and can see the surface now. Wulf holds Jilly clamped against his body with one of his huge arms while he holds the knife to her throat with the other. Levi stands on the steps with the rifle pointed at Wulf.

I quickly look around to make sure there is no one else about to foil our plan to rescue Jilly. The explosions we heard were the guard towers. Now they are nothing but smoking piles of wood. The *Quest* hovers overhead. I hope they recognize us and don't shoot us. I think the chances are good they will. There are not many with Levi's golden hair. I am sure Zan is up there, making sure we are not shot. I do not glance up to see. Levi's eyes flick my way. He is waiting on me to make his move.

I place the gun on the platform as quietly as possible. Then I leverage my body up with my arms until I can swing my legs up. So far so good. I pick up the gun and creep silently toward Wulf and Jilly. I can still hear the heavy *thump-thump* sound and the angry, scared screams and yells of the rovers. What is making that noise?

"Let her go and we will leave your people alone," Levi says.

"She's staying with me," Wulf says.

I slide my hands into what I hope is the proper position to hold the gun. It is so much longer and awkward than the gun Levi taught me to shoot with. I look down at it and realize I have no idea how to shoot it. I recognize the trigger, but there's supposed to be a safety on it. I don't know what to do.

Levi comes up the rest of the steps so he is completely exposed. I'm not ready but Levi does not know that. I do the only thing I know to do. I switch the rifle in my hands like it's a club and swing at the back of Wulf's head. He either has eyes in the back of his head or he senses it because he turns as I swing. He shoves Jilly away and catches the rifle before it strikes him. Jilly falls to the platform and manages to scramble away on her hands and knees.

Levi shoots Wulf. So why do I feel it? I look at Wulf, who somehow has a hole in his stomach, and then down at the blood that blossoms forth on mine. Wulf staggers for me, but Levi brings the gun down on the back of his head and he crashes to the platform.

"Damn things are only good for one shot," Levi says. Then he sees me and the color drains from his face. "Oh God, Wren."

All I can do is look at the blood spreading on my clothes. Levi snatches up the shawl that still lies on the platform, folds it many times, and places it on my stomach. "Hold this here," he commands. I place my hands over it and hold it in place. Levi rips off his shirt and ties it around my body.

"I was shot," I say.

"I know, love," he says. "I was the one who shot you. The bullet passed through him and into you." He looks at Jilly. "You're going to have to walk. I've got to carry her." Jilly scrambles to her feet. I can tell she is still in shock, and I wonder if I am. Levi picks me up in his arms and my hands instinctively go to my wound. Levi takes off down the stairs, and each step jars me. Over Levi's shoulder I see Jilly following us as best she can with her injured foot.

How does he know which way to go? For some reason he does

and takes off. I reach out my hand to Jilly. "Keep up," I say, or I think I say. I cannot be certain.

Levi must have heard me. "Grab on to my belt and don't let go," he instructs Jilly. She grabs on as we take off again.

"Pace," I think I say. "Where is Pace?" My mouth feels like it is disconnected from my brain.

"He'll be along," Levi says.

"Colm? Tobias?"

"Let's worry about you now."

"Wait!" A girl calls out to us. She's thin, small, and pretty with pale blond hair. Another younger girl is with her, along with three boys who don't look more than ten. "We're from the dome. Take us with you."

I see her over Levi's shoulder. "Wait," I say. Something Jon told me surfaces in my mind. "Bess?" Levi swings around to look at them.

"Yes, I'm Bess."

"Come on," Levi says. "Help her," he says, and Bess takes Jilly's hand. "Stay close and do what I do."

Levi takes off at a trot, and each step sends pain shooting through my body. I've been shot. I still can't believe it. Will I die? *God, don't let me die.* I might have wanted to die last night, but now I very much want to live.

We wind our way through the huts. The village seems empty. Where have the people gone? Are they huddling inside, away from the shooting? I still hear shots. Then someone shouts.

"Levi!" It is Colm and Tobias. They run up to us. "What happened? What is that thing in the sky?"

"My family," Levi says. "Wren's been shot, Pace went to find his mother. We've got to get to the ridge while they're covering us. Oh, and these kids are coming with us, they're from the dome."

"Climb on," Colm says to Jilly, and she hops onto his back. Tobias picks up the younger girl and we take off again only to stop short. I twist my head around to see what stopped us.

Ragnor, Janna, and his brother whose name I still don't know.

"She's hurt?" Ragnor asks.

"Shot," Levi says. He leaves out the details. "Let us go and we can help her. Save her."

Am I going to die? "Pace," I say. "I need to see Pace."

"Shhh." Levi bends his head. Is he comforting me or maybe he just wants me to keep quiet. I don't. Instead I speak to Ragnor.

"Come with us. You don't have to live this way."

"Go," Ragnor says. "I will ah-look for your ah-man."

"Thank you," I say, and Levi and Jilly echo the sentiment. We take off again. There is no direct route through the village, so Levi continues to weave his way around the huts until suddenly we are clear.

I now know what was shaking the earth. Standing before us, in the field we walked through when we were brought into the village, is a huge machine. It is as tall as my father's building and looks like a box with four huge legs attached to it. The front of the box has a long extension. There are windows on the front and side that I can see and guns extend from each one, aimed at the area behind us.

Everyone stops and Levi lets out a whoop. A hatch opens on top and Alcide pops out and waves. "Woohoo!" he yells with a wide grin on his dear, sweet face.

"Wren's hurt," Levi yells. "Where is Dr. Stewart?"

"In here," Alcide yells back. "Wait." He disappears and pops back out. "Go find James." He points up the ridge. "He's on a cycle. We'll cover your back until everyone is safe. Then we'll transfer you to the *Quest*." Levi nods and starts to run. "Wait!" Alcide yells. "Where are Pace and Zan?"

"Zan?" Levi yells back.

"Isn't she with you?" Levi looks at me and the color drains from his face. "Go, go, go!" Alcide yells as a bullet whines over our heads.

"Watch for Pace!" Levi yells back, and we take off again. I keep my hands on my stomach. I can feel the blood seeping through the shawl and I am growing cold.

"Where is Zan?" I ask. I feel confused. Why did Alcide think Zan was with us? She was left behind on the roof of the dome. She should be with her family. Maybe Zan went into the village to find us. That sounds like something she would do. But wouldn't James be with her? Surely her father would not let her go in alone.

I don't know how he does it, but Levi keeps running, straight up the hill that shelters the rover village with Colm, Tobias, and the rest following behind. I hear gunshots ringing in the distance. Where is Pace?

We finally crest the ridge. James is there, with Jon, David, Harry, and the steam cycles. Behind us we hear the heavy *thump-thump* of the machine following us up the hill.

Confusion starts as everyone is talking at once. Somehow I wind up being held by David as Levi simply hands me to him and picks up a gun. Everything seems as if it is happening at a distance. I see the shadow of the big machine loom over us. I watch as James, Colm, and Tobias hug one another while Harry embraces Jilly, who finally bursts into tears. Jon gathers the children who escaped with us into a fierce hug. They all must be from the scarabs.

"We thought you were dead," David says to me. "My God, Wren," he exclaims when he sees the blood on my hands. "Please don't die now."

"I'll try," I think I say. My mind is having trouble taking everything in. Seeing everyone safe makes me wonder if I am dreaming, or, worse, if I've died. Maybe we are all dead. "Thank God you got out." Even though he seems far away I can plainly see the concern on David's face. "Lucy?"

"She's fine," David says. "Will be glad to see you."

"Where's Pace?" I hear shouting in the distance and more shooting.

"It's Pace!" Jon exclaims. "He's got a woman with him. Rovers are following them."

"They're friends," I say. "David, please put me down."

"Take cover," James barks. "Get behind the cycles." James and Harry kneel and aim their guns while Colm and Tobias lead the children and Jilly to crouch behind the cycles. David puts me down. My legs nearly buckle, but I am stubborn if nothing else. I brace an arm on a cycle and look down the hill while David picks up his rifle. Levi pounds on the leg of the machine, and Peter sticks his head out of a window. "Don't shoot the people with Pace," Levi yells up.

Pace and Ellen are running from the village. Ragnor, Janna, and Ragnor's brother are with them.

"Don't shoot them, they are friends," I call out to the men. Ragnor's brother pitches forward and falls on his face. Ragnor and Janna stop, while Pace and Ellen keep running. I see Wulf coming out of the shelter of the huts with two rifles in his hands and his men right behind him. He has a bandage wrapped around his stomach. How is it he is up running around and I can barely stand?

Because the bullet is still in you . . .

Ragnor's brother must be dead. I watch as Janna pulls at Ragnor, and they once more start up the hill behind Pace and Ellen, who is faltering. She has her skirts gathered and Pace is nearly dragging her. Wulf drops to his knee and raises his rifle.

"Shoot him!" I yell. "Shoot the man with the gun. Shoot him, shoot him, shoot him!"

The men start shooting. But they are in the wrong place to get a line of sight and Wulf has made himself into a very small target. I am more worried about them hitting Pace and the rest.

"Shoot them!" Levi bangs on the machine and points down the hill. Where is the *Quest*? All they have to do is fly in between them. I search the skies but don't see it. It must have circled behind us and is lost in the trees.

Levi moves to the other side of the machine and gets a better line. He shoots and dirt sprays up in front of Wulf. His men start shooting back at Levi's position. I know their guns can't shoot as far as ours, but it is still dangerous. Pace and Ellen, Ragnor and Janna are still well within Wulf's range. Ellen falls and Pace is pulled backward and nearly falls himself. Ragnor bends to help Ellen up along with Pace, and Janna runs ahead. They pull Ellen to her feet.

Wulf shoots.

I scream for Pace.

Levi shoots again, and the men in the machine shoot at Wulf's position.

Ellen falls between Pace and Ragnor, and Pace drops beside her. And then I slide into darkness.

· 19 ·

I am floating. Does this mean I'm dead? I can't be dead, I hurt
too much. "Jane?" I recognize the face looking down at me. For
some reason she looks very sad.

"You're safe now," she says. "On the *Quest*." I look up. I'm in a
very soft bed beneath clean sheets in a very nice room.

"Zan?" I say. I meant to ask if I am in Zan's room because that's
the only place I can think of that would be this nice.

"We don't know where she is," Jane says. She wipes her eyes and
smiles tremulously.

I am confused. How could they not know where Zan is? "In the
fight? Pace?" I ask as my last memory comes to me.

"He's fine, dear," Jane says. "Unfortunately his mother did not
make it."

"Ellen . . ." I screw my eyes shut. I am so confused. What happened to Zan? How is she lost? And Ellen is dead. I need to see
Pace, but the thought of moving is more than I can handle at the
moment.

"Get some rest," Jane urges, and tucks the blankets up under my chin. I drift away, wondering which part of my life is real and which is a dream.

◆

I wake the next morning to sunlight streaming through a window. I ache all over. I put a hand to my stomach where I was shot. There is a thick pad over my wound and a bandage wrapped around my torso. I am dressed in a short gown. Zan's, I am certain. I am also remarkably clean, except for my hair, which is braided and wrapped around my head like a crown.

And I'm hungry, which I take as a sign that I am not going to die. I slowly and tentatively sit up, because I am also thirsty and there is a carafe of water on the table next to the bed.

"Good morning." Levi leans in the doorway. He's dressed in a white shirt and tan pants, and he looks absolutely wonderful. He also seems sad.

"What happened?" I ask.

"That's my girl, straight for the throat," he says as he comes into the room. "How are you feeling?"

I take a mental inventory of my body. Of course I am sore where I was shot, and I have more bruises than I can count, along with another scar on my temple. But I am alive and we are safe. That goes a long way to making me feel better. "Okay," I say, and Levi smiles his glorious smile.

He comes in. "May I?" he asks, indicating the side of the bed.

"Yes."

He pours me a glass of water and hands it to me as he sits. I drink it greedily, knowing that it is pure and clean. I hand him the empty glass, and he fills is again with a sweet smile.

"Tell me what's happened."

"First of all Dr. Stewart removed your bullet and said it did not hit any internal organs." He picks up a small vial from the table and rattles it. The bullet is inside. He hands it to me and I hold it up to the light.

"It felt much bigger when it was in me," I say.

"I'm so sorry, Wren. I never expected that to happen. That guy is so thick I never dreamed it would pass through." He looks wretched as he apologizes, and I almost feel sorry for him.

"We made it," I say. "That's all that matters. Did we all make it?"

"Everyone but Ellen," Levi says sadly.

I put my hand to my heart as it aches at Levi's news. "Where is Pace?" I ask. Where else would he be but grieving for his mother, but the thought of him alone at this time is more than I can stand.

"Building her a coffin."

I look at him in confusion. "He wants to bury her." Now I understand. Pace told me about people burying their dead in the ground before the dome.

"Lyon moved everyone to a safer place after we went into the dome. A place on higher ground that was easily defensible. That's where we are now. They accomplished quite a bit while we were inside. They built a large stockade with a cabin and shelter for the animals and . . ."

Suddenly a gray striped ball of fur leaps onto the bed and bounds for me. "Jonah!" I exclaim and gather him to me. His purr rumbles as he butts his head beneath my chin.

Levi reaches out and rubs Jonah's back. "He's been right beside you ever since we carried you in. And your pony is fine also. I know you worry over them."

I smile my gratitude. "He's been on the *Quest* the entire time?"

"Jane couldn't stand to leave him behind after . . ."

"After what?" Jonah moves from my hands to sit next to me on the bed. He presses his back against my hip and begins to groom himself, purring loudly as he does so.

"They thought we were dead," Levi says. "Which is why they didn't rescue us. When Lyon went to the dome there were three burned bodies staked outside the dome that resembled us in size. A few of my personal items were there with them."

"My father's work," I say. Then I ask. "Where is Zan? I remember something about her being missing."

Levi picks up my hand. "Zan has been missing since the night we went into the dome."

"What? How?"

"Lyon doesn't know. She simply disappeared. It took them two days to get out of the mines. There was a lot of backtracking because the tunnels had changed. Zan was not here when they finally made it out. Since all the gliders were still on top of the dome, Lyon flew the *Quest* over and they went down on the ladder. The gliders were there, along with Zan's fur coat and hat, but Zan was simply gone."

"Could she have fallen off?"

"They searched everywhere. There was no sign of her. Not even a scrap of clothing."

"She went inside," I say. "That's the only logical explanation."

"I hope so," Levi says. "Thank God there were only three bodies out there."

"You don't think one of them could have been Zan do you?" I ask, panic suddenly filling me.

"She's got several inches on you, heightwise. Lyon said the body and clothing style matched you. Plus the victim had brown hair that wasn't burned off."

"I wonder who they were," I say. "Probably more of the poor scarabs."

I think about the scarabs we saw imprisoned when we were

taken outside. The poor people, left there to starve and be tools in my father's games. Then another memory comes to me. One from the cells. "Levi. I think I know where Zan is."

"What?" he asks in disbelief. "Where?"

"When we were put in the cells, Pruitt asked if Jilly and I should be put in the same cell as another girl. Findley told him no, to put us in a cell by ourselves and to take the girl up to my room. That night I heard them move her. She was raising quite a ruckus, but I couldn't make out what she was saying." I squeeze Levi's hand. "It has to be Zan. Who else could it be?"

"You're right," Levi says, and his smile lights the room. "It has to be. I'll go tell Lyon and Jane." He jumps up from the bed and drops a kiss on my forehead before he leaves, and I am alone once more, except for Jonah. I lean over, somewhat painfully, and bury my nose in his fur. I immediately get dizzy and lean back on my pillow.

I need food, but, more importantly, I need to see Pace. His mother is dead and he has to be grieving. I will not let him go through this alone. I wait for the dizziness to pass, and then slowly and carefully I rise from the bed. My legs are wobbly but they hold, and I make my way to the water closet with Jonah trailing behind me.

My boots sit on the floor. My goggles are on a small table. Zan's leather pants are there also. That is when I realize that my boots and my goggles are my only possessions. I've lost everything. My home, my family, and the few meager things I owned. Yet I have so much. My freedom, good friends—I smile at Jonah, who sits on the edge of the tub—and two outstanding young men who claim to love me. I have so much to be grateful for.

I lean on the sink and look in the mirror. I have a bruise on the left side of my face that stretches from my cheek up into my hairline and a cut that will add another scar to my collection.

I ease the gown off over my head. My stomach is tightly bandaged and the tightness gives my wound a sense of comfort although it does make it hard to move. I turn around to look at my back in the mirror. It is peppered with bruises, as are my upper arms and the back of my right hand. My legs are in much better shape that the rest of my body, so I have great hope that they will continue to support me.

I am grateful to be alive. I am also grateful that we were rescued, that for the most part we survived this. That David, Lucy, and Harry managed to escape the dome also.

Now we just have to find Zan, convince the people inside the dome that the only future there, for everyone, is if we tear down the walls and prepare for another rover attack, because I know Wulf will not let our escape go without some sort of retribution.

"It's going to be a busy day," I tell Jonah. "No time for laying about for us."

I hate raiding Zan's things for something to wear, but I don't have much choice. I go into the living area of the Hatfields cabin to find Levi, Lyon, and Jane talking.

"Wren," Jane exclaims. "You shouldn't be up. I was just going to bring you a tray."

"I need to see Pace," I say. "But first I wanted to say thank you, for everything. Especially for rescuing us from the rovers."

"You should thank Peter also," Lyon says. "He's the one who saw you. We could not believe it when he said you were alive."

"How did he know?"

"We've had someone posted at the entrance to the dome every day, hoping for news of Zan. We were certain you three were dead, and I tried everything I knew of to get in or to get someone to respond, but there was nothing. If not for those three bodies we found outside I would have thought the dome empty," Lyon says. "I knew Zan had to be inside and knew that when we went inside it would have to be with a show of power. That's when Jethro came to me with his idea for a walking fortress."

"That's the big machine with the guns," Levi explained as I perch on the edge of a side table while I listen to the news. Jonah makes himself at home on the back of the sofa, purring loudly while I listen to the news.

"Actually, I call it a tank," Lyon says. "Because the top looks like a big water tank to me. We made it from metals we scavenged from the area's castle ruins. Old suits of armor and things like that. While searching for supplies we found our current location. A fortress originally set here. Dr. Stewart thinks it dates back to medieval times. It is easily defensible with a good supply of water."

"Dr. Stewart was just testing the tank when Peter showed up, out of breath from running the entire way, to tell us that he saw you three, along with the rest, given to some rovers outside the dome," Jane says. "We were overjoyed when he said one was Rosalyn's husband and the other his uncle. David and Lucy knew the other young woman had to be Jilly, and of course we had no idea who Pace's mother was until you were rescued. I'm so sorry that we lost her."

"But thank God that you were able to rescue us," I say.

"We also came across a few other people while we were escaping through the mines," Lyon adds. "And we managed to round up several chickens and bring them out with us," he says with a grin.

My heart swells with gratitude. More shiners are alive. I can't wait to see who survived. But first I ask. "For what purpose did Dr. Stewart build his tank?"

"To break the glass," Levi says with a grin. "And we're going to, now that we know where Zan is."

◆

Jane would not let me leave the *Quest* until I ate something, which I did, heartily. Levi waits for me and when I am done we walk outside. The *Quest* is moored to a stone tower on a hillside. From the deck I can see the top half of the dome in the distance, to the south and west of where we stand.

"How far is it?" I ask as a gentle breeze teases my hair. I take a deep, albeit painful breath of the fresh, free air.

"Five miles or more."

"And Peter ran the whole way," I say in awe. "Before we left the mines, I was certain he would die soon of the black lung."

"Leaving probably saved his life," Levi says. He squeezes my hand that sits on the railing of the deck, and then we walk to the steps that lead to the top of the tower, where a platform has been constructed for easier access. The tower has an opening where a door probably stood before the fires; now it just yawns empty.

"Over there is the rover settlement," Levi says and points to the south and east. "Six or seven miles." I cannot see anything but my innate sense of direction tells me where it is located. "And the channel straight south."

The *Quest* is suspended just about the trees, but we are so much higher than everything else that I feel as if I can see forever. Indeed I can; to the west, I see a long stretch of gray that has to be the ocean. I know anyone looking this way would be hard pressed to see anything beyond a trail of smoke. With her shiny surface the *Quest* is nearly impossible to see from a distance, as the sun would just reflect back the sky. I look to the north and see green hills rolling into the distance, a land as immense as the sea, although I know differently after seeing it on the map.

"And this is what we call the enclave, until the lot of you decide on a name yourself."

I look down at the castle ruins. They sit on top of a large rolling knoll and trees have been cleared around the area, no doubt by our group, since everywhere I look I see newly cut wood used in building. Beyond the walls are neat rows of dirt, and just a touch of green peeps up from the ground. A stream of water runs around the ruins, and I remember Pace calling it a moat when he told me about castles from the days long before the comet. The tower has two walls that run from it, forming half of a square. The rest of the square is made of wooden posts placed side by side and lashed with rope. The square is large, nearly as large as our cavern down below. The stone walls have a wide ledge, big enough to walk safely on. The wall comes up some four feet above the ledge on the outside, and I realize the wall is there to hide behind in battle. The same thing is repeated on the walls built of wood. Boards run around the interior walls as a walkway and shelter from attack. It is well thought out. We will be safe here.

One stone wall has a house built against the entire length. The other holds smaller sheds. I hear noise coming from one of the sheds. Hammering. That must be where Pace is. One of the wooden walls has pens built against it and the pens hold the goats and other animals. "Sheep?" I ask Levi when I see the short and stout fluffy animals.

"They found them grazing nearby and rounded them up using the steam cycles," he explains. "There's also a herd of wild horses around. I can't wait to see them."

I've never seen a horse before; to think they survived all these years. I can't wait to see them myself.

"I can't believe the rovers have not made use of them," Levi continues. "They would be a lot more deadly on horseback."

That was not something I wanted to even consider. "Where are the ponies?"

"Outside grazing," Levi says and points. I look beyond the walls and see them on a nearby slope and quickly recognize Ghost among them. Two people are with them, a boy and a girl. I recognize Freddie and Nancy, still drawn to each other after losing their parents.

There are two stone rings in the square, and Colm and Tobias are busy at work putting a shed over them. Chickens peck in the grass of the square, and Rosalyn and Lucy hang laundry on a line. Everywhere I look I see cats lying about, on the wall, on the rooftops, around the yard. And of course, Jonah, who winds between my legs as I look around. There is also an abundance of plants, growing in every imaginable container that was scrounged from the ruins. It is good to see that we will not starve, if the newly planted rows outside and the plants growing inside are any indication.

Levi sees where I am looking at and explains. "Dr. Stewart was able to identify many indigenous fruits and vegetables growing wild, and they have been transferred here. We also carry packets of seed with us on the *Quest* just in case we are ever grounded for long periods of time and to help those who may need it."

"It's a wonderful thing that you do," I say. "I know without you we would have been lost."

"It is worth it," he says, and I know he is not talking about helping us as a group. "Every minute of it."

I choose to ignore his hint and instead focus on the things around me. "Where is everyone else? Adam, James, Alcide?"

"Most of the men are with our troops, scouting for rovers and learning how to operate the tank," Levi explains. "Since we won't be able to take it with us when we go." His voice trails off, sadly.

I can't think about that now. I always knew that the day would come when the Hatfields would move on, but I've put it to the back of my mind, like so many other things. For so long my life has consisted of just staying alive and living day to day, that I've not taken the time to think of the future and what it will bring.

"This way," Levi says, back to his usual cheerful self. He leads me into the tower, which is nothing more than a winding staircase. We are about five stories up and the wall of the tower has tall and narrow windows that let in the light. "Arrow slits," Levi explains. Along the wall lanterns have been hung to light the way at night. I smile at the thought that has gone into this place. I have yet to see the details but I am confident we will be safe here. That we have found a new home.

Jonah skips down the stairs with his tail straight in the air and meows when he gets too far ahead of us. Levi walks slowly for my sake. I am weak from my wound but I press on. I must see Pace.

We come out in the yard between the cabin and the sheds. I was wrong about Pace; it is George, who is the oldest of the shiners that survived, doing all the hammering. The sheds hold an assortment of things I've never seen before. More treasures left by the former inhabitants of this land.

The cabin is built of logs that are notched together. There is a door in the center and three windows on either side with wooden coverings raised above them on hinges. An overhang runs the length of it with posts every so often to keep it upright. Pip's cage hangs from a hook beneath it. The door is open and he is gone. With Pace, I hope. I will never forget the sight of him flying over our heads at the rover camp. As if he'd come himself to rescue us.

Lucy runs to me as soon as we come out while Levi moves on to where Colm and Tobias are working. "Wren, oh Wren," she says and pulls me into a hearty embrace. "It is more beautiful than I could imagine." Tears fill her dark and lovely eyes. "I just wish Alex could have seen all this . . . and my parents." She hurriedly wipes away the tears and hugs me again. "Thank you. For everything."

"It wasn't me, Lucy," I say. "It was all of us, working together." She is still so beautiful with her dark hair and eyes, although her skin is not as white as it was before, due to her time in the sun. "I was so worried about you. I am so glad you made it out." I look around. "Where is Jilly?"

"She's inside helping Sally with the children's lessons." Lucy takes my hands in hers as we step apart. "I have something to ask you," she says. "David and I are to be married. Will you stand up with me? Harry is going to stand with David."

I smile. "I would be honored." Then I ask. "Who is going to marry you?"

"Lyon says that all ship's captains have the legal right to marry people. So Captain Manning will do it. We are planning on having it tomorrow if you feel up to it. We're also going to build our own cabin close by, as are Rosalyn and Colm."

"That's wonderful news," I say, genuinely happy for her. "How is Adam, by the way? Last I saw him he was recovering from his injuries."

"He is fine," Lucy assures me. "His arm is still in a sling and he wasn't able to participate in your rescue, which made him angry, but he is out with the men today, learning how to work that giant war machine and teaching David and Harry how to shoot."

"I heard that more shiners were saved when you went through the tunnels."

"Yes, my cousin, Joe, and his wife, Nell. Their little boy was with the children. Little Joey. They are building also."

"That's wonderful news," I say. "We will have our own little village here. Was there anyone else?"

Lucy shakes her head. "That's it, except for all these chickens. We came upon them and just herded them out before us once James found the way. Oh, and the canaries."

I had forgotten about the canaries. I have gotten so used to Pip, especially after Pace tamed him. But there were several more, all kept in cages in a chamber close by our village so they could be picked up and taken to whatever tunnel was needed.

"I freed them," Lucy says. "Those that were still alive. Some of them had starved, poor things, but the rest . . . After knowing that Pip was the reason you came back in, I couldn't stand the thought of abandoning the rest, so when I saw that we were close by I just turned them loose. The last we saw of them they were flying up out of the place where the dome caved in."

"And hopefully they made it outside. The only birds I recall seeing when we went back in were some pigeons. I bet the bees have all left the dome too." Bees were kept on one of the rooftops to keep our gardens pollinated. "I bet my father doesn't even realize it."

"He'll realize it when they don't have any fruit or vegetables," Lucy says.

I look around the yard, at all the progress that's been made in the two and a half weeks that we were gone, and I am amazed. We shall do well here. I know it. We can plant gardens and build homes and grow strong on our own. We don't need the dome, and as long as we can stay away from the rovers we'll be fine. But I can't forget the faces of the scarabs who were held prisoner, or the workers who are deemed worthless because of someone else's actions. Or the fact that my father is holding Zan prisoner. These things cannot go on.

Rosalyn comes to me and gives me a hug. "I knew my Colm was alive," she said. "If you had not gone in, we might never have found him." Rosalyn, along with Adam, was on the council that governed us when we lived in the tunnels.

I realize now that our trip inside, even though disastrous for the three of us, and Zan, was a godsend for Colm and Tobias, Lucy, David, and Harry. Perhaps even Jilly, if she is happy now. "I'm so glad," I say to Rosalyn. "What are they doing?"

"Making a cover for our wells," she explains. "I believe the water comes from the underground river. It tastes the same."

"It could run beneath us for miles," I say. "It's hard to even imagine how many."

"Here's hoping we never have to find out."

"Wren!" Jilly calls to me from the door of the cabin. Rosalyn gives me another quick hug and goes back to her work with Lucy. Colm grins at me before I turn to go to the cabin with Jonah in his usual spot, trailing after me.

"Thank God you're up and about," Jilly says as she hugs me also. "I was afraid we'd lost you."

"How is Pace?" I ask. "Where is he?"

"Digging a grave for his mother," she says. I follow her as she limps into the cabin. She's dressed in some of Zan's clothes also. "James is with him."

"James?" I ask.

She nods. She'd seen the animosity between James and Pace herself. I look around the cabin. We stand in a large room with a two long tables and benches built from split logs. The children sit at one of the tables, intent on their lessons, while Sally, who was their teacher when we lived beneath the dome, works with them on their lessons. A stack of books sits on the table, courtesy of the Hatfields' immense library.

The back wall is made of stone, and there is a fireplace built into it. A long shelf runs across it, and more shelves are built on either side and full of the things we managed to recover from our village, including some odds and ends of clothes. A spinning wheel much like the one we used in our village sits in the corner.

"I wonder where they found that?" I ask.

"In one of the ruins, I suppose," Jilly says. "I cannot wait until I can go out exploring. As soon as this foot heals."

"How is it?"

"Fine since Dr. Stewart cleaned it up. He put some sort of medicine on it, an herbal mixture, he said, and it started feeling better immediately. Didn't even need a stitch to close it."

On either end of the large room is a staircase that leads to an open area. Beyond the staircase are rooms with doors.

Jilly leads me to one of the rooms off to the left. "Pace went looking for a nice spot to bury her and said he found a church with a graveyard nearby. James went back with him to dig the grave. Ellen is in here," she says, and leads me to the room off to the left.

Ellen lies in a box that is supported on two cross pieces of wood with legs attached to them. She wears the same dress she had on since we were captured, but it is clean now, and her hair is neatly combed. Someone took great care with her.

"Jane helped him ready her," Jilly says.

"It should have been me that helped him," I say.

"Don't be ridiculous, Wren," she replies. "You could have just as easily died."

"What happened after I fainted?" I ask. "Where are Ragnor and Janna?"

"They just disappeared. One minute they were there and the next gone. I just know they didn't go back to the village. Pace wouldn't leave Ellen, so David and James went down to help him while Levi and that big walking machine gave them cover. The *Quest* swooped down and took some of us while the rest came back on the cycles and the machine."

"Lyon calls it a tank."

"The tank," Jilly says with a smile.

"Where is it now?"

"Somewhere behind us," Jilly says, pointing behind the stone. "The men all act like it's a big toy to be played with. They are all learning how to drive it and such."

"What about the scarab children and Bess?"

"Jon took them out with those two big dogs to give them a day to recover from everything."

"Belle and Beau are the dogs." I walk over to Ellen's coffin to look closely at her. She looks so much younger now; her face is relaxed and not twisted up with tension and hatred. I am so happy that we had the chance to talk things out and she did not die hating me. I am especially glad that she told me about my mother. The fact that she knew her gave us a connection that I am so sorry we did not get to explore more. We both love Pace. Surely from that common ground we could have built a relationship.

Jilly puts an arm around my shoulder, and I lean my head against hers. "I feel like I've failed him," I say. "Because I wasn't there for him when she died."

"We all have our own ways of grieving," Jilly says. "He was worried about you too, until Dr. Stewart assured him that you would be all right. You can't blame yourself for not being there. You were shot too. You could have died."

"It's just that he was there for me when I lost my grandfather. I know how he feels."

"He hasn't gone anywhere," Jilly says. "You can still help him through this."

"First I must find him."

"Then go," Jilly says. "Find him."

I nod. But I have something to do before I leave. I touch Ellen's hands that lay folded across her stomach. They are still and so very, very cold and empty. I squeeze them gently. "Thank you for raising such a wonderful son."

· 20 ·

I am weaker than I thought. I don't know what I expected. I
suppose the best thing for me to do would be to remain in bed
until I can recover my strength. But since the past few weeks of my
life have consisted of doing nothing but waiting, I carry on, through
the wide gate that protects our enclave and over the flat-planked
bridge that is as new as everything else. Jonah pauses to look at the
water and reach out a tentative paw to test it. Huge rocks sit in the
moat, and more are scattered about in the high grass that covers
the gentle slope that leads down to the forest. They must be the remnants of the original walls. Given enough time, we could move them
back into place to make our walls stronger.

Wouldn't it be even better if we did not need the walls to stay
safe? If we could all live together in peace? I feel that, for us, it will
be a long time coming.

I have no idea where to find Pace. But I hear plenty of noise
about, and there is a path between the neat rows of plantings, so I
follow it with Jonah now scampering ahead. He will lead me to
someone eventually.

"Wren! Wait!" It is Levi, coming through the gate. I stop and wait for him to catch up.

"Do you know where Pace went?" I ask. "Jilly said he went with James to dig a grave."

"I don't," Levi says. "But I will help you find them since I know you are not going to stay in bed and rest."

"No, I'm not," I say with a smile. "It's hard to believe all they accomplished in such a short time."

"My uncle is driven under even the most normal of circumstances. He tends to do a lot when on land because there's not much to do during flight."

"You never doubted him," I say.

"No," Levi says. "But I did wonder what was taking him so long at times." We go to the bottom of the slope and he plucks a stem of grass as we walk and sticks it in his mouth. "Patience is not one of my virtues either."

"I know I was going crazy during the time we were locked up. At least I had books to pass the time. What did you do?"

"You mean when I wasn't getting punched around by dear Mr. Pruitt?" Levi laughs as if it were all a game. "I did my daily calisthenics. I looked for ways out of the cell. And I thought about you quite a bit."

"Levi . . ."

"No pressure, Wren," he says cheerfully. "You know how I feel."

Do I . . . Yes, I know Levi is attracted to me, and I know he likes to kiss me because he does at opportune moments, but has he ever told me his feelings? Has he confessed his love like Pace has on numerous occasions, even when he knows I am not sure about mine? Strange that this is the first time I've even realized this.

"I also had quite a talk with Findley one day. He was quite interested in the outside world," Levi adds.

"But not interested enough to help us escape the rovers."

"He's biding his time, waiting for the right moment." Levi speaks as if Findley's actions are perfectly acceptable. I, meanwhile, am still angry with him at deserting us, as if he decided we were not strong enough to win this battle.

The trail leads into a section of forest, and we follow it through the thick trees while birds and squirrels scold us from the branches and Jonah stalks before us, ignoring the chatter. The land moves down and then up again, and we come out of the trees in the pasture where the ponies graze.

Ghost's head comes up and he scents the air, then with a neigh and a toss of his mane he comes straight to me, with the other ponies following behind. It is amazing to see them move so confidently, even though they are blind from being born in the mines. He butts his head in my chest and snuffs heavily. His head jars my wound and nearly staggers me. Levi catches me before I can fall.

I'm so happy to see my favorite pony. "Ghost." I wrap my arms around his neck, even though my wound pains me. "Oh how I've missed you and worried about you."

"We took care of him for you," Nancy assures me. "We bring them out to graze every morning and make sure they are safe at night."

"We're making carts for them too," Freddie says. "So they can help with the chores. They also did the plowing. All of them."

"They need to work," I say. "They are getting fat from the grass." Ghost snorts as if he understands me, and we all laugh.

I noticed the change in the world when we came out of the dome, but I was too busy trying to stay alive to enjoy it. Now I take a moment to really appreciate it. The blue of the sky, the green of the grass, the new leaves on the trees that are so much brighter than the evergreens. The way Jonah jumps and starts as if he is fighting an imaginary battle. The constant chirping of the birds and the small bursts of color among the grass that I suddenly notice.

I kneel down in the field and cup my hand around a pale violet . . . I look to Levi for the answer. He drops down beside me. "They are flowers." He grins and plucks it from its stalk and places it in the braid around my head. "It is sad to think that you've never seen one, but such a joy to watch your discovery. This is just the first of many that will bloom here." He touches one that is still closed up. "They'll be in all their glory in a few more days."

"I dreamed about it," I said. "In my dream I knew what they were. I was in a field like this, and it was covered with flowers of so many different colors. And there were butterflies everywhere. I think that's why I always knew I'd escape. Because of the dream I had, seeing it in my mind's eye."

"That is one of the best ways to accomplish something, by seeing it in your mind," he touches my head. "And in your heart." His fingertips graze the top of my breast. The way he looks at me I know he wants to kiss me again. But I won't kiss him. Not today and especially not now when Pace is somewhere hurting.

Thank goodness for Nancy. She appears beside us with a fistful of flowers. "Can I put them in your hair?" she asks.

"Please do," I say, grinning at her as Levi laughs.

She begins, humming a song while she weaves in the flowers. Jonah places a paw on my thigh and rises up to sniff the strange things in my hair. When Nancy is done, she steps back with a smile on her face. "You look like a princess," she says, and pirouettes off through the waving stalks of grass.

"Girls," Freddy says, with a roll of his eyes. Still he chases after her, and Levi and I both grin at their play.

"Jane has been reading them fairy tales," Levi explains.

"I read some too, while I was held prisoner," I say. "The princess always needs saving by the prince. I thought the princess should just get up and save herself."

Levi bursts out laughing. "You sound exactly like Zan. God help your father if that's all the books she has to read in there."

"There were others," I say. "Reading them gave me a better understanding of how the world was. I especially enjoyed Jane Austen's stories."

"I imagine the lot of them were first editions," Levi says. "Dr. Stewart will never want to leave when he realizes all the treasures that must be inside."

"Is that all you are worried about?" I ask. "The treasures that are inside? What about the people, Levi? A lot of them are suffering. Aren't you worried about them?"

"Now where did that come from?" Levi asks. "Haven't I proven myself to you over and over again?"

"You have," I say. "I'm sorry. I just feel foolish, wasting my time here in a meadow of flowers when Pace needs me."

Levi opens his mouth to say something, and then shuts it. He stands up and extends his hand. "Let's go find Pace," he says somewhat sadly. I feel wretched now, after spouting off at him. Or maybe it is just that I'm already tired and the day has just barely begun. I take his hand and he pulls me to my feet.

I give Ghost a good-bye hug, and we leave the lovely meadow and go back the way we came. We follow the path in another direction when we return before the enclave. Jonah comes galloping after us and flies by, intent on the new sights and smells before him.

"You've got to realize, Wren, that right now finding Zan is our first priority," Levi says when we enter the forest once more.

"Of course it is," I reply. "I wouldn't expect anything else." I feel the need to explain myself, especially since Levi has been nothing but kind. "It's just that there are so many people inside who are suffering.

You didn't see the things I saw when I was out in the city. You saw the scarabs and that was only a part of it. Everyone inside the dome is at risk, including the royals. Jilly was just the start of it. Now that my father has found that he can touch them, he will eliminate anyone who gets in his way."

Levi stops and grabs my upper arms as if he wants to shake me. "Wren, how many times do you have to be told that you are not responsible for everyone in the dome? How many more times are you going to risk your life to save someone you don't even know? We went back in to save your friends, and it turns out the only one you really knew was Lucy. Isn't it true that you only met the rest the one time?"

I cannot deny it. Still it sounds so callous the way Levi says it. "I could not abandon any of them."

"How many more do you feel the need to save before you are satisfied? How many more chances do you think you have to cheat death?"

I know he feels guilty about shooting me, even if it was accidental. I don't blame him. I've risked my life plenty on my own by rushing into situations without much thought. "Hopefully once more is all I'll need."

"Wren." Levi shakes his head. "Do you know how lucky we were yesterday?"

"Believe me, I know, Levi. I know very well how close I came to dying. Or just wanting to die. But the people who are inside deserve a chance too. The right to chose has been taken from them."

"Yes, by your father," Levi spouts impatiently. "You are not responsible for him, either. The man didn't even want you, and yet everything you do is because you want to win his approval."

As soon as he says the words Levi knows they are wrong. I look at him in stunned silence for one long moment, and then I punch him in the jaw.

Punching him was a mistake. I should have just slapped him. My fist feels like I punched a cave wall, but I do have the satisfaction of knowing that I surprised Levi and may even have hurt him. His hand goes to his face and he tests his jaw by moving his mouth.

I turn to go. I don't know where I am going but I do not care. I just need to get away. I need to find Pace. Before I take two steps Levi grabs my shoulder, wheels me around, puts his hands on my face, and kisses me.

I don't want to kiss him. I just want to go. I could fight him, but I know that will just make him want it more. So I go perfectly still and wait.

He stops. He moves his head back but keeps his hands in place as he studies me, intently, his warm brown eyes searching mine until, finally, he sees the answer that he does not want to see.

"You choose Pace."

"I do." Once I say it my heart lurches in my chest. It feels as if I've been keeping my love for him locked away and suddenly it floods me, filling my soul with such a yearning that it hurts.

"Wren . . ." Levi moves a flower that's come loose from my braid. "There is so much more out there. So much I want to show you. You don't have to settle. Don't you know that?"

"I'm not settling for Pace," I say. "I love him. And he loves me. Don't you realize that's something you've never said to me? You've danced around the word, but you've never said it to me. Sure you want me. And you've asked me to run off and see the world, but you never said 'I love you.' Don't you think that means something?"

He looks more stunned now than he did when I struck him. I

step away, and his hands drop to his side. "I've got to find Pace," I say, and I go, leaving him alone on the path.

◆

Striking out on my own might not have been the best decision I've made, but since my recent history is full of bad decisions I carry on, even though each step is painful. I really should have reconsidered staying in bed. My wound throbs with every move I make. I also have no idea where I'm going. Jilly said something about a church with a cemetery. It seems like it would have to be close by if it served the people who used to live in our enclave.

The path comes to an end on a wider trail, similar to the one that ran close by the catwalk. Jonah turns west and gallops ahead only to stop and turn and look at me. I decide he knows more about this area than I do, so I follow him with my hand pressed against my wound. I have a horrible feeling that I am bleeding again.

We continue down the road, and another smaller one turns off to the left. Jonah makes the turn, and I follow along until I see a stone tower, much smaller than the one at our enclave. I continue on the path until the road curves, and suddenly I am standing before the stone remains of a small building. The roof is gone, but the frame is still there, four stone walls that form a peak on either end and a stone tower beside it. Beyond it is another stone building, small and cozy, in spite of its state; it probably was the residence for the minister.

I see the remnants of a fence also, twisted and rusted iron bars. Jonah trots through an opening, his tail the only thing showing through the tall grass, and I once more follow along. As I go through the gate I see slabs of stone sticking up in rows, and I stop to squat before one, bracing myself on it as I kneel down to look at the words carved into the stone.

The letters are faint and the stone is green with mold, still I run my fingers across them, as if touch will help me decipher the faded words.

Kathleen Simpson
Beloved Wife and Mother
B. June 22, 1803 D. March 9, 1854

She died three years before the comet came. But what about her children? Were they left outside to die, or were they lucky enough to make it into the dome? I suddenly realize that I am standing on her grave, and I stand and move off to the side, memories of Pace's tale of how the dead were placed in the past coming back to me.

I am in a cemetery. This is where Pace came to bury Ellen. It's a beautiful spot. At one time it was probably a lot more open, but now the trees are encroaching on it and weeds have overtaken the gardens. But the sunlight dapples through the leaves in a very pretty way, and somewhere close by a stream runs, and the flow of the water is soothing.

Pip flits to me and lands on the grave marker. He warbles a song and preens his feather and takes off. I follow him, weaving my way around the markers around the back of the church until I see Pace and James standing beside a pile of dirt. This is something I never thought I would see, the two of them working together and talking together as friends. They both have their shirts off and their backs glisten with sweat, and dirt is smeared on their faces and arms. Jonah rushes up to them, meowing as he goes and both look up and see me.

"Shouldn't you be in bed?" James asks. Pace says nothing.

"Yes," I say. "But some things are more important right at the moment." Even though I have walked the entire way, I am out of breath and my wound pains me terribly now. I know I am bleeding, I just don't know how bad it is.

James sticks his shovel upright in the dirt and picks up his shirt, which is hanging on a bush. "I'm glad you survived, Wren," he says. "I'll go back and tell everyone we are ready," he says to Pace. "We will need help getting her down here."

Pace extends his hand to James. "Thank you for helping me," he says.

James looks at Pace's hand and then grasps it in his own. "It was the least I could do," he replies. James pauses by me, as I have not moved from my spot since James spoke to me. "I was scared when you dropped on us yesterday that I wouldn't get a chance to say this." His green eyes are clear and for the first time in all our lives I see his sister and my best friend, Peggy, in them. The innate kindness that she had, and her love of life and everyone she met. "I owe you an apology for how I treated you before. You were right, and you never stopped believing it. Maybe if I had believed it too, so many people wouldn't have died."

"James," I say, and then I don't know what else to say. He puts his hand on my shoulder and smiles at me, and then with another look at Pace he leaves.

Pace sticks in shovel in the dirt also, picks up his shirt and puts it on without buttoning it. Pip floats down and perches on the shovel handle. Pace comes to where I stand, and I have to concentrate on staying on my feet, as the world seems to be spinning around me. I look up into his beautiful blue eyes and I see the sadness in them.

"I couldn't save her," he says.

"I know."

He looks around, at the sky, at the trees, at the ground, even at Jonah, who is busy stalking something through the high grass. I know he's not looking at me because he's trying not to cry. I step closer to him; close enough that I can feel the heat rising from his body. There is a streak of dirt on his cheek, and I touch it with my thumb, smoothing it away. His eyes flit to mine and then away, as if he is shy.

I know why. Because he is not sure where my heart lies. I step closer, sliding my arms around his waist and resting my head beneath his chin, feeling the slick moisture on his chest soaking into my shirt.

Pace raises his arms and wraps them around me.

"I love you, Pace. I want to be with you. Only you."

And then he weeps.

· 21 ·

I should have been there when you woke up," Pace says. Somehow we wound up on the ground. I don't know if it was because my legs gave out or because he was crying. I just know that now we now lay curled up together, Pace on his back, me on my side, and we are completely surrounded by the tall grass with a patch of blue sky above us. We might be lying on a grave. I don't really care at the moment. For the first time since we came out of the dome, I feel a sense of peace, and I don't want to move because I am afraid if I do, I will lose it.

"And spend all that time just watching me sleep?" I ask. "It doesn't matter that you weren't there. All that matters is we are together now."

"I don't know what I would have done if I'd lost you too," he says and his arms hug me just a bit tighter.

"You would go on, Pace." I rise up a bit so I can see his face, even though it is painful to do so. "You'd have to. For me. Just like I would go on if something happened to you. No more dwelling on what has happened for either of us. From now on it has got to be making the most out of the moment that is right in front of us."

"Because we are still not safe out here."

"No, we are not. And who knows if we ever will be. After the time I spent with Wulf, I know he will want revenge for our rescue. I know he will not stop until we are all dead."

"What did happen when you were with him? I have never seen you as frightened as you were when you came back."

I think about what happened, and I know when Pace hears he will be angry, but I also want him to know what a serious threat Wulf is too all of us. "He planned to buy me from Ragnor. Then he promised me that he would rape me. He pinned me on his bed so I would know he was serious. Then he questioned me about the dome. He thought the *Quest* and the dome being at war caused the damage. I didn't bother to tell him differently. I didn't want him to know that we were the ones they'd fought against for fear of his retaliation against all of us. He threatened to scar me with a hot poker if I didn't tell him the truth. That is how I got the burn on my cheek. I am just grateful he didn't ask me about the *Quest* because I know he would have seen through my lies. Are far as he knew, our first time out of the dome was that day."

"The next time I see him I will kill him," Pace says simply, yet it surprises me. I know he will fight when needed, but I have never heard him say anything so violent. I lower my head once more to his shoulder and trace a lazy pattern on his stomach with my finger. "Did they tell you about Zan?" he asks.

"I think she's a prisoner of my father." I explain to him my reasoning behind this, and Pace agrees with my conclusion.

"So we'll be going back into the dome," he says. "But this time, it will be with a show of force."

"With Dr. Stewart's tank?"

"It has a battering ram you know."

"To break the glass."

"To break the glass," he echoes. "I hope he marches it right down the promenade."

"Pace," I say. "I need to ask you something, and I want an honest answer."

"I've always been honest with you, Wren."

"Do you think the reason I am doing all this is to gain favor with my father?"

"What?" he spouts indignantly. "Whatever made you think that?"

"Levi said it. He said I'm trying to get my father's approval and that's why I keep putting myself in dangerous situations, because I need his attention." Those weren't Levi's exact words, but it is the intent I got from his comment.

"This all started way before you knew who your father was. Finding out he is Sir Meredith is just a coincidence, nothing more. You would be fighting this battle no matter who was in charge. That's how passionately you believe in what you are doing. The fact that Sir Meredith is in charge is what saved our lives when we surrendered, which was genius on your part." I feel him move his head so he can see my face, and I twist mine to look up at him. "What did you do when he said that?"

"Punched him in the face."

Pace laughs and it is such a joyous noise that I can't help but grin. "I would love to have seen that." His laughter brings Jonah and Pip both over to investigate. Pip lands on a grave marker and Jonah stretches on his back legs to sniff at the bright yellow canary. Pace smiles at our friends and then he shifts, bringing us both to a sitting position. "Is that what made you make up your mind between me and Levi?"

"No," I confess. "I knew when Wulf had me. Yours was the face

I wanted to see. You were the one I needed to talk to. You were my regret, that I had hurt you. I never wanted to hurt you."

"I would rather go through the hurt to have you be certain of us, than never have pain and have you live with the uncertainty," Pace says as he caresses my cheek and sticks a flower that has fallen out of place back into my braid.

"I am certain of you. You are the one thing in my life that I am certain of." He lowers his mouth to kiss me, and it is so gentle, and so sweet, full of promise for our future. A future that we are going to fight for. When he finally pulls away he looks at my hair and grins. "I like it like this," he says. "Even with the flowers."

"Don't get used to it," I say. "And the flowers are courtesy of Nancy. She worked very hard getting them arranged just right."

"I shall be sure to thank her," Pace says. He looks up at the sky, placing the sun to get an idea of the time. "We should get back. Are you strong enough to walk?"

"Do I have a choice?" Pace helps me to my feet, and we set off back the way we came. "How did you find this place?" I ask.

"Jane told me about it," Pace replies. "She spotted it when they were looking for a safe place to move everyone. When I told her I wanted to bury Mother like they did in the before time, she told me what to do and suggested I look for the churchyard. I thought I'd come back and cut back the grass and clean up the place when I got a chance."

We are just out of the cemetery, and I turn to look at the ruins of the church. It really is a pretty setting. It is obvious where the new growth begins and the old ends. Tall evergreens wave to and fro in the breeze, and around ground level is an explosion of shiny green buds, just waiting to burst into bloom like the wild flowers in the meadow. The building itself is so interesting, with its peaked stonewalls and the tower beside it.

"It would not be that hard to put a roof on it and make it livable," I say.

Pace takes my hand, and I look up into his beautiful blue eyes. "I was thinking the same thing." He kisses me again. I do not know what I did to deserve him, but I know in my heart I will do everything in my power to make sure I never hurt him again.

◆

By the time we reach the turn in the path to return to the enclave, I am having a hard time keeping up with Pace. My legs feel as if they are made of wood, and it takes every bit of my concentration to determine where my feet should go with each step. It doesn't take long for Pace to realize my difficulty, and he kneels down so I can get on his back. He carries me the rest of the way, with Pip swooping over our heads and Jonah trotting along beside us. I am so exhausted that all I can do it lay my head on Pace's shoulder and hang on.

As we turn up the slope that leads to the enclave I see that everyone has returned. The tank sits by the gate that leads inside, and I get my first look at it up close. Pace sets me on my feet as we come to it, and I reach out to touch the cold hard metal of its leg. Jonah takes one look at it, puts his ears back, hisses, and runs through the gate as if his tail is on fire. Pip flutters around it and then lights on the top of one of the wooden posts that forms the wall of the enclave.

I am amazed at the mind of Dr. Stewart. That he was able to create this from the pieces of armor they found among the ruins in the area. I look up the leg and see how it hinges at the knee, much like my own. It also hinges where the leg meets the body. The body, which looks a lot like a rectangle, only with curved edges, easily stands five stories high. There are eight narrow openings, large enough for someone to maneuver a rifle from the inside, yet small enough that only the best marksmen would be able to shoot inside of it. In the front, over the long cone that protrudes, are two more openings. There is a hatch in the belly that opens only from the inside, and a rope ladder hangs down from the top and can be rolled up and taken inside once everyone is in.

"There's a seat for whoever is driving it inside." Pace points to the windows over the cone. "The nose is like a battering ram. Lyon is certain that a combination of explosives and the tank pounding on the glass will shatter it."

"And we just walk right in." I look at the tank in wonder. "Can you imagine how powerful the rovers would be if they had someone like Dr. Stewart among them?" I say to Pace. "There is so much available to them, all they had to do was put it to use."

"Levi said if they had tamed the horses that run wild they would be a lot harder for us to beat in hand-to-hand combat," Pace replies. "I think you were right about them. The strongest takes control and continually keeps the rest beat down so they won't over throw him. Progress is impossible when it isn't nurtured."

"They are more like us than we originally thought," I say. "Like us, they never had a choice."

"Ragnor and his wife chose to leave," Pace says. "At least we think they did. They disappeared. For all we know they could be spying on us and going back to tell Wulf where we are."

"Or they could be biding their time, waiting to see who is going to come out the winner. I believe they are hoping it will be us. Did they help you find . . ." The last time I saw Ragnor, he said he would help Pace escape. But since that escape is how Ellen got killed, I hesitate to mention it.

"He found me and led me to the hut where she'd been taken," Pace says. "I never would have found her without him. Of course if I hadn't found her she might still be alive."

I put my hand on his arm. "No. Don't think that. From what I know of Wulf, he would have used her or anyone else he thought we knew as bait to get us back. He would have tortured her, and even if you surrendered it would have not changed what happened to her. At least she died with you there. At least she died knowing that you would be safe."

"She didn't even know what hit her. Dr. Stewart said she died instantly."

"So she did not suffer. That's all anyone can ask for, for the people they love."

Pace smiles sweetly. "I guess that's all anyone can ask for when they die. Not to suffer." He shakes his head. "I wish you could have known her before all this. When she wasn't so full of hate and confusion. I wish you could have known her the way I did." His voice breaks and Pace pinches the bridge of his nose between his fingers to keep from crying.

"I will know her," I say. "I'll know her because of you. Because she raised you and she taught you to be kind, and strong and patient, and oh so very wise about things. She taught you to keep calm, even when the world is exploding, and to love passionately and to be fair to everyone. She taught you to believe in things beyond the dome and to act on what you believe. I cannot even begin to imagine how proud of you she must have been, but I can imagine how much she loved you."

Pace blinks back tears. "Thank you, Wren."

"There you are!" Jane exclaims as she comes through the gate and across the footbridge. "I have been worried sick about you. I never dreamed you would take off across the country. When Levi came back without you, I wanted to shake him."

"I had to find Pace," I say simply.

Jane looks at the two of us standing there, side by side, and she smiles. "I'm glad you did. But please, Wren, come inside and let me check on your wound. Your tromping across the country cannot have been good for it."

I realize that Jane is right when I take a step to follow her inside the enclave and nearly sink to the ground. Pace catches me and picks me up, this time in his arms and carries me. I feel foolish for having almost fainted again and embarrassed because I am so weak, especially when Pace carries me into the cabin with Jonah meowing loudly behind us. Everyone is inside and they all turn to look at us. There are more people than I can count gathered around the two long tables.

"Wren!" Jilly exclaims

"What happened?" Lucy chimes in.

"She just overdid it," Jane says. "Now please, everyone; let her rest." Pace follows Jane down the hall to the right and they go into the first room. It is small, barely big enough for the bed and a set of shelves. An opening in the stone serves as a window, and shutters hang on either side. The bed is nothing more than a simple box of wood with blankets and quilts recovered from our village. Pace sets me down and the sweet smell of fresh grass comes from the mattress. Once more I am amazed at how much was accomplished while we were held prisoner inside the dome. Jonah jumps onto the bed and immediately starts sniffing everything in sight.

Jane unbuttons my shirt and pulls the bandage away from the padding. "You're bleeding," she says.

"I thought I might be." My skin is tender, and I'm not sure if I want her to touch me.

"And you didn't say anything?" Pace explodes.

I look at him over Jane's shoulder. "I wanted to be with you," I say simply.

"What's done is done," Jane says. "Pace, please go up to the

Quest and ask Dr. Stewart if could come check on Wren. I don't want to subject her to the stairs in the tower at this time."

"Yes ma'am," Pace says, and takes off.

Jane leaves as well, and I gingerly lay back on the bed and try to relax. There is so much to think about. Going into the dome to find Zan and the worry over the rovers attacking again. The morning was so beautiful and the world seemed so peaceful. We cannot be lulled into a false sense of security, especially when Wulf is out there. Jane returns in a short time with a bowl full of water and some towels and sits on the edge of the bed.

"You're going to have to sit up so I can remove your bandages," she says. I am weaker than I thought. Jane has to help me up. "Silly Wren," she says. "Still trying to save the world by yourself?"

"No," I say. "I know I need all the help I can get."

"You will have it," she says. "They all will follow you anywhere."

I shake my head as Jane unwinds the bandage from my torso. "It is not me," I say. "It's this." I wave my hand to encompass the room, but I mean it for the world outside. "We all want the same thing."

"But you are the one who is willing to go the distance to get it," Jane says. "You are the one who saw beyond the glass and had enough gumption to stand up and say, 'There is a world out there and I want to see it. I want to live in it.'"

"Why are you saying this?" I ask.

Jane smiles. "Possibly because you broke my nephew's heart, and I want you to know the impact you have on the people around you."

"I didn't break his heart," I say. "Levi doesn't love me. Not the way Pace does."

"Just because he didn't say it doesn't mean he doesn't feel it. Levi has lost so many people that he loved. His mother, his father, and his brother . . . he feels like he should have been with them when they died, that he should have died too. He guards his heart very carefully."

"Are you saying that I should be with Levi?"

Jane shakes her head. "No. It is obvious that you and Pace are very much in love. Perhaps Levi was meant to come along to reinforce your feelings for Pace." She is down to the padding and I can clearly see the bloodstain that has soaked through. "I just don't want you to leave things as they are with him. If you feel that you must close that door, then do it gently so he may leave here with some closure between you. If you don't, I am afraid he will not take a chance on loving again for a long, long time."

I understand what she is saying. "I can do that," I say. "I care deeply for Levi. He's saved my life more times that I can count, even if he did shoot me." Jane laughs. "He's taught me so much, about myself. Things that I never realized. He's made me see how strong I can be, and how to fight, which is very helpful considering the circumstances."

"Thank you," Jane says. "I just want him to be happy."

"So do I," I say. "And Jane. I am sure that Zan is okay. My father is way too curious, and too bored with everyone else, to hurt her."

She tilts her head, and her eyes turn inward as if she is thinking about something. And I realize she is. She is thinking about Zan. "I know you are right," she says with a smile. "I know I would feel it here," she places her hand over her heart, "if something had happened to her." She looks at the padding on my wound. "This is probably going to hurt." She pulls the padding off and I feel as if my skin is coming with it. She immediately places the wet towel on my stomach and presses it against my flesh to clean away the blood and soothe the rawness.

When she pulls it away I get a good look at my wound. It is just to the right of my navel and puckered with the stitches Dr. Stewart closed it with.

"You are lucky it wasn't any deeper," Jane says. "It could have hit a vital organ. It nicked some of your blood vessels, which caused you to lose quite a bit of blood, but it wasn't that deep and was fairly easy for Jethro to remove. All your moving around today probably damaged the stitches on the inside, which is why I want Dr. Stewart to look at it again."

"I guess I am lucky that Wulf is so thick," I say. "When it passed through him it probably slowed it down enough that it didn't have enough power behind it when it hit me."

Jane smiles. "Yes, Levi does feel terrible about that too."

"I don't blame him," I say. "His saving mine and Jilly's lives is worth taking a bullet for."

"That is an excellent way to look at it," Jane agrees, as Pace comes through the door with Dr. Stewart in tow.

"I hear you've been running around the countryside instead of resting as I instructed," Dr. Stewart says as soon as he comes in. I give him a sheepish look as Jane buttons the top few buttons of my shirt for modesty's sake. She moves away so Dr. Stewart can sit beside me, and Pace moves to the foot of the bed. He holds fresh bandages in his hands.

Dr. Stewart presses on my stomach on either side of the wound. A bit of blood seeps out and Jane hands him the cloth to wipe it away. "You have to give this time to heal," he says. "No moving for at least twenty-four hours." I open my mouth to protest. I need to be with Pace when he buries his mother. "No excuses," Dr. Stewart says with an uplifted finger. "I am certain your young man here understands."

"I do," Pace says. "Your health is more important than anything else." I don't agree, but I can tell that I am not going to get any support from anyone here. Dr. Stewart has his bag with him, and he takes out a jar of some sort of ointment and rubs it across my wound and places a stack of padding on it. Pace hands him the roll of bandages and he winds them around my stomach and ties them on the side.

"Food and rest," he says. "I will check on you again tomorrow and let you know if you can rise from this bed."

I nod my head. "Thank you for everything," I say. "Your tank is amazing. I felt the earth shaking beneath my feet during the attack."

"It was my design," Dr. Stewart says. "But your friends are the ones who brought it to life. George's work on the forge and the rest of them pitching in to do whatever it takes. There's nothing we cannot accomplish with such determination and desire. And speaking of tanks, we're going to use our walking tank to raise the hot water tanks into place as soon as everyone is done with lunch." He takes out his pocket watch and looks at it. "Then we are taking the *Quest* to explore some ruins about an hour north of here," he says. "Busy day," he says with a grin and leaves.

"Hot water tanks?" I ask.

"We have water closets on either end," Jane explains. "This side for the girls, the other for the boys. Dr. Stewart is placing tanks up on the stone and the sun will heat the water for us."

"Amazing," I say.

"I will fix you some lunch," Jane says. "And if you promise to do as Dr. Stewart says, I will allow your friends to come in."

"I promise," I say. Jane leaves, and Pace sits down in the place recently vacated by Dr. Stewart. Jonah curls up beside my thigh and goes to work on his bathing ritual. I rub his ears affectionately.

"Please don't feel bad about not going back with me to bury Mother," Pace says.

"How can I not feel bad about that?" I ask. "I want to be there for you."

"Just knowing you want to be there is enough. It isn't worth your getting worse. There's a lot that still has to happen. We need you healthy for that."

"For marching into the dome?"

"I know you don't want to miss that."

"No," I agree. "That is one thing I do not want to miss."

Pace leaves to go bury his mother, and, in spite of what he says, I am filled with guilt. Most everyone goes with him, to help with Ellen's coffin and to pay their respects, including the children who are excited about an outing, even if it is a sad occasion. Lyon leaves his guards in the enclave in case the rovers show up. Jilly stays behind because of her foot, and we both fall asleep, quietly lulled by the soft breeze that comes through the window and the varied songs of the birds. It is such a peaceful sound, one I missed when I was inside and one Jilly has never experienced until now.

I sleep so deeply that it seems like only a few minutes have passed when we hear the noise of everyone's return, but I can tell by the way the sun shines through the window that a couple of hours have passed. Jilly rises from her nap and goes to check on everyone, leaving me alone once more, except for Jonah, who mews sleepily and rolls over on his back, contorting his body in an impossible position yet looking very comfortable as he does so.

I ache to see Pace because I want to comfort him. Yet I do not know how. I think back to when my grandfather died in a cave-in and how Pace comforted me. He was the only one I had, and our private little cave by the river the only place I had to go. And thankfully, he was just there for me. To hold me, and to let me talk or to just share the silence when I needed it.

But I also recall the sensations of how he kissed me and how we almost got carried away and made love that night. Luckily we didn't, because I certainly wasn't ready then. And as sure as I am of my love for him, I am still not sure if I am ready now.

He has never pressured me. Not once. Which leads me to recall my experience with Wulf, the vulgarity of it and how close I came to being under his power.

We are still not safe, not any of us, as long as Wulf is out there. I know he will not leave the attack that freed us unanswered. But there is nothing we can do. We were so lucky that we escaped with only the one loss. Even with our superior weaponry and machines, we are not a match for their sheer numbers. They were caught by surprise the first time. I know it won't happen a second time.

A knock on my door brings me out of my thoughts. Lucy comes in when I answer.

"You are supposed to be sleeping," she says.

"I was," I reply. "How was it?"

"Sweet," she replies. "And sad. A lot like ours were, except instead of lighting a fire they lowered her into the ground."

I nod in understanding. "Pace?"

"He's helping with the tanks. Do you know we will have hot water just by pulling on a chain?" Lucy says without much excitement. Something is on her mind.

"Dr. Stewart is a genius," I say. "There is no end to the things he can create."

"I guess you know that they are planning an attack on the dome to get Lyon and Jane's daughter back," Lucy says. "It is planned for tomorrow . . ."

"Tomorrow," I echo. "Which means you have to postpone your wedding until after."

She suddenly tears up and sits down beside me on the bed. "I'm scared, Wren. We just got out two weeks ago, and now David says he is going back in to fight. What if something happens to him? What if he ends up dead . . . like Alex?"

"You can't live your life on what ifs," I say. "And you also cannot expect David not to fight because you are frightened. He has to do what he believes is right. Isn't that what made you fall in love with him in the first place?"

Lucy nods through her tears. "I just don't know what I'll do if I lose him," she says. "He is all I have."

Now I remember that Lucy's parents were killed in the flood, and she probably didn't even know until James told her when he and Lyon brought her out, along with David and Harry. It all seems so very long ago. "It's funny," I say. "Pace and I just had the same conversation this morning. If something happens to David you have to carry on, for both of you."

Lucy grips my hand as she nods, then swipes at the tears. "It's just so hard."

"I know." I shrug. "Loving someone is hard. But it is also worth it."

"It is," she agrees. "I just never dreamed that we would have all this danger out here. David learned how to shoot a gun the morning after we got out and then a week later he's going on an attack to help free you."

"It was the same with us," I say. "If not for the Hatfields, we would either have died or been captured in those first few days."

"David says if it's not worth fighting for then it's not worth having."

"I don't think freedom has ever come easy for anyone," I reply. "Because the people who keep us from being free do not want to have to replace us by doing the work we did themselves. It is easier for them to keep us oppressed."

"You are right," Lucy agrees. "Do you think Lyon would be doing this if he didn't think his daughter was in there?"

"I don't know," I say after I think on it a moment. "He abhors slavery of any kind, and he felt that we were kept as slaves. When he found out about the note you sent out by Pip, he was adamant about getting you out, but since everyone we were concerned about is out . . . I just don't know. I don't think he would desert us as long as he felt we were in danger, which is why he's gone to such lengths to make sure we are protected and can survive." I rub my hand over Jonah, who has awakened to watch our conversation. "Why did you put the note on Pip? How did that come about?"

"He just kept showing up, every morning, like clockwork," Lucy explains. "We had no idea what had happened to you. We didn't know if you were alive or dead or trapped. But every morning Pip was there, sitting on the kitchen windowsill, and we let him in and gave him some crumbs, and then he'd peck on the window and we let him go. Harry was staying with us then because the streets were so dangerous going back to his home. The scarabs had all disappeared and we had no idea what happened to them, and there were riots from the workers who lost their jobs when the furnaces were destroyed. Then one day I was out delivering laundry to the royals. Before I got to that part of town someone yelled out 'Shiner!' and they started throwing things at me. Rocks, rotten food, even dog shite. It was horrible. They blamed the shiners for everything that happened because that was what Sir Meredith told everyone. People started watching our house day and night. They threatened to burn us out. They wanted to punish me for everything that happened. We tried to go out through the sewers but couldn't find our way. I never worked in the tunnels, so I didn't know them the way you did. When the route I'd taken was blocked, I was afraid we'd never find our way out. It wasn't until James showed up with Lyon that we were able to escape. I don't know how he made it unless it was because the sight of the filchers scared the crowd away."

"We had no idea." I didn't. If I had I would have gone back in myself to find a way to get them out.

"It was Harry's idea," Lucy says. "About the note. He remembered reading something in a book about pigeons who carry messages and we tried it. We weren't even sure if you were alive, we just had to do something."

"Well, it worked."

"Funny that," Lucy says with a smile. "Harry's father hated it because he was always sneaking off to the library when he was supposed to be making deliveries and learning to be a butcher."

"I didn't think any of the working class was allowed in the library."

"They could go in, they just couldn't take anything out. The shiners weren't let in because, naturally, we were filthy from all that coal."

"Stupid gits," I say, and Lucy laughs. She has forgotten her fear for David. I know it will come back again when they prepare to go into the dome, and I lay a reassuring hand on hers. "Lyon will do everything in his power to make sure no one gets hurt," I say. "You just have to trust him and David to do their best."

"I will." She looks into my eyes. "Are you going in? If they let you?"

"I'm going in whether or not they let me."

◆

I sleep again after Lucy leaves, but only because I am so bored and lonely that it is the only option left to me. Jonah does not mind at all. He stays pressed against my side the entire afternoon. I finally wake up after another dreamless sleep. The sky outside is dim with dusk, and the smell drifting into my room lets me know that it is dinner time. The sounds I hear are peaceful. The scrape of wood on wood. Footsteps on the stairs. Quiet voices and the higher sound of a child's laughter and the creaking of floorboards overhead. Once more I am amazed by how much was accomplished in such a short time. But when everyone works together for a like purpose, there is no limit to what they can do.

I feel as if I can lay there forever in quiet contemplation. The sound of the door opening stirs Jonah, and I turn to see Pace. His hair is wet and he's wearing clean clothes.

"We have water now," he says. "But it hasn't had time to get hot."

"Kind of like taking a bath with the glowfish?" I ask.

"Colder." He grins. "Dr. Stewart said you can come to dinner if you promise to sit still."

I slide to the edge of the bed and start to stand. Pace is at my side before my feet hit the floor and picks me up. "Is this part of sitting still?" I ask.

"It is if you want to come to the meeting."

"There's a meeting?" I ask.

"Lyon's sharing his plan to go into the dome."

"For tomorrow." I am already forming a plan to be a part of it. I just have to be.

"He wants his daughter back."

"Can you blame him?"

"No," Pace replies as he carries me through the door. "Not a bit. Just like I don't blame you for wanting to be a part of it."

"You don't expect me to stay behind do you? Not after everything that has happened."

Pace stops in the hallway. I hear the excited chatter of everyone in the main room, but his words are only for me. "I don't. I know you have to go. Just remember that you are wounded. Please don't do anything foolish."

"I won't," I promise, knowing that when the time comes I cannot give him any guarantees. "I know my limitations."

"And here I didn't think you had any," Pace says with a grin, and we resume our journey to the main room of the cabin.

It is the first time I've seen everyone together since our return. I haven't had a chance to talk to most of my friends since I was banished to the bedroom. Now it seems as if everyone is talking at once. Pace places me in the one chair that sits at the end of a table and goes to fix me a plate of food.

"Where are the little ones?" I ask.

"Fed, washed, and sent to bed," Rosalyn says as she walks by. "So that we may have a few peaceful moments."

By the serious look on Lyon's face, I doubt if he is contemplating peace at all. He stands next to Dr. Stewart in deep discussion. Not everyone is here yet: some must still be cleaning up after the activities of the busy day. James is still missing, along with Jon, David, Harry, and Peter. And Levi. I see Joe and Nellie for the first time since I returned and they come by. Nellie hugs me and bursts into tears. "Thank you for taking care of little Joey," she says.

"I'm just glad you found each other," I say, recalling the little boy who had no qualms about telling Rosalyn's daughter Stella about the facts of life.

"How are you feeling, Wren?" Alcide asks after Joe and Nellie leave.

"Better," I say. "I was lucky it wasn't worse."

"I can second that," Adam says as he sits down next to me. I notice his arm is now out of the sling. "Once is enough for me," he adds. "Next time you can get shot," he says to Alcide.

"Not me," Alcide says. "I'm staying inside the tank, where it's safe. And where I get to shoot guns."

"Sounds like you enjoy that part," I say.

"It's better than sitting in a tree and waiting for them to shoot me," he says, reminding me of the night we were attacked. Alcide sits beside me on the other side from Adam. "There's something I need to tell you, Wren." Alcide is usually saying something funny, so his serious tone catches me off guard.

"What is it?" I ask, dreading that something else will go wrong.

"The Hatfields have offered to take two of us with them to replace the men they lost. I'm going with them when they leave."

"Alcide," I say, too surprised and saddened to say anything else. I look at Adam.

"I'm staying," he says. "There is a lot that needs doing right here. But James is considering it."

"It's a chance to see something of the world." Alcide talks as if he is seeking my permission. "And it won't be forever. Just to America and back and then I can decide if I want to stay on." He looks at me hopefully.

"I think it sounds amazing," I say, and he grins. "When are they talking about leaving?"

"That all depends upon when we find Zan," Adam says. "But soon I think. They can't take care of us forever. We have to learn how to take care of ourselves." I am so grateful for Adam, for his steadiness and his ability to lead. He was on our council, along with Rosalyn, before our world and the others in it were lost. Knowing he is here, and that he wants to stay, gives me great hope for our future. I would not blame him if he wanted to leave, since he lost Peggy.

Pace returns with my plate, and Alcide slides down the bench to make room for him. Jilly joins us, and Adam slides down for her so she won't have to climb over the bench with her bad foot. I notice that she is blushing a bit when Adam helps her, and I can't help but smile.

Harry, David, and Jon, with Beau by his side, come in. Jon sees me and comes straight away with Beau following. Jonah pops out from beneath my chair and sniffs at Beau. Jon was captured with me when the filchers mistook him for Pace. He was the first of us to leave the dome, taking his chance when James, Adam, and Alcide blew up the fans. Beau found him and the two became fast friends.

"We all made it," Jon says with a grin. "Even Bess," he adds.

"I'm glad we were able to help them," I say. "But Jon . . . your people who are on the inside. It doesn't look good for them."

"I know," he says. "Levi told me. Hopefully we can save them when we find Zan."

"Are you joining the attack?" I ask.

"We all are," Jon says. "Every one of us."

"We all have someone or something to fight for," Harry says as he joins us. David is behind him and Lucy comes over and everyone fills in the empty places on the benches.

"Of course Harry is excited," Alcide says. "He gets to drive the tank."

"We all have something we're good at," Harry says with a big grin. "Yours is eating. Mine is driving the tank."

"Alcide is good at talking too," Peter says.

"I'm also good at looking good," Alcide says. I can't help but agree. He looks more and more like his cousin Alex, who I had a crush on, every day. We all laugh at his comment. It is such a good feeling. We are all together in a way that I never thought we would be when all of this started. I really did not know what to expect when we got out, except that I hoped it would be better than the life we had below. To see where we are now compared to a month ago amazes me. I look at the people around me, at this table and the other. All are smiling, chatting, passing food around, and helping one another. I see the underlying worry on the faces of some of the women. Rosalyn, Nellie, and Lucy, all in dread of the coming battle. I know we can get through it. We truly have a chance to be happy here and to build a home and a life, all of us together.

James and Levi come in, both with wet hair and clean clothes. Levi glances my way briefly and smiles sadly.

I promised Jane I would talk to Levi. It is not something I am looking forward to.

· 23 ·

*O*ur dinner is much simpler fare than what we had before. The
strain of feeding so many people must be wearing on the
stores aboard the *Quest*. The Hatfields have been so generous with
us, sharing food, clothing, medical supplies, and their endless
knowledge of the world. Even without the fancy settings we enjoyed
before, the meal is still cozy and comfortable. There is a fire in the
stone fireplace that warms the room and fat candles are set about. I
decide then and there to talk to Adam later about using water to
make power for the enclave. We had a waterwheel below and it provided us with light. I do not see why we can't do the same with the
nearby stream.

The dogs, Belle and Beau, lay before the fireplace. Pace has
brought Pip's cage inside and it hangs by one of the windows that
face inside the enclave. Pip has his head tucked beneath his wing,
resting up from his travels. How much does that little bird see, I can't
help but wonder. Jonah lies in the windowsill behind him, looking
outside and flicking his tail.

When we are done eating, Lyon stands. He is at the opposite

end of the long table. Jane sits to his right, Dr. Stewart to his left, and Levi beside Jane, then Peter, James, Adam, and Jilly. Harry sits beside Dr. Stewart, then Lucy, David, Alcide, and Pace. Jon and Bess, Tobias, George, Sally, Nellie and Joe, and Rosalyn and Colm sit at the other table. If the children were here they would fill in the rest of the spaces. By now the giggles and thumping from the loft above have subsided, and the children are either asleep or quietly spying on us. If it were me up there, I would definitely be doing the latter.

"The first thing I would like to say is that no one here should feel obligated in any way to participate in this attack."

"We are all going to help," Adam says. "To the last man."

And woman, I want to add but don't. There will be time for that later. Right now I want to hear Lyon's plan.

"Thank you," Lyon says as he places his hand over his heart. Jane bows her head and dabs at her eyes. I am amazed at how well they hold themselves together, even though they are worried sick about Zan. Yet they have carried on, still helping us, even risking their lives to save us from the rovers. I hope the rest of the world is made up of people like the Hatfields instead of those like Wulf and my father. My little bit of experience has taught me that it is not likely. There are all kinds out there, I am certain of it. I can only hope that those who do good are stronger than the ones who do evil.

Dr. Stewart stands and Jane moves the plates aside. Lucy sees that they need more room and moves to help, along with David and Harry. Dr. Stewart unrolls a large piece of paper and places it on the table and those of us on the end and everyone at the other table gather round, with Harry insisting that I sit in his place.

The large piece of paper has a drawing of the dome with the interior bits filled in. There is not much detail; it's just an approximation of where things are, like the hole blown in the mines over the river, the promenade, the door that leads out, the stockyards, and my father's building.

"Thank you, Pace, David, and Harry, for giving us the layout inside," Lyon says. "From this we have formulated our plan of attack." He points to the spot where the promenade ends. "This leads to the royals?" he looks at Jilly, who nods. "This is where we are going to break the glass. Jethro has found the remnants of the road on our side of the glass. So it is just a matter of driving right through. Harry and Jethro will man the controls of the tank, Alcide and Peter will take the guns, along with two of my men."

"How long to you think it will take to break it down?" Pace asks.

"Not long at all," Dr. Stewart says. "I have examined the place thoroughly and have found a weakness that should lead to complete breakage after a few well-placed blows."

We grin. Every single one of us.

"The tank will enter and the cycles will go along to provide cover," Lyon continues. "We expect their main force to concentrate on this attack. Levi, Pace, and David will be on the cycles since they are the best shots and excel at hand-to-hand combat." Lyon looks at me. "I don't suppose there is any way we can convince you to stay out of this, is there?"

"No sir," I say.

"Wren will go in with the cycles. I expect her father will show up, so her presence should be helpful."

I seriously doubt that, after our parting, but I don't want to say so. Besides, if my father is there, Findley should be also, and I think I can bring him to our side when he sees the force we bring to the fight.

"Adam, Jon, Colm, and Joe will go in here." Lyon points to the glass tunnel that leads inside. "Adam and Colm are familiar with explosives. If charges are set here and here," he points, "They should be able to enter and set another charge at the door into the dome and get inside. Jon. Your people are imprisoned there. Can you convince them to join in the fight?"

"That shouldn't be a problem," Jon says. "They will gladly join in."

Lyon nods and smiles. "From there you go to the stockyards and free every animal there and drive them through the dome. They should cause enough confusion and distraction that James and I can get to Zan here."

"How are we going in?" James asks.

Lyon points to the hole on top of the dome where we came through before. "We will fly, just like we did the first time." James grins. "Everything will be coordinated by time, to give James and me a chance to get into position to move when the animals are released."

"You will come off the catwalk here," I say, pointing to a place close by to where my father and I were attacked by the frustrated workers. "This is where the workers live. They could be convinced to fight. But they might just decide to attack you. We have no contact there, no one to help. They are frustrated and hungry."

"We can try to convince them after we release the animals," Adam says.

"The animals will likely need to be convinced," Lyon says. "They have spent their entire lives in pens, they might not know how to run."

"We'll convince them," Jon says. "We can get every scarab in there to drive them out."

"Jon," I say. "They might not be able too. They are starving. They haven't had food in days, possibly weeks."

"They will come through," Jon assures me, and Bess nods her head in agreement.

"What about the filchers?" Lucy asks. "The bluecoats will rally to the royals, but the filchers will do whatever profits them."

"Shoot them," Lyon says. "Everyone will have a weapon. They don't. Now is not the time for diplomacy. If they surrender, then let them be, but if they don't, then shoot them and don't feel guilty about it."

"Give me a gun and I'll shoot them," Bess says. "And I promise I won't feel guilty about it either." The look on her face shows her hatred. "Filthy filchers," she adds.

"What about me?" George asks.

"People will be coming out," Lyon says. "We can't have them running crazy over the countryside without knowing the dangers. We need to set up a holding area here," he indicates the ruins where we first camped. "And here." Lyon points to the dome entrance. "Tobias can man this one since he is more familiar with this area." Tobias nods. "Just remember what you tell them when they come out is important. This place is more than adequate for you. You will have to decide how much of it you want to share."

I hadn't thought about that. We are a community here. How many more people do we want to bring into it? How many more people can we support? I just assumed that once the glass was broken, people could stay in their homes and just use the resources outside for gardens and such. I didn't think about the entire population moving in with us. Is it true what Ragnor said? That there isn't enough for all of us to survive out here? Why wouldn't there be? We have gardens, and there is livestock in the dome. With all the land there is outside, they will be free to breed and multiply. There is plenty of pasture. The orchards and other gardens on the rooftops can be transplanted to the outside. And with all the trees around, the buildings that are in disrepair can be fixed.

Everything in moderation my mind warns me. You can't just start chopping down trees. There has to be organization. There has to be rhyme and reason about the decisions we make.

"We found another ruin similar to this not too far from here," Jon says, as my mind whirls with the repercussions of freeing the inhabitants of the dome. "We can duplicate what's been done here, for the scarabs. It might be that we'll do so well that you'll have to find something else to call us."

"As long as we can continue to call you friend," James says, and everyone nods in agreement.

"Not everyone will want to come out," Lyon continues. "But we need someone to calm them when they do. George, Tobias, Rosalyn, Lucy. Can you do this?"

"We will," Rosalyn says. "Sally and Nellie can watch the children."

"I'll go with them," Bess says. I can tell she is dying to be a part of the attack. "I can stay with Tobias since that's where my people will be."

"I should be there too," Jilly says. "I know my foot makes me not much use, but believe me, the royals will not listen to any of you. I will have to be there to make them see reason."

"We'll take care of you, gel," George assures her. "One of the pony carts is ready. You can ride in it, and I'm sure Freddie will volunteer to lead you. It's best we just let him come with us because I know he'll be sneaking out if we don't. At least this way we can keep an eye on him."

"Wherever he goes, my sister will follow," Peter says about Nancy.

"We'll take care of them," Rosalyn assures him.

"I will station one of my men with each of you," Lyon says. "And the rest will be on the *Quest*, which will scout for rovers. Our flank will be exposed, and I do not put it past them to attack."

Something else to consider. "What about after?" I ask.

"After what?" Lyon asks.

"After we find Zan and the glass is broken and there are more people outside. After you leave. What happens then? What will we do? We need to protect this world. We all have to live in it together. There has to be some sort of organization, some sort of leadership or else we all end up fighting one another for the resources."

I can tell Lyon has not thought much past rescuing Zan. Freeing the people in the dome is not his purpose; it will just be a side effect from his attack. Lyon and Jane both look at me in astonishment, and then Dr. Stewart pipes up.

"Parliament."

Now we are the ones confused, until both Jilly and Pace straighten in their seats. "From the before time," Jilly says. "England had royalty, which was basically a figurehead. The governing body of the country was parliament. I don't remember all the basics. Some were Lords, or such, and inherited the position, but others were elected by the people."

"And there was a prime minister who was like the king, only elected," Pace adds.

"Like our council?" Adam asks.

"Yes," Pace says. "Sometime after the dome was closed they must have done away with it officially and just had representatives of each faction meet with the governing committee."

"Except we didn't have a representative," Jon says.

"The governing committee must be what was left of parliament."

"And the master general enforcer at some time must have been the prime minister," I say. "Funny how my father thinks he is protecting our history when in fact it's just been twisted to suit the needs of a few people so they can stay in control."

"It's a farce," James said. "A joke of what it once was."

"That is why we must make sure that this new world doesn't turn out to be a farce too," I say. "You have built a home for us here. A new place for the shiners . . . and our friends. The others who choose to come out will need a place also." I want to make sure that what I am saying doesn't sound selfish, but I also want everyone to know that I want to protect what they worked so hard to create.

I can tell everyone is thinking hard about my words. Freeing the people of the dome will affect us all in different ways. I know Jilly wants to see her parents, but she doesn't expect them to live with us, not when they have a perfectly wonderful house inside. And Jon's comment about building an enclave for the scarabs makes perfect sense. They have never had anything but the scraps.

But what about the workers who are now starving? I remember the mob from the street. Banded together they would be a force to be reckoned with. I know we can defend the enclave. I just don't want to have to fight against them, especially since we have the rovers to deal with.

I know Harry has family inside also. If the animals are driven out, what does that mean for them? There is so much to think about. So much to deal with, and I am suddenly overwhelmed.

We all are.

"We will keep it all under control," Lyon assures us. But I am not sure if he means it, or if he is afraid of losing our support in freeing Zan. He grins, and it looks so much like Zan that I can't help smiling. "We will put into force a thing called martial law. It means the army with the biggest guns is in charge. And that would be us. It should be a simple matter after that to form a parliamentary government."

Not if my father is involved, I think.

"Don't forget you have the tank to back you up," Jane adds.

"Talk about a master general enforcer," Alcide says, and we all laugh, and some of the earlier tension, regrettably created by me, subsides from the room.

"We will strike at dawn," Lyon says. "Is everyone sure of what they are supposed to do?"

We all nod and voice our agreement.

"James and I will go in before the sunrise," Lyon adds. "James, you might as well sleep on the *Quest* tonight."

"I don't think I'll be doing much sleeping," James says. "But I'll try my best."

"I best make sure the tank is ready," Harry says.

"I'll go with you," Alcide adds, and they both leave. Everyone else rises and goes to prepare.

Levi was silent throughout dinner and the planning afterward. I see him talking to Adam and Jilly. I know I am responsible for his silence and for his seeming so sad. Jane was right. I misjudged his feelings for me. That does not take anything away from what I feel for Pace. It just means that I treated Levi badly, and he does not deserve that.

"Are you ready to go back to your room?" Pace asks.

"I left things in a bad way with Levi," I say. "I need to talk to him tonight." I don't add the "just in case something happens to one of us tomorrow." Lyon might act as if the attack on the dome will be easy. We all have learned since we came out that life is fragile. One or more of us could easily die tomorrow.

"Of course," Pace says. "Just take it easy, please? Because I know you won't tomorrow."

"Help me up?" I ask. I am stiff from my wound, from lying about all day and from sitting too long. Pace helps me climb from the bench and Jonah jumps from his perch and stretches, making me envious at the ease with which he moves.

Even though Levi is talking to Adam and Jilly, I see him glance my way out of the corner of his eye. "Can we talk?" I ask.

He nods. "Outside? Can you walk that far?"

"I can," I say.

"Not too far," Pace says.

"I promise."

"I'll watch out for her," Levi assures him.

"I know you will," Pace says, and there is no malice in his words, no jealousy. I love him even more because of it, if it is even possible for me to love him more. And I find I can't wait to find out.

But first, I must resolve things with Levi.

We go outside, silently, because I don't know where to begin. Jonah follows, as I knew he would, and takes off through the gate and stops to sniff in one of the freshly tilled rows.

"Fertilizer," Levi says as we see him squat.

"Is that what they are using to power the tank?" I ask. The *Quest* is powered by human waste, recycled from the water closets in the cabins. A remarkable invention, as far as I am concerned, and very practical.

Levi grins. "No. He's come up with something he calls solar power. Somehow he draws energy from the sun. You can't see it from here, but there is a series of panels that move and catch the sun's rays. They charge a power pod inside and that's how the tank moves."

"Amazing," I say. "Is that how our water tanks are heated too?"

"Yes," Levi says. "Hot water with the turn of a knob."

"I am anxious to try that out." I say. "Hopefully it will take some of the stiffness out."

"I never should have let you go out today," Levi says. "But it was a way to be with you."

We've been walking slowly the entire time we've talked and have arrived at the gate. The land falls away down the slope, and our view is unrestricted because of the clearing. Crickets chirp and the peepers add to the chorus and off to the right I hear the hoot of an owl.

"I missed this, inside," I say. "All the sounds that you don't really hear unless you want to."

"It is peaceful," Levi says. He looks up. The moon is just a sliver in the sky. It is not missed, as the stars feel as if you can reach up and touch them. Behind and above us the ropes that keep the *Quest* moored in place creak as the airship gently shifts on an air current that is too high to touch Levi and me. Beyond I can hear the hollow sounds of the tank and Harry's and Alcide's voices in conversation, too distant for us to make out their words.

Jonah pounces on something and I hear a squeak. "A mouse," Levi says. It must escape him because he suddenly takes off down a row, darting one way and the next, and we both grin at his antics.

"I'm sorry for what I said today. About your father. I don't know why I said it. I know nothing about your relationship with him." He sighs. "I guess I really don't know that much about you. I just wanted to pretend like I did."

"You know me better than a lot of people, Levi. I've told you things that I've never said to anyone else. Not even Pace."

"Sometimes distance makes that easier, I think," he says.

"It does," I agree. We don't look at each other; instead we keep our eyes on Jonah, who is still after the mouse.

"Wren, I don't want you to think that I don't love you, because I do."

I feel his eyes on me so I turn my head to look at him. "I love you too, Levi," I say. "But it's not the same love I feel for Pace."

"Would you be surprised to hear that I understand?" He shrugs. "I just didn't want you to think that I didn't love you."

"And I didn't want you to leave thinking I hated you."

"Can you tell me where I messed up? Besides the stupid thing I said today."

"You didn't mess up, Levi. You are wonderful and kind of scary, when I think about it. Because you've lived so much and done so much. But Pace——"

"Pace was there first," Levi interrupts.

"No. Pace was just there. For me. Through everything. With no questions and no regrets. There was this moment . . ." I search for the words to try to explain. "It was when the filchers were after him. I was supposed to meet him to find out about Alex. He needed help and I asked him to trust me, and he took my hand and we just came together, as one. We didn't know it at the time, but we figured it out. Through everything that happened, it wasn't just me or him, it was the two of us together, fighting for our lives. For everyone's lives. I guess I forgot that part because I was feeling so sorry for myself when the sunlight blinded me. But Pace kept on, doing what I couldn't do. He never gave up on us or on our beliefs, while I was second-guessing myself on everything. What happened between us shouldn't have happened. I'm not saying that I'm sorry that it did." I stop. I don't know what else to say, and I certainly don't want to hurt him any more than I have.

"Thank you for being honest with me," Levi says. He looks back at the cabin. "And if you ever——"

"Stop," I say, and playfully punch him in the chest.

He laughs and his teeth flash in the darkness. "You can't blame me for trying."

"No," I say. "I won't."

He stops laughing and looks down at me with such a sweet look on his face that it tears at my heart.

"You saved my life, Levi. In more ways than you'll ever know. You helped me realize things about myself. I can never forget that. I won't ever forget you."

"You're pretty unforgettable too."

"Wait, pretty or forgettable?" I say, pretending like I misheard him.

We both laugh and Jonah jumps straight up in the air at the noise, and we laugh at his antics. But then I see someone standing amidst the trees at the bottom of the slope, and I grab Levi's arm.

"We're being watched," I say, and of course he turns. "Don't bother to look. You can't see them." He bends his head close to mine as if we are talking quietly.

"Hug me and look over my shoulder," he says. "Do they have weapons?"

I do as he asks and stare off into the tree line. The man is tall and straight, and he has a rifle slung over his back. The figure behind him moves to his side, and I recognize them both at that moment. "It's Ragnor and Janna."

Levi breaks the hug and looks into my eyes. "Maybe we should talk to them."

"I think that might be wise." I say. "If they wanted to hurt us they could have shot at us."

"You better stay here." Levi turns and takes off down the hill. He hasn't gone more than a few steps when Pace steps through the gate and comes to my side. His pistol is on his hip and he holds a rifle.

"You were listening?" I don't know if I should be indignant or happy.

"Yes." He keeps his eyes on Levi as he walks down the hill. Jonah stops his hunt and watches also. "I trust you, Wren. I just don't trust him with you."

"Yet here you are, covering his back."

"Just because I don't trust him with my girl doesn't mean that I don't like him or that I want him to get hurt." He spares me a glance and his eyes are hot with possession. A thrill runs through me and I tingle at his nearness.

This is not the time for tingling. Levi's life could be in danger. All our lives could. For some reason I trust Ragnor, and because I do, Levi chooses to also. "I thought Lyon had his men posted to watch for rovers," I say.

"There's been no sign so he brought them in to prepare for tomorrow. Besides, only a shiner would have been able to spot them."

"We are going to have to do better," I say. "If we are going to protect this place. We need to make a schedule and take shifts."

"We'll figure it out," Pace assures me. Levi is close to the bottom of the slope, and Ragnor and Janna step out of the trees. They speak for a moment, and then Levi turns and waves us down. "Do you feel up to it?" Pace asks.

"Right now this is more important than how I feel," I say, and we start down the slope. Jonah decides to follow us and trots delicately through the tender shoots of the rows.

Ragnor dips his head in my direction when we arrive. I know he respects me for what I did, running for Jilly and Ellen, and possibly for the fact that I survived my meeting with Wulf.

"Ragnor has news," Levi says.

"Wulf is dying," he says simply. "He has ah-fever from his ah-wound."

Can it be that simple? Our trouble with the rovers could be over because their leader is dying. "Are you certain?" I ask.

"Aye," he replies. "I have spies. The ah-fever came upon him that ah-night."

"So what happens then? If he dies?"

"Ragnor will challenge." Janna says.

"Can you win?"

Ragnor nods. He feels confident. I have no idea who he will have to fight. I can only pray that he is right.

"What does this mean for us?" Pace asks. "Can we have peace?"

"I ah-want peace," Ragnor says. "I want to ah-learn." He stops and clears his throat. "I want to . . . learn," he says forcibly, and I realize he is trying to mimic our way of speaking. "I want . . . better." He looks at Janna and puts his arm around her, drawing her close. "For our child."

"Congratulations," Pace says, and they look at him in confusion.

"It means we are happy for you," I say. "Would you like something to eat? We have plenty." I really don't know the state of our food stores, all I know is I cannot send them away without something. Ragnor did not have to come to us. Or he could have an ulterior motive. I choose to believe that we can be friends and offer each other something in this new world.

Ragnor looks at Janna and she nods. They seem to know what each other is thinking at all times. We start back up the slope to the enclave.

"I have always thought," Ragnor is careful with his words, as if he is measuring them before they come out, "that the high ground would be a wiser place to live."

"It is," Levi says. "When we were taken to your settlement I knew you were at a disadvantage should the *Quest* attack."

"Quest?"

"The airship," I say. "The boat in the sky."

"They are your friends?"

"They are my family," Levi says.

"Did you fight?" Ragnor asks. "Were ye . . . you with them?"

"We all did," I confess. "And all of your people were killed and the bodies taken out to sea."

He nods once more, taking it all in. I wonder if he had friends who fought, and then I think not. He would have been there with them. Wulf sent them. He sent the ones who he didn't care about. He sent them as a sacrifice to test our power and learned from it, which is why he did not attack again. "You are at war with the dome?" Ragnor asks.

"We are," Levi says. "They have a member of my family inside, and we are going in to get her."

"How did you find us?" Pace asks.

"The big cart with guns," Ragnor says. "We heard it and followed it. Then we waited."

"For you," Janna says to me. I am flattered that they trust me and also encouraged by their actions. If we can have peace with the rovers and free Zan and find a way for us all to live together and prosper . . . It is a dream I haven't dared dream until now.

Ragnor and Janna pause at the gateway into the enclave. They look at the walls as if it is a trap, and then they step through, together. "You have nothing to fear here," I say, as they look at the walls around the inside and the walkways above them that serve for protection. At the wells and the pens of goats and ponies and the chickens, all contained in their little yard for the night. They also look at the gate that is now in place that will be shut once we settle down for the night.

Some of our group might say that it is unwise to bring Ragnor and Janna into our enclave. They could say that they are here to spy on us and find out our weaknesses. I think not, and I know Pace and Levi agree with me, or they would have said something before we came in. As I watch them look around I know that they will know that we are prepared to fight to stay here. That we can survive.

I see nothing wrong with Ragnor knowing that at all.

· 24 ·

I did not sleep well after Ragnor and Janna left, since I had slept most of the day. It could not be because of the apprehension over what we are about to do. Or so I told myself over and over again throughout the night. I tried my best to stay quiet so as not to disturb Jilly, who shared the bed with me, and Pace, who slept beside me on the floor, but it was hard. For a long time I lay on my back and rubbed Jonah's ears and listened to the sound of Pace's steady breathing and the tiny noises that Jilly made, as if she were talking in her dreams. Beyond, I heard the chorus of the night and the continued hooting of the owl outside the window.

I wished several times that Pace shared my bed and Jilly was on the floor, and finally, in the middle of the night, I slipped from beneath my blankets and joined Pace. He only stirred enough to roll to me and place his arm around me, pulling me firmly against his stomach. "I love you," he murmurs into my ear. He is wearing his pants but his chest is bare, and I feel the heat of his body through my undershirt. Jonah joined us, curling into the place between

Pace's arm and my knees, and I finally fell asleep only to be awakened in what seemed like minutes.

"The *Quest* is on its way," Pace says. He is already dressed and is wearing his weapons. I glance out the window. It is still dark outside, but I rise even though Jonah protests sleepily. "Maybe you should lock him in," Pace suggests.

"I think I will," I say. Jilly hears us talking and stirs. Pace leaves, and Jilly and I dress quietly, both of us thinking of the day to come and wondering if we will all survive it. I shut the door firmly in Jonah's face as we leave, and I hear the cat digging at the door to escape. I should have shut the window too. I hope it is too high for him to jump to.

No one speaks as we pass through the large room to go outside. One small candle is lit for those few of us who cannot see in the dark. Pip is still asleep in his cage and the door is shut.

"Something to eat?" Rosalyn asks. Jonah meows loudly from my room.

"No thank you," both Jilly and I say. We go out on the porch. I hear the sound of the tank as it walks away with Harry, Alcide, Peter, and Dr. Stewart inside and feel the slight tremors of its passage beneath my feet. Adam, Jon, Colm, and Joe wear packs on their backs. They have the explosives. George, Tobias, and Freddie stand beside a cart with one of the ponies hitched to it. It's not Ghost, it's the one I call Blue. I rub his nose as George helps Jilly into the cart and Ghost whinnies from his pen. Rosalyn, Bess, and Nancy come out of the cabin, and the cart takes off with Freddie leading Blue. George and Tobias both carry rifles and Adam, Jon, Colm, and Joe have pistols strapped to their hips. I wonder when Tobias and Colm learned how to shoot. So much has happened in such a short amount of time, yet it seems like it has been forever since we left the dome.

Levi, Pace, David, and Lucy are with the steam cycles. The engines *putt-putt* quietly in the darkness, and the lights are on so that they can see to drive. I hold up my finger, asking for a few seconds, and run to the ponies. "This will soon be over," I tell Ghost as I rub his head. "No more battles, no more worries. Just peace and sunshine and green pastures." I look up at the sky that has turned a shade lighter with the coming dawn. "Please God, let it be so," I add. I run back to the cycles and climb on behind Pace, who looks at Levi and nods. I wrap my arms around Pace's waist and we take off.

We ride on what was once a road. Occasionally we have to detour around a fallen tree, but for the most part it is clear, much like the road Levi and I rode on the night we went to save Lyon and Pace from the rovers. If only this morning will be the end of our battles. My stomach twists in anticipation and once more I have that feeling of being on a precipice, about to step off.

When we lived belowground there was this great chasm that was found when a tunnel was made. The young men would tie a rope around their waists, and while their friends held it they would leap out into the darkness and let the wind carry them upward as if they were flying. I was never brave enough to do it, because I was afraid of falling, or it was more I was afraid of the unknown.

Yet I feel as if I am about to do it. Only I know I won't be flying alone. I will have someone by my side who will be there to catch me when I fall. If I fall. We have come too far to fall or to fail.

The dome rises before us, blocking out the night. It is lighter than the sky, a gray presence that looms over the wildness of the nature that surrounds us. Does it sense us? Does it know that its rule is about to be over? Will it die quietly or will it scream in agony?

We will find out the answer soon enough.

The tank waits for us. It is already in position, standing right before the dome, close enough to touch it if it moves another step. Dr. Stewart's head sticks out from the top. Lucy hugs David and kisses him and goes to where George, Jilly, Rosalyn, Freddie, and Nancy wait. Bess joins Adam, Jon, Colm, Tobias, and Joe, and they take off around the dome to their position.

We wait. I keep my arms around Pace, and he lays his hand on mine. Levi checks his weapons. The rifles stuck in the stocks on the cycle. The pistols in his belt. The knives in sheaths on his back. The cross bow that is strapped to the seat behind him. After a while we see the *Quest* coming in from the direction of the sea. The night is so quiet that I hear the hum of her engines. Where are all the creatures that sing at night? Do they sense the coming battle, or is it just that time before dawn when they go to sleep and the day creatures are yet to wake up?

We are too close to the dome to see James and Lyon drop off the *Quest* and float down to the dome on the wings. I remember the sensation of flying with Levi. It was scary and thrilling at the same time. I know James loves it, no matter what the purpose.

Finally a red flare flies through the air.

"Ten minutes everyone," Dr. Stewart says. Ten minutes is the time Pace and James decided it would take James and Lyon to get inside the dome, traverse the catwalk, and come down into the streets. Ten minutes hopefully will give Adam and the rest enough time to get into place. They might need longer. We don't know how long it will take us to break through the glass. All that matters now is that James and Lyon are in place.

No one talks. We just wait. Pace gently runs his fingers over the back of my hand and it is hypnotic. I keep my head against his shoulder and wonder if I could actually fall asleep.

"It is time," Dr. Stewart announces, and lowers back into the tank. Levi revs the engine on his cycle, and David does the same. Suddenly a blast comes out of the front of the tank and it careens into the glass of the dome. A splintering sound echoes off the glass. The battering ram retracts and then shoots forward, and we hear a definite crunch. It does it again and again and again, and then it goes all the way through.

I gasp and Pace squeezes my hand. George lets out a whoop of victory. Harry moves the tank forward. One step, then another, and it pushes against the glass and it splinters away and the tank moves onward, inside, with the next step.

Break the glass. It is done. The tank keeps moving. Levi's cycle is beside us. He takes the crossbow from the back and gives it to me. "Just in case," he says, and takes off, following the tank. David follows, then Pace and I. I clutch the crossbow in one hand and hang on to Pace with the other as we ride into the dome.

The last time I was on the promenade I was coming from the other direction. From here it looks much the same. The tall and skinny houses with the painted lawns lined up in neat rows on either side of the street. A few lights shine here and there. The people for the most part are still asleep. Each footstep of the tank echoes ominously and windows open and people stick their heads out. Someone screams.

And then the alarm sounds. I would not have thought it possible without any power, but it goes off, screaming overhead. The last time I heard it was the day Alex died. The day this all began.

How long before somebody shows up? How long before James and Lyon can reach Zan? How long before I see the look of complete shock on my father's face and the amusement on Findley's?

Harry seems determined. The tank keeps on trudging onward,

down the promenade, and we follow. Royals come out of their houses, dressed in their nightclothes and robes while holding their fancy little dogs that loudly yip in panic. Larger dogs give chase while the royals stare slack-jawed at us and then at the hole in the dome. I wave and Pace laughs.

"Harry's going to walk right up to the government building and pound on the door," Pace says.

"If my father is smart he'll let Zan answer it," I reply.

We continue on. I wonder how Adam and his group are doing. Are they in yet? Have they freed the scarabs? Are they on their way to the stockyards?

A cat races by us with its ears pinned back, and then another and another. A dog runs by and outpaces them. We reach the gatehouse; Harry stomps right through it, and the guards dive out of the way. What could they do? They are unarmed, only there for show, nothing more.

We move into the shopping district, and I hear a shot ring out. Then a rumble and the ground shakes beneath us and a large cracking sound rings overhead. Pace and I both look up and then immediately cover our heads as shards of glass rain down on us.

"Find cover," Levi yells. "Get beneath the tank!" The three cycles pull up close, and we hop off and take cover beneath. Levi takes a pistol from his holster and pounds on a leg. Alcide lifts a hatch.

"What?"

"The dome is shattering," Levi says, just as Alcide ducks back in for safety's sake. "There must have been a fault in the glass from before. The explosion Adam set shattered it!"

Glass continues to rain down as the dome creaks so loudly that I feel as if the girders will fall in and smash us beneath their weight. I hear screaming coming from the royal end of the promenade, and shouts of confusion sound before us. Whoever is out on the street is at risk. The glass tinkles against the tank, and we hear the guys whooping for joy inside.

This is more than I ever dreamed of when Lyon said we would break the glass. I cautiously look up and see the sky above me. For the first time in two hundred years the sun will touch the buildings and the streets. Dawn will truly come to the dome, and I will be here to see it.

Finally the glass stops falling, and we move out, looking up to make sure there is nothing left to fall. The tank moves forward again. We scrape the glass off the seats of the cycles and climb back on.

The people who live above the shops are now sticking their heads out of their windows and looking at us and at the sky in shock. Some come out. "What's happening?" a woman asks.

"You're free now," I say. "Free to go outside."

"Where are the flames?" she asks.

"There are no flames," I say. "Look up! Look at the sky!" She does and her jaw drops open in shock and she covers her mouth. We move on. What she does next is up to her.

We hear another gunshot and it ricochets off the tank. "This is it," Pace says. A line of bluecoats comes into view, all with weapons. Twenty, maybe more, it is hard to tell as things get really confusing all at once. They fire at the tank and bullets whine around us. We are in danger of being hit, not from the bluecoats but from the bullets that bounce off the tank. David points down an alley. "Go around them," he yells. Pace and Levi nod. Levi follows David, who goes left, and Pace and I go right, and the tank keeps on moving, even though the bluecoats fire repeatedly at it.

"They're just following orders," Pace says. "You'd think they'd just lay down their guns and go outside."

"My father won't give up, because giving up means admitting

he's wrong." Pace doesn't answer and I suddenly know why. I realize what I said. My father won't give up. He won't give up Zan, and he won't give up his position, because he has staked everything he has on keeping the people on the inside from knowing that the outside is safe. He would rather die than admit he is wrong. Giving up is not an option.

We have got to get to Zan. Pace must realize it too because the cycle suddenly speeds up, and we zip through the alleyways and across the streets, daring anyone to get in our path. I loop the crossbow over my shoulder and wrap both arms around Pace's rock-hard stomach.

Pace takes a corner on two wheels and I see the fountain ahead of us. I also see a cow. "Watch out!" I say in his ear as we come to another corner. Pace slams on the brakes and we slide sideways into the intersection. There are cows coming toward us. And pigs. And goats. They lumber awkwardly with the whites of their eyes showing. They've never run in their lives, much less walked, and they are in a panic. Pace puts the cycle in gear and the wheels spin as we get out of the way of the animals.

"We better try to get across on foot," he says. "We might have a better chance." We dismount and peer around the corner. The remaining animals are milling about more than running. Behind them I see a mass of people coming our way. I hope Adam and the rest are safe.

"It's the workers," I say. "We've got to move before they get here. There is no telling what they will do."

Pace draws his pistol and takes my hand with the other. I take a good grip on the crossbow. "Let's go," he says, and we dash out into the street. A cow bumps into me, and I stagger a step but manage to keep my feet as we reach the fountain. The workers are getting closer. We duck low and continue on. In the distance I hear the engines of the steam cycles and the heavy clanking of the tank. We are all about to converge on my father's building. I wonder what we will find there.

We dash down another alley and turn a corner, taking the same route we did when we surrendered a few weeks earlier. I press my hand to my wound and gasp for air as we arrive at my father's building.

My father stands on the top step. His arm is around Zan and he holds a pistol to her head. Her hands are tied and her mouth gagged, but her eyes speak volumes. She is angry. Very angry. My heart sinks into my stomach. This has got to stop.

Lyon and James both stand on the steps below him. Pace slows to a walk as we come closer. Levi and David both arrive on their cycles. They dismount. Levi draws both his pistols, and we all four walk to the building and join Lyon and James on the lower steps.

"I should have known you couldn't leave it alone," my father says when he sees me. "Why couldn't you just go away?"

"You sold me into slavery," I say. "You expect me to just live with that?" I put my foot on the next step and something in his eyes tells me to stop. "Do you know what he wanted to do to me?"

"It was better than burning, wasn't it?" he says.

"You are one sick and twisted man," Levi says.

"Just let her go," Lyon says. "None of this would have happened if you'd left my daughter alone."

"None of this would have happened if you hadn't come snooping around. The rovers would have taken them." He moves the gun away from Zan's head momentarily to wave it in my direction. Levi flinches and it immediately goes back to Zan's temple. "We could have continued to live as we were. In peace."

The workers are getting closer. Their footsteps fill the air. For some reason we can't hear the tank anymore. That worries me, but not as much as Zan's and the rest of our situation does at this exact moment. I really believe my father has gone insane. How could he not be? He's told so many lies and manipulated so many people that he could not possibly keep up with it.

He looks haggard and old. He looks beaten. Yet he does not know it. He will not accept it. We have got to do something before the workers get here. There will be another riot. Where is Findley? Surely he can make my father see reason. Surely he can do something.

"Let her go, and we will leave," Lyon says. "Just let her go."

The workers pour into the street and run when they see us. They run right for us. They begin yelling and screaming and shaking their fists in the air. Some of them carry stout pieces of wood. We immediately turn around, all six of us, and form a barrier between my father and Zan and the workers. We aim our weapons outward.

My father needs us now. Yet he will not let go of Zan.

The crowd presses closer and we move up a step. And then another one. The area is full and more people are coming. Royals and shopkeepers and scarabs all converge into the alleyways until they are full, and they keep pressing toward us. The noise is deafening. Everyone is shouting. I see the king in the crowd, along with Jilly's father. They try to force their way through to the steps without any luck. I cannot help them. All I can do is watch as the king is shoved to the side. I feel sorry for Jilly's father. Hopefully he will know soon enough that Jilly is safe.

We need the tank, and we need Findley to bring the bluecoats. We need more weapons to keep this mob from rioting.

Where are Adam and Jon? Colm and Joe? *Please let them be safe. Please God, help us.* I look out over the angry and confused crowd and wonder how we are going to get out. The tank is the only thing that will convince these people to let us go, because right now they see us as the enemy.

Maybe I was wrong. Maybe they didn't want to be free because they are not taking advantage of it when it is right in front of them. They are angry, and I can feel their anger like the heat from a flame. They want someone to pay for the misery they've experienced. And that someone is my father.

"Let her go," Lyon says over his shoulder. "And we will protect you."

"You can't protect me," my father says. "Not from this mob. You'll be lucky if you escape yourselves."

"Please," I say. I turn to look at him, imploring him with every part of my being. Begging him to free Zan. Zan should not have to suffer for us. Lyon, Jane, and Levi should not have to suffer for us.

My father does not respond to me. As he has never responded to me. The door behind him opens and Findley steps out. He is covered with sweat, his uniform is dirty, and there is a streak of blood on his face. My father glances at him, and I can see the relief plainly written on his face until Findley raises his gun to my father's head. The crowd responds, roaring their approval, their faces showing their hunger for my father's blood. They want revenge. They want atonement.

My father realizes that he is betrayed. The look on his face is one of desperation.

"It's over." Findley presses the barrel against my father's temple. "Let her go."

"You can't do this," my father says. "None of this."

"I already have," Findley replies. "Look around you. It's over. There is nothing you can say or do to change it. But you can make things better. For the girl. For your daughter."

"That's all I ever wanted to do," my father says. He releases his hold on Zan, and she dashes to Lyon, who throws his arms around her quickly and only for a moment before releasing her because the crowd is pressing closer, screaming for blood. For the master general enforcer's blood. Findley reaches for the gun my father holds, but before he can grab it, my father jumps back against the door and levels the gun on Findley.

"Wren." He has to shout to be heard, and the look in his eyes suddenly terrifies me. "If ever I was capable of love, it would have been with your mother. I just want you to know that."

"Father?" I say and take a step toward him. Before I can blink he puts the gun to his temple and pulls the trigger. Blood sprays over me. My father falls to the ground. I stand there like I am made of stone and shake because of what I've just seen.

My father killed himself. I hear the screams of the crowd behind me. I feel the press of the bodies as my friends step closer, pushed on by the mob. I hear shots being fired, and somewhere in the distance I hear the tank and know it is coming because the stone steps shake beneath my feet.

"Wren!" Pace yells above the voices. He shakes me. "We've got to go before they kill us."

"This way!" Findley says. He shoves my father's body out of the way with his foot and opens the door. Pace pulls me inside, and the rest of my friends follow.

"Find something to block this door," Lyon commands as he and Findley lean against it.

I shake my head. All around me is chaos. David and Levi run to do Lyon's bidding. James takes the gag from Zan's mouth and unties her hands. Then he puts his hands on her cheeks and kisses her. She throws her arms around his neck and kisses him back. "Let's see if we can find another way out of here," James says to Zan, and they take off, hand in hand.

Pace is standing before me. From somewhere he got a handkerchief, and he is using it to wipe the blood from my face. I can see the mob through the window. Some of them beat against the doors.

Lyon and Findley push all their weight against them to keep them from getting in. My father's body is out there.

"We shouldn't have left him," I say.

"There's nothing we can do for him," Pace says. And then through the window I see my father's body, moving through the air, carried over the heads of the people as if he were a dead fish floating on the surf. There is nothing they can do to him. He is dead, yet the knowledge that they have him, that they will defile him, sickens me. Pace continues to dab at the blood on my face while David and Levi return with a large table.

The mob beats at the door. They are organized now, working in unison while shouting vile things at us. They don't know who we are. They don't realize that we are trying to free them. They are angry and full of hatred and looking for someone to blame and since my father took the coward's way out their hatred is now centered on us.

"I just wanted to help," I whisper. "Don't they know that?"

Pace puts his hands on my face, but I continue to stare out the windows at the people pressing against it. David and Levi struggle to push the table into place while Lyon and Findley try to hold back the mob.

"Wren. Look at me." Pace puts his hands on my face, forcing me to stop looking out the window and to look into his beautiful blue eyes. "We're not done yet. We've come so far. You've got to stay with us." He kisses me quickly. "You've got to stay with me."

I understand what he's saying, but I can't seem to keep up with him. I feel as if my mind and body are completely out of sync, as if time, for me, is going at a different speed. I know that I still hold Levi's crossbow in my hand and it feels as if it is a part of me, an extension grafted to my bone.

I see James and Zan come back to where we stand. James shakes his head. "We're surrounded," he says. "It's as if everyone in the dome is out there. It's only a matter of time before they make their way in the other entrance."

My mind and body come together again in the time that surrounds me, and suddenly everything makes sense. "Everyone is." I look at Pace, and he smiles as he runs his thumb beneath my eye, catching a tear that I did not know was there. "We've got to talk to them."

"We can't go out there," James says. "They'll kill us."

"We've got to," I say. "It's the reason why we're here."

"We're not going to have any choice," Levi announces. "We can't hold them off much longer."

"Everyone have your weapons ready," Lyon instructs. He hands Findley one of his guns. "This is a lot better than the one you have. It shoots more than one round."

"Thank you," Findley says, and shakes his head as Lyon pulls another gun from a shoulder holster so that he once again has one in each hand. Levi hands one of his guns to Zan and fills his empty hand with one of the long knives he carries on his back. David and James are both armed, as is Pace, and I have the crossbow.

"Keep your heads and try to stay together," Lyon says. "Try to make for the tank." Before his words fade into the noise outside the door splinters and the glass breaks. Hands reach through, trying to grab us. Behind us are the sounds of voices raised in victory and the pounding of footsteps. They are coming at us from both directions. The table screeches across the floor as the crowd beats on it and finally the door flies open as it clears the table.

"Shoot at them to discourage them," Lyon yells, and he aims at the first man who comes through the door and drops him. More people press through, stepping on their fallen comrade without thought. More shots are fired but there are so many of them and suddenly we are all outside, surrounded by pushing and pulling and screeching voices. They will tear us apart. All of us.

Somehow I am torn away from Pace. I see him, reaching for me. Calling my name. I raise the crossbow and shoot the man who drags me away from Pace. I hear gunshots and screams and the heavy steps of the tank. Somehow I find myself at the fountain and I try to step onto the dais. I notch another arrow into the crossbow and look above the crowd for Pace. Instead I see my father's body, hanging by the neck from a lamppost and it sickens me. Yes, he deserved to pay for his crimes, but this, this is so very wrong.

More gunshots sound, and I realize that all my friends are fighting for their lives. We have the superior weapons, but there are so many people. Where is the tank? As if in answer to my prayer, I feel the vibration beneath my feet that means it is close. It storms into the square and people scatter as a volley of gunfire bursts from the windows.

Suddenly Pace has me and is rushing me away from the fountain to the tank. Lyon is there, along with Findley.

"Where are Zan and James?" Lyon shouts. We all shake our heads. More shots are fired into the crowd from the tank. People fall to the ground, some wounded, others in fear, screaming and covering their heads. More shots sound on the other side of the square. James and Zan? I can't see who is shooting. Pace presses me against one of his legs and shields me with his body. Lyon fires his gun into the air and the noise subsides as the crowd quiets down, knowing they are outmatched. I can feel them trembling in fear. No matter how angry they are, they don't want to die.

It grows so quiet that I can hear crying. Who is crying? It sounds like Zan. Is it Levi? Oh God, please no, don't let it be Levi.

Pace gasps, and then he turns to me and his face is stricken. I am too short. I can't see over the people. I can't see over the crowd. "Who is it?" I ask. "Who is hurt?"

"James," he says. "It's James. I think he's dead."

· 25 ·

The crowd parts for us as we walk through. I don't know if it's the weapons we carry or the looks on our faces that humble them. We move until we come to the steps of my father's building. Zan sits on the top step with James's head in her lap. Lyon dashes to her side. Behind us I hear the heavy clomping of the tank as Harry pushes through the crowd to stand between us and the mob.

James.

Our friends appear. Adam runs up the steps, followed by Jon, Colm, and Joe. Levi appears and then David. They are both bloody and their mouths set in a grim line. Bluecoats line the steps, and Pace and I pass through them. I kneel beside Adam.

"He saved me," Zan says. Tears run down her face. I look at James and see the hole in his chest where his heart lies. I see the blood seeping out of his chest.

"One of them took my gun from me," Zan says, and I see that she is bloody too. "He didn't know what he was doing. It went off and James stepped in front of the bullet. If not it would have struck me." Lyon puts his hand on her hair, and she crumbles into him.

"It's my fault," she wails. "It's all my fault."

James.

James apologized to me yesterday morning. They were the last words we spoke. He can't be gone. He just can't. Yet he is.

The hatch opens on our side of the tank. Alcide and Peter.

"No," Alcide cries out.

Adam looks up at him and then at Lyon. "We've got to get him out of here," he says.

"We will," Lyon says. "I promise you we will." He rises and looks out over the crowd. "But first we have to take care of this. Someone needs to talk to these people." He looks at me. "Wren?"

I shake my head and look at Pace. "Not me," I say. "You should do it. You can say it so much more eloquently than I."

"But this was your battle. Your belief. Your resolve that got us here."

"We all have our parts to play," I say. "This was not just me, it was all of us. This part of it is yours."

Pace nods. "Then we'll do it together." He takes my hand and smiles at me.

"Together," I say.

"Help us up," he says to Levi and David. They put their hands together to form a basket. Pace puts his hands on their shoulders and his foot in their hands and they push him up to the back of the tank, where Alcide is waiting to pull him up. They do the same with me. Alcide jumps down and Dr. Stewart comes out of the hatch as Pace and I move to the front of the tank.

The crowd turns to look up at us. The questions are on their faces. Some people are weeping. Some are dead or wounded, and their friends and family kneel beside the bodies, but all have their eyes on Pace and me. And I quickly realize that I have no idea what to say, but I should say something, so I begin and pray that the words will come to me.

"Look above you," I say. "Do you see the sky? Do you see how blue it is? There are no flames out there. There is blue sky and fresh air and rain and an ocean that stretches on forever. There is beauty out there." The people look up and understanding lights their faces.

"We were lied to!" Someone yells out, and others murmur in agreement.

"The man who lied to you is dead," Pace says. "His body is hanging there from the lamppost. You can't hurt him now, and he cannot lie to you any longer. But know this. He not only lied to you, he lied to everyone. In this everyone in the dome was treated equally. The king down to the shiners and scarabs were all told the same lie, and the lie was carried for many generations." As Pace speaks I search the crowd for the king, but I do not see him. Is he among the fallen, or was he wise enough to escape when things got out of hand?

"So what do we do now?" someone yells. "Who is going to give us food?"

"You'll have to work for it, like you always have," Pace says. "But you can choose the work you want to do. You can grow your own food. Tend your own gardens. You can trade with others. But that doesn't mean you can just go out there and take what you want. We have to preserve the world out there and the resources it offers, just like we had to in here. But we are going to do things differently now."

"Says who?" someone yells.

"Says all of us," Pace replies. "I want each of you to elect someone to speak for you. Someone from the tradesmen. Someone from the workers. Someone from the gardeners, the butchers, the weavers. Someone from the royals and someone from the scarabs."

"Everyone will be represented," I say. "Everyone will have an equal vote."

"Why do you get a say?" someone yells out. "You're nothing but a dirty shiner!"

"Leave her be!" a voice yells out. I recognize it and look out in the crowd to see Max, the dome cleaner, taking my side. "She was the only one brave enough to see this through," he says. "She's earned the right to speak."

I smile my gratitude at Max.

"Pick your representatives," Pace says. "But, remember, these are the ones who will speak for you. Meet us at the library at noon, and we will tell you what we have learned of the outside world. If we all work together, then we can survive."

"What if we don't want to talk?" someone yells out.

Pace stomps on the tank with one foot. "Then this will talk to you."

"As will we!" Findley yells out, and I realize that the bluecoats have gathered around the tank below us and Findley is now the man in charge of them.

It strikes me then. There are no signs of filchers. Did they all run for it once they found that they could get out, or did they simply remove their masks and blend in with the crowd? I cannot believe they will change just like that.

We will have to watch out for them. No, not we, them. Us. The parliament. The new government that will be put into place. We will also have to watch out for the rovers. Just because Ragnor expects to take over doesn't mean it will be peaceful.

"Can we go out?" someone yells. "Can we see?"

Pace points down the promenade. "Indeed you may," he says.

"There are people waiting to answer your questions. But remember this. This world is for all of us. We all have an equal share. Treat it and those around you as you would want to be treated. Respect this world and the people you share it with, and we will all survive and prosper."

I was right. This was Pace's part. The people disband, moving quietly as if they are in shock. Perhaps they are. I know I am. They take their dead and their wounded and they go, some silently, some still crying, until the street is empty.

Except for my father's body, hanging on the lamppost, slowly swaying back and forth. Findley sends some men to cut him down.

Findley joins me on the stairs. "Now what happens?" he asks.

"That is up to you," I say.

He looks at Lyon. "I want to go with him."

◆

I have no use for my father's body. I tell Findley to burn him with the rest of the dead. James is my only concern now. Findley brings two sheets from the building. My father is wrapped in one and James in the other. Adam, Alcide, Colm, and Joe lift James to their shoulders to carry him out, back down the promenade, the way we came in. The tank follows them, escorting them out.

"I've got my people to take care of," Jon says. "Some of them are starving."

"Tell Jane," Lyon says. "We will have to go hunting, but it will get done."

"Thank you," Jon says, and he goes back the way he came in.

"I'm so sorry, Poppa," Zan says to Lyon. "I was curious, and I decided to come in and look around. I had no more than landed on the catwalk when two of their policemen found me. They brought me down and threw me in a cell. I thought for certain you would find me before you left. I was left in that dreadful cell for days and then finally I was moved to a room. I had no idea what had happened to everyone. I was afraid you were all dead. And now James is because of me."

"Please, Zan," I say. "Don't blame yourself. It was an accident."

Levi pulls her to him in a bone-crushing hug. "Wren would know, love," he says. "I accidentally shot her."

"What?"

"So much has happened," I say. "We can talk about it on the way out."

"Mother?" Zan asks.

"She's fine. Waiting above and probably beside herself," Lyon says. "So much has happened." He shakes his head, and I know he feels responsible for James.

"Come on, then," Levi says. "You can ride out with me."

"Do you think the cycles are still there?" I ask.

"They best be," Levi says. "Or we are going to have a long walk."

Miraculously, they are. Lyon rides with David, Zan with Levi, and Pace and I find the one we rode in on intact.

"Did you ever think you would leave the dome this way?" Pace asks as we ride back down the promenade to the entrance we made.

"Never," I say. "I always thought that the only way I could escape was by my ashes. To do this. I never dreamed it would happen."

Pace squeezes my hand that holds tightly to his waist. "Yes, you did, Wren. You dreamed it and it came true. You dreamed it for all of us.

· 26 ·

I still feel as if it's not real, as if the past few weeks have been a dream, but the sight of James's body, lying in the same place where Ellen's was just the day before, makes me realize that it is very much real. The battle has been won, but at such a cost.

James's funeral will wait until after the meeting. For now we need to regroup, and decisions must be made. Jilly decided to stay with her parents to help them adjust. The Hatfields, along with Levi, went back to the *Quest*. Dr. Stewart stayed inside the dome to visit the library, while Findley tried his best to restore order to the earlier chaos. We have three hours to recover before the meeting. Most of us sit around the table. Adam, Alcide, David, Lucy, Rosalyn, Colm, Tobias, and Joe.

"It should be Adam to represent the shiners," I say as I rub Jonah's ears. Jonah was very displeased with me for locking him up, and he voiced his displeasure loud and long when I let him out. "And we need someone to represent our group here."

"It should be you, Wren," Adam says. "Without you, none of us would be here."

I open my mouth to protest, but then I realize, Why shouldn't it be me? I have felt the responsibility of the lives around me, especially those who died. I have tried to deny my role in all of this, because I thought by denying it I would not bear the guilt of the deaths. But I cannot deny the fact that people have died. That people I loved died. Shouldn't I honor their lives by making sure that what they died for survives? Shouldn't I strive to make this world we created a better place in their memory?

"I will represent the enclave," I say. "If everyone will agree to Adam representing the shiners. But Pace should be there also. He was the one who talked to the people. They will be expecting him to be there."

"As he should be," David says. "The people inside have to be shocked at what happened to them. They should have some continuity."

"Works for me," Alcide says, and everyone else voices their agreement, and then we disband. There is work to be done. Jon's people are on their way here, and they need to be fed.

"And here I thought I was going to have to argue with you," Pace says before I can rise from my seat.

"Why?" I ask, even though I know the answer.

Pace leans into me and kisses me. "It's about time you realized how important you really are," he says. "To all of us."

Pace goes to let Pip out of his cage while I go to the door to see the preparations being made for the scarabs' arrival. The children are helping with the work, and I pray that the ones we rescued from the rovers will find their parents in the lot that is with Jon.

"Wren! Pace!" We hear Peter's voice calling from the tower where the *Quest* is now docked. "Come quick!"

"What is it?" I ask, shading my eyes as I look up at Peter.

"Smoke." Peter points to the east. "Looks like the rovers' camp."

"That can't be good," I say. We go to the staircase.

"Maybe you should wait to hear from Ragnor before you decide," Pace suggests as we climb. I am not moving as fast as usual, and I have to put my hand to my wound to ease some of the pain I feel. I've already done too much today, and the day is far from over. Jonah scampers up the steps and then turns to look at me as if to say hurry up.

When we get to the top Levi is waiting for us. "Lyon says to come aboard. We're going to go investigate the smoke." Four of Lyon's men come off the *Quest* with rifles and take up positions along the wall. Lyon is always thinking and always looking out for us. It has yet to sink in to my mind that we will have to use the same caution, especially now. We have relied too much on Lyon's generosity. We have to start looking out for ourselves.

The *Quest* casts off, and we remain outside on the deck. Jonah goes inside the cabin as Lyon, Jane, and Zan join us. We have gone no more than ten feet when Pip lands on the railing and then hops to Pace's shoulder.

Zan's eyes are red and her skin blotchy. I know she's been crying for James. "I've felt like such an idiot these past few weeks," she confesses. "If only I'd done what I was told, James would still be alive."

"You don't know that for certain, Zan," I say. "You can't blame yourself."

"You must think me a horrible ninny, crying like this," Zan wipes her eyes, "when you've lost so many."

"I don't," I assure her. "I am glad James has someone to mourn him. To mourn what could have been." I push a lock of her golden hair behind her ear. "We will not forget him."

"Nor will I."

We stand together at the rail as the *Quest* makes for the plume of smoke. In the distance I can see the dome. The glass is gone around the top, leaving nothing but a skeleton of rusty girders that are ugly against the sky.

"We should break all of it," Levi says as he joins Zan and me. "And tear down the girders."

"It no longer serves a purpose," Zan agrees.

"Maybe it can still," I say. "Maybe it can serve to remind us to never give up. To never stop looking for answers. To always believe in your dreams."

Levi gives me a lopsided smile. His hands squeeze the railing, and I know he wants to touch me, but he won't. Not now. For a brief moment I wish there were two of me. One to stay here and live the life I fought so desperately to have and another to sail the skies and explore the world with Levi.

But there is only one of me. And I chose Pace with every fiber of my being. That is one decision that I am sworn will have no regrets.

"There are people down below," Pace says. He is on the opposite side of the deck with Lyon, so we hurry to where they stand. Lyon has a spyglass to his eye. The wind is blowing in from the east so the *Quest* sailed south and then north to avoid the smoke.

"They have to be from the rover camp," he says. "It looks like they are scattering."

"Because of the fire?" I say. I am worried about Ragnor and Janna. This looks like a lot more than merely challenging Wulf's successor for leadership. This looks like out-and-out rebellion. But on whose part?

"More than likely." Lyon hands the spyglass to Pace. I look down and can barely make out the movement beneath the trees. Lots of people going in different directions.

"We're almost to their camp," Levi says. I don't know how he can tell. The smoke is so dense I have no clue where we are.

"Are any of them heading in our direction?" I ask.

"We'll have to circle around to see," Lyon says.

"I see flames," Pace says. He still has the spyglass. "It looks like the entire village is on fire."

We come over a rise and I can plainly see the rover camp below. The entire thing is on fire, and people run in every direction, carrying their belongings in a haphazard way and not going back for the things they drop.

"Oh those poor people," Jane exclaims. Lyon gives her a look, and I know that the rovers will not be getting any help from the *Quest*.

"What if some of these people make their way to the dome or the enclave?" I ask. "There will be fighting." I can't imagine that there wouldn't be, and the people in the dome are not prepared for it.

"Nobody said it was going to be easy," Levi reminds me.

"We are going to have to make a guard schedule for the enclave," Pace says.

"I wish we could find Ragnor."

"If he's alive, he'll find you," Pace says.

The *Quest* dips a little lower, and I study the ground beneath us, hoping, or maybe not hoping, to see Ragnor and Janna. "That's Wulf's hut," I say. I point to a pile of smoldering ruins off from the rest, only identifiable because of the ring of stones that surrounded it.

"I would say its safe to guess he's not in charge anymore," Levi says.

"There's nothing we can do here," Lyon says. "Our time is better used making sure the enclave remains safe." He goes to a pipe that runs down from the flight cabin in the *Quest* and tells Captain Manning to take us back home.

"Any sign of Ragnor?" I ask Pace as the *Quest* makes it turn.

"No," he says, and hands me the spyglass. I have no need for it. I believe him.

◆

We return to the enclave and pick up Adam before we go back to the dome for the meeting. Lyon insists on taking us in the *Quest* so we can get a feel for how the people are reacting to their freedom.

We see so many people just milling about outside the structure. All the livestock that were released stayed fairly close. We find them clumped together in the sweet grass that the ponies grazed on the first night after we made the climb up the cliff.

Many hands point up when the *Quest* flies overhead, and several follow us to where we dock on the catwalk by the sea. Their faces show their wonder at everything that surrounds them. I am pleased to see that the people gathered at the catwalk are from all the factions of the dome. Royals stand alongside workers. It is a good start for us, I believe.

"Should I come with you?" Levi asks as Adam, Pace, and I leave the *Quest*.

"No," Pace says. "If we get into trouble in there, we're going to need someone we can count on to get us out."

Pace and Adam move onto the catwalk, but I stop to talk to Levi. "Thank you for offering," I say. "But it's time we started doing things on our own. We've got to learn how to take care of ourselves, or all this was just a waste of everyone's time."

"You're right," Levi says. "But that doesn't make it any easier to let go."

"Keep an eye on Jonah for me?" My cat beat on the door with his paws to be let out of the cabin.

"I will," Levi promises. "Be careful in there."

I turn to go.

"And, Wren." Levi adds. "Don't back down. Be strong and be fair."

"I will," I say. "I will remember everything you taught me."

He smiles at me, and I join Adam and Pace. The crowd parts as we come off the catwalk. They look at us with the same curiosity that they study the *Quest*. I find it funny: before all this happened they would have looked at Adam and me with contempt because of our shiner eyes and at Pace with fear because he was a bluecoat.

We see more and more people as we walk to the dome. I realize I should have warned them about what the sun will do to their skin and their eyes. But then again, I cannot be responsible for every person inside the dome. I tried that burden on, and it was too much for me.

"They are following us," Adam says.

"They want to know what's going to happen to them," Pace says.

"For the first time in their lives, it is up to them," I reply.

We go inside. For the first time ever, I notice how drab everything is. How old and worn compared to the brightness of the colors outside. It feels as if the clean and fresh air from outside is warring with the staleness inside. It won't last long. Soon every part of the dome will be cleansed. I cannot wait to see how everyone will react when it rains.

Children of all the factions run and shout on the promenade. Bringing down the glass also brought down the internal barriers. I am fairly certain the majority of the royals are hiding within their homes. I wonder who they will send to represent their faction, or if they think they are above needing representation.

My answer awaits us when we reach the library. A large and angry crowd stands outside and bluecoats line the steps. It doesn't look like a good start to our parliament.

We make our way through the crowd. When they see Pace, they let us through. They must recognize him from earlier this morning. We go up the steps of the library, where a group of men and women are arguing with one of the bluecoats, who immediately salutes Pace when he sees him. That's when I realize Pace is wearing his enforcer uniform with the captain bars. Did he do it on purpose or just because we just don't have that many clothes to choose from?

"They won't let us in," one of the people on the steps says. "For the meeting."

"Why not?" Pace asks the bluecoat.

"Because the king is inside."

"Where is Mr. Findley?" Pace asks.

"Dealing with some problems, sir."

"Send someone to find him," Pace says. "We're going inside. And let the representatives in also."

Pace walks by the bluecoats and we follow. I am amazed by how calmly he is handling everything. He has taken complete control of the situation, and the bluecoats obey him, over what I am certain were the king's orders. When did he become this person walking beside me?

"Ah! There you are!" Dr. Stewart says as soon as Pace and I walk into the large main room of the library. I look up at the soaring ceiling and the rows and rows of books that cover the walls. They go all the way to the arched glass dome of the building, a miniature replica of our dome. Balconies go around the perimeter of the room, each with several ladders, so the books are easily accessible for those with library privileges. The middle of the room holds row after row of tables, all highly polished so that the sunlight that comes through the domed ceiling makes them glow. Each table has six high-backed chairs with deep cushions upon them. It truly is a luxurious room. It has been many years since I've been inside the library. I am filled with wonder at the knowledge that surrounds me and with anger that it was kept from me for so long.

Before Dr. Stewart can wave us over, a man in a suit with a large silk scarf tied around his neck intercepts us. "Only those invited in by the king may be inside," he says.

"I guess the king wasn't paying attention," Adam says as we walk by the man as if he doesn't exist. Dr. Stewart smiles and waves, and as he moves aside a few steps we can see that he was talking with the king when we came in.

"Excellent!" Dr. Stewart exclaims as we approach. "I was just explaining parliamentary procedure to his highness." Dr. Stewart's exuberance is contagious, and I cannot help but grin at the excitement that plainly shows on his face.

The king's face also shows his emotion, and it is obvious to the three of us that his highness is not pleased with this turn of events. I have noticed that Dr. Stewart gets so excited about things when he is talking that he really does not pay attention to other people's reactions.

"I must say it was rather impertinent of you to make decisions for everyone," the king begins, aiming his tirade at Pace. Behind us I hear the clamor of people entering the library, along with the protests of the same man who tried to stop us.

"You misunderstand," Pace says. "The purpose of this meeting is for all of us to make decisions together to benefit everyone."

"It is no longer all about you and the privileged," I add. "But you are welcome to stay and share in the decision making. After all, you will be affected just like the rest of us."

"I will not stand for this," the king spouts. "I will have all of you arrested and tried for treason."

"Oh dear," Dr. Stewart says.

Pace shakes his head. "You can be a part of this if you choose. A new future for everyone. Or you can decide not to, and you will be on your own. I think if you look around, you won't find anyone to support you. Everyone here is looking to the future."

Voices rise around us, most of them in wonder at the library. I did not realize how many more were excluded from coming inside. I always thought it was just the shiners who were penalized. Now I realize there were so many more. We all may find that we have more in common than we thought.

"The time of living in the past is over," I say. "It was over the second the glass came down. The time has come to look to the future."

"Is there anyone here to represent the royals?" Pace asks. "Wouldn't you like the privilege of doing so, to really be a part of making decisions instead of letting someone else do it for you?"

"The only way we will survive is if we all work together," Adam adds.

The king opens his mouth to protest once more, but one look at the people milling around inside the library silences him. "I suppose I should listen to what you have to say and voice my opinion on matters," he says instead.

"Stupendous!" Dr. Stewart says. He grabs the king's hand and pumps it up and down while clasping his other hand against his back. I know the king is not used to being manhandled in this way, and I put my hand to my mouth to cover my grin. "Can I be of any assistance to you during your meeting?" he asks.

"I think we would all appreciate anything you have to offer," Pace says. "Should we get this under way?" he asks me, and I appreciate his doing so. He doesn't need me. He should be the one representing our enclave, not me. Then I remember what we learned about parliament, and I realize that perhaps instead of representing just one faction, he should be the one who heads up all of them.

But will this group see his potential, or will they dismiss him because he is young?

"Can everyone find a seat please?" Pace calls out. People move to the chairs and the sound of wood scraping over wood fills the space as they settle in.

An arm raises to get my attention, and I see Jon coming toward us. "Are you here to represent the scarabs?" I ask.

"I am," Jon says with a smile. "And we are searching for a new name for our group. We will no longer be living off of everyone else's castoffs. We will be making our own way."

"I'm so happy for you, Jon," I say. "For all of you. Of us all, your people have suffered the most."

"I'm not so sure about that, Wren." Jon takes my hands into his. "I am so sorry about James."

"So am I," I say. "I truly believe he could have done great things if given a chance."

"That is all any of us wants," Jon says. "A chance. And now we all have one. I hope we will appreciate it."

"If everyone looks at it the way you do, then they will."

Most everyone is sitting now, so Jon and I sit down at the table closest to us with Adam and Dr. Stewart. I see that Findley has come in also, and he sits at the table next to us. No one has enough courage to join the king at his table, except for the man with the scarf who chastised us, and he stands behind him, instead of sitting down.

Pace stands before the tables and waits until everyone quiets down. "I know you have questions about what has happened to our world," he begins. "Questions about the world outside. Questions about how this all came to be."

A few voices rise, some with insults directed at the king, others with questions. Pace waits until they quiet again, and I watch him, amazed and proud at the easy confidence he displays as he stands before everyone.

When the crowd is quiet Pace introduces himself and tells them the story of how we escaped the dome. He begins with Alex's death, because they all saw it or knew someone who did. The way he tells it does not make either of us sound like a hero, instead we just seem determined. He also does not speak ill of my father, even though he was responsible for so many deaths. They listen, enraptured, as he speaks, until Pace tells them about the rovers. That is when the concern plainly shows on their faces.

"So by breaking the glass you have condemned us to death," someone says.

I shake my head. They sound just like my father, living in fear.

"We can beat the rovers," Pace says. "I have not mentioned them to make you frightened. I am telling you this so you will be prepared. We have high hopes that we will have peace with them." He glances at me, and I smile my encouragement. We still have not heard anything from Ragnor. "Now," Pace says, "tell us who you are and who you represent and then Dr. Stewart, who is from America, will tell us about a thing called parliament."

"I think it would be helpful if all this was written down," Dr. Stewart adds. He must not know the value we put on paper, but then I realize, paper is something we can have plenty of now.

The king clears his throat. "My man, Snowdon, can record everything, if that is agreeable," he says. Everyone agrees, or else they are too taken aback by the fact that the king is here with us to protest.

Snowdon goes in pursuit of paper and pen, which is provided to him by a woman who I missed before. She must be the librarian, and for a brief moment I envy her position. Snowdon nervously sits down beside the king and holds the pen aloft, waiting for Pace to proceed. Pace looks at me and smiles.

"My name is Wren MacAvoy, and I represent the enclave, a settlement outside the dome."

"My name is Adam Reid, and I represent the shiners."

"My name is Jon Monroe, and I represent those you called the scarabs."

And to my amazement, the king stands. "My name is King Henry of Hanover-Saxe-Coburg and Gotha, Duke of Kent and Windsor," he continues to rattle off titles that have absolutely no meaning to the rest of us, but we listen in fascination. "And I represent," he pauses and then grins so widely that he looks like a small boy who has just discovered a rare treasure, "the royals!"

The voices ring out around the room. I did not realize how many smaller factions there were. The butchers, the bakers, the metalsmiths, the gardeners, the shopkeepers, the launderers, and those who serve the royals. The workers from the fans who attacked us. The teachers and the doctors and nurses and those who cared for the animals. The street sweepers and lamplighters and Max who represents the dome cleaners. The last to stand is Findley. I am surprised when he does not; instead the bluecoat next to him stands and declares his name as Pierce, while Findley just sits and smiles. So many groups to make up the whole. So many to care for, but so many who can work to make this new world succeed.

The future is ours if we want it bad enough. I know I do.

The meeting continues for hours, hours in which I realize that I have not eaten anything at all today. Hours in which I fight the urge to lay down and sleep because I am still so weak from my wound. I have to pay attention. There is so much these people need to know to survive and so much I need to do to ensure the safety of the people who I represent in the enclave.

They ask question after question. All of them having to do with their survival. I had not realized how safe we were inside. There was no question of food or shelter. We might not have had much, but there was always that assurance that we would not starve or be in fear of outsiders for our lives.

Pace answers their questions with an amazing amount of patience, even when it seems like the exact same question is being asked again.

At least they are happy about parliament and what it represents for the future. Finally, when I do not think I can keep my eyes open any longer, Pace draws the meeting to a close.

"The dome was not built in a day," he says. "So we should not expect to solve all our problems in just a few hours. Can we all agree to meet back here again tomorrow?"

"I have one more question," Jon says. "If we are to implement parliament, shouldn't we go ahead and elect our prime minister?"

"I agree," the king says to my surprise. He rises from his chair. "I would like to volunteer my services."

"And I would like to nominate Pace Bratton," Adam says before the king sits down again. By the look on his face, I am fairly certain the king thought the job would be his.

"If it is acceptable to everyone, I can act as a facilitator, since I am impartial," Dr. Stewart interjects.

My eyes meet Pace's. I can tell by looking at him that he is surprised yet flattered. Yet he wants my approval. I give it to him, gladly, willingly, with my smile and a nod of my head. Why shouldn't he be prime minister? He is fair, he is honest, he is patient. He has a way about him that soothes people.

This is why I fought this battle, why *we* fought this battle. We should be able to aspire to things that are greater than expected. We should dream about things that are out of reach. We should not be afraid to reach for the sky, and if we find it is glass we should break through it. Without reaching we cannot achieve anything.

Pace is made for greater things. I never would have thought it the first time I saw him, but as he said, "Things are not always what they seem."

The vote is quick. Pace is elected. The king is not happy, but he offers his congratulations. It is a good start. The noise of talk among the factions is loud, and then it suddenly quiets to a hush. We look to the door.

Levi and Lyon are there, and with them, Ragnor and Janna. They both are bloodied and bruised, and I fear for the worst. I run straight to them.

"What happened?" I ask. "We saw the smoke."

"Wulf is dead," Ragnor says. "The village is no more."

"What about the people?" Pace joins us. Everyone around us is listening. There has to be good news, Lyon would not have brought them here if there wasn't.

"My husband challenged Timor for power after Wulf died," Janna says. "He won, but he spared Timor's life."

"I should have killed him," Ragnor says. "I told him to leave. Some chose to go with him. They fired the village."

"What will you do?" Pace asks.

"We will build again. Better this time. Will you show us?"

"We will," Pace says. "For a trade. Show these people how to hunt. What plants they can use for their gardens. Where to find water. How to fish." He extends his right hand to Ragnor. "Do we have a trade?"

Ragnor nods and takes Pace's hand in his. They shake. "We have a trade."

I feel a great weight lift from my shoulders. There are still dangers out there. Timor's faction. The filchers who disappeared. The certainty that not everyone will be happy with how things are. Luckily my hope for a better future is stronger than my fears.

*W*e have always burned our dead. When we lived inside the mines we placed them on a litter in the stream that ran through our village and lit them on fire and let the ashes carry them beneath the wall. I used to wonder where the water would lead. Now I know that it leads to the sea, as we followed the river out after the explosions that destroyed our village.

That evening we do the same for James. Adam, Alcide, Pace, and Peter hoist his body to their shoulders and carry him to the ridge behind the enclave as we all follow with Jonah and a few other cats trailing us, along with the dogs, Belle and Beau. Ragnor and Janna follow us, and they stay off to the side, curiously watching as we continue to our destination.

The children spent the day gathering wood under Rosalyn and Colm's direction, and a large pyre, higher than my head, awaits James's body. The men place him on top, and as the sun rises in the sky I look out at the land that surrounds us.

We are slightly higher than the hilltop where we live. Only our stone tower and walls make it higher. The top of this ridge is nothing more than a large boulder, smooth and scarred from the fires that left it barren and lonely. A few small depressions hold water from the rain that fell overnight, and there are a few crevices of dirt where wild violets have taken hold.

The land rolls off, endless and beautiful, hill after hill, covered with trees and grass, while the valleys below are filled with the blazing colors of the wild flowers. So much beauty, at such a cost. Another life lost because of men's selfish desires.

There is no more time for what ifs. There is no changing the past; all we can do is learn from it and hope for the future. Hope that it is better, that we are stronger, that we will survive and our children and their children will appreciate the sacrifices that we all made so that they could choose their own paths.

I will make sure that James, Peggy, and all the rest who died in our struggle are not forgotten.

Pace comes to my side. Adam and Alcide light the pyre, and we all watch as the flames lick up around James's body and the sheet catches and he is suddenly engulfed in flame. Lyon and Jane stand across from us, with Zan between them, and she weeps as they both hold onto her hands. Levi stands behind them and to the side, and he looks so alone.

I cannot help him. It is not for me to do. I watch the smoke rise as the flames consumes James's body, and I know that what was James is already gone, to be with Peggy so she will not have to be alone. Adam speaks, and I slip my hand into Pace's as the words wash over me.

Do not look for me in the morning, for I will not be there.
Do not seek me at the table or by your side, but know I care.
For you will find me in the wind that rushes through the trees.
You will find me in the bird song as it carries on the breeze.

You will see me in the ocean, as it tosses upon the shore.
You will hear my voice at sunset as I whisper your name once more.
For I will always be with you as long as you remember me.
I will wait for you on the other side, until your face I see.
Then we will journey together, to the world that awaits us there.
Do not look for me in the morning, for I will be elsewhere.

Such beautiful words, and I know they came straight from Adam's heart. When he is done he bows his head, bidding a final goodbye to his best friend and brother of his heart. His last tie to Peggy. Jilly slips by his side and takes his hand, and I see Adam squeeze hers, and my heart swells with the hope that they may find happiness with each other. The possibility is there. The seed has been planted, and with care it will grow.

One by one, people drift away. Ragnor and Janna disappear into the forest. Sally and George gather the children and head down the hill. Rosalyn, Colm, Joe, and Nellie follow, along with Freddie and Nancy. The Hatfields and Dr. Stewart leave, and Levi lingers for a moment, with Belle by his side, patiently waiting, and then he turns to go without a word. Harry and David are next, and Lucy takes my hand for a moment before they leave. Peter and Jon with Beau following along are next. Then Pace squeezes my hand, and Jilly joins him, and they go, leaving me with Adam and Alcide and Jonah, of course. He is determined never to let me out of his sight again.

We three are the last of our generation. We stand there close by the pyre, the three of us, letting the heat wash over us and not speaking. We have to step back as the pyre collapses inward and the fire burns higher and brighter until, slowly, the flames begin to subside and there is nothing left but a few charred logs and a pile of ash.

"Let the wind take him," Adam says as a benediction. "Take him to a place where there is no fear or pain. Where there is only laughter and love." He looks up to the heavens. "I will always love you, Peggy. I will always remember you, James. At least in death, you have each other. That gives me comfort."

I place my hand on Adam's back, and Alcide steps to his side. And with one last look, we move on, together, back to the enclave, where our friends are waiting.

♦

The evening was full of sadness, but the next day is a cause for celebration. We are determined to make Lucy and David's wedding full of joy, despite our loss of James. Zan takes on the project wholeheartedly, and Lucy, Jilly, and I, with Jonah the only male allowed, go to Zan's room on the *Quest* to prepare for the wedding.

"I can't believe I am nervous after all the time David and I have spent together," Lucy confesses as Jilly bushes her hair.

"It isn't nerves," I say. "It is excitement. You are starting a new chapter in your life."

"We all are," Jilly agrees. "I cannot believe how excited my parents are. About everything. I think they might even try to have another baby," she says with a grin.

"I know I am," Zan says. "From now on, no more foolish impetuous decisions. I hate myself for going into the dome when I knew I shouldn't. If not for me, James would still be alive."

"Don't think that, Zan." I go to her and put my arms around her. "If there is one thing I've learned from all this, it is that you cannot live your life by regret."

"We all have regrets," Lucy says. "If not for me, Alex would still be alive."

"But we would still be inside the dome," I say. "Because Alex proved to us that the outside existed. That it was safe."

"Isn't it funny how one thing leads to another and then another and then something bigger," Jilly remarks. "If not for me being in the kitchen by chance one day, when Harry made a delivery to the cook, I never would have known that there were other people as unhappy with their lot as I was. I never would have met all of you, my true friends."

"James could have died just as easily fighting the rovers. Or by falling off the cliff like Eddie and his son. We have no way of knowing what fate had in store for him," I say. "I knew James well," I continue, thinking about the trouble between us and how, in the end, we were together as friends. "I know that he would rather die fighting and knowing that he saved a life. He died well, and he lived passionately, and he made a difference in his life and his death."

"Here, here," Jilly says.

"Remember him always here." I touch Zan's breast above her heart. "Keep him there always. But do not live your life with regret, or else he died in vain."

Zan nods tearfully and smiles. "I will never forget what he did for me. And I will live a life that will make all of you proud. For James."

We come together, the four of us, with arms around one another and heads together. We share our misty eyes and watery smiles, and then Zan breaks away and turns to her closet.

"The bride shall wear white," she says, and pulls out a dress for Lucy. She hands me the yellow one I wore before and Jilly a soft pink and selects a blue one for herself. And for the next few hours I put away thoughts of revolution and death and just concentrate on being a girl whose dear friend is getting married.

And I think of Pace.

◆

The ceremony is in the meadow where the ponies grazed. The grass is shorn, but the flowers are tall and a riot of color, more than

I ever imagined seeing. An arch built from tree branches and deco-
rated with ribbons and sprays of pink blossoms stands at the top of
the gentle slope. The children chatter and frolic barefoot as everyone gathers. We may not possess much, but what we do have in the
way of clothing is shared among us all. It is clean and mended and
everyone has taken great care to make sure that they look their best.
Lyon, Jane, Zan, Dr. Stewart, and Levi are dressed more grandly
that everyone else, of course, but I know they would shine just as
much without the fancy clothes. Zan does. Levi always will.

Still I only have eyes for Pace, who stands off to the side, wearing his enforcer uniform, without the gold bands and medals. Pip,
on his shoulder, is the only gold adorning his uniform.

I gave Freddie and Nancy the chore of getting Ghost ready. They
washed him and braided flowers into his mane and tail, and Lucy
sits sideways on his back as we wait for David, Harry, and Captain
Manning to take their places before the arch.

Captain Manning nods and I step forward, leading Ghost up the
slope until we come to the place where they are gathered. David
lifts Lucy from Ghost's back, and I hand the lead to Freddie, who
takes Ghost to the side, and then I move to my place beside Lucy.

I listen to Captain Manning as he speaks the words that will join
them in marriage, and suddenly the meadow is filled with butterflies. The colors are wondrous and beautiful. Lucy laughs gaily and
David picks her up by the waist and they spin around.

It is just like my dream except I am not alone. And I realize that
what I set out to do came to fruition because I had these people
around me. They gave me strength and they gave me courage. They
gave me a purpose. They supported me and they followed me.

Without them I am nothing. With them, I can do anything. I
have done everything I set out to do. Yes, I grieve for those we lost.
But looking around me today, at this beauty, at this happiness that

302 • Kassy Tayler

fills all of us, I can say with all honesty that their deaths were not in vain. Not my grandfather's, not James's, not Peggy's, and most definitely not Alex's.

Pace grins at me from where he stands, and the butterflies take off, filling the sky with their color. Jonah leaps into the air to try to catch one, and Pip jumps from Pace's shoulder and swoops over his head to chastise him for his actions.

I laugh. My heart swells with joy beneath the beautiful blue sky. Pace comes to me and takes my hand into his, leans down and very gently kisses me.

◆

The time has finally come to say good-bye to the Hatfields. The *Quest* has been docked at the catwalk for the past several days to make it easier to load the supplies they will need for the trip back to America. Nearly everyone from the dome has come out to look at it, and Lyon even let the king and queen tour it, along with all the members of parliament so they can go back and report the wonders they've seen.

It is strange to see so much activity outside now. The road, which was once covered with thick grass, is now a hard dirt track as people venture farther and farther out of the dome. Fences have been built to keep the animals that once lived inside from trampling the newly planted gardens. What was once wild is turning civilized as the citizens spread out, no longer confined by the glass.

It makes me very happy that we found a place away from the dome to settle where we can be on our own. It makes me even happier that our good-byes are to be said in private, as we have gathered at the catwalk at dawn, before the dome stirs to life.

"Are you sure you want to stay?" Jane asks Dr. Stewart yet again.

"Of course I do," he replies. "There is so much to study, and help-ing these people build a brand-new society is such a wonderful op-portunity. Just think of the possibilities. Besides, you'll be back in a few months with my supplies, so it's not like I will be here forever."

Jane touches his cheek with her hand and looks to me. "Take good care of him," she says. "Don't let him get so engrossed with what he is doing that he walks off a cliff."

"I will," I say.

Jane turns to Jon, who stands nearby with Beau at his side. "Take good care of our sweet Beau too," she says as she stoops to ruffle the fur at his neck.

"You know I will," Jon replies. "Thank you so much for letting him stay."

"It is his choice," Jane says. "Dogs know in their souls when they find their person. Beau found you, and there is no denying that he is your dog. I know he is in good hands." Jane returns to Pace and me. "I cannot wait to see what you make of this brand-new world of yours," she says as she takes my hands into hers. "I am certain it will be something special."

"We could not have done any of this without your help," I say. "You saved us when you came."

Lyon joins us. "We will be back before you know it," he assures us. "With plenty of supplies."

"Thank you, sir," Pace says. "For everything"

Lyon and Jane leave us, and Levi walks up. "Do you mind if I have a moment with Wren?" Levi asks Pace.

"That is up to Wren," Pace says.

I nod and follow Levi a short distance away. He takes from his shirt a package wrapped in brown paper, and once again I marvel at the extravagance that I will never get used to. "I wanted you to have this," he says.

I open the paper and find a circle made of twigs. It is amazing how perfect the circle is for what it is made of. In the middle of the circle is an ornate weaving of different colored threads that leave an open circle in the middle of the larger circle. A loop is on one side and the other has a hanging of beads and feathers that trail down.

"What is it?" I ask.

"A dream catcher."

"From the story you told me about the talking spider?" I ask.

"Yes," Levi says with a shy smile. He takes it from my hand and holds it up by the loop. "It catches the good dreams here, and the bad ones fall through the hole," he explains, pointing. "I only want good dreams for you, Wren." He glances at Pace. "For both of you." His eyes return to me, and I see the longing in the depths of his warm brown eyes.

I hate that I hurt him. Unfortunately, someone would be hurt no matter who I chose. All I can do is hope and pray that he finds someone who will love him in return, the way he deserves to be loved.

"Please come back someday," I say, and am surprised to hear the tears in my voice. "I can't stand the thought that I might not ever see you again."

Levi takes my upper arms in his hands and squeezes them gently. I know he wants to do more, and I also know that it would hurt him too much if we did. "I will," he says. "I promise."

I smile through the mist in my eyes and nod, because I believe him with all my heart. He will come back. "Time to board," he says. "When Lyon is ready to go, he's ready to go. No more dilly-dallying for anyone."

We walk back to Pace as I keep a tight hold on the dream catcher. Levi extends his hand to Pace and they shake, and then to my surprise they embrace and pound each other on the back, the way men are prone to do, as if they are embarrassed at their show of emotion.

"Be safe," Levi says.

"You too," Pace says. "I'll take good care of her."

"You better," Levi says, and grins at both of us before turning to go up the steps to the *Quest*.

"I shall miss you terribly," Zan says. She gives me a bone-crushing hug and moves on to Pace. "I promise to take good care of Alcide," she adds. She looks back at the group gathered to see them off and then looks beyond, at the trees and the hills rising in the distance. I know she is thinking of James. I hope she will never forget him. I know I will not. Just as I will never forget Peggy.

Alcide is next. His grin is contagious. "Are you sure you can manage without me?" he asks.

"Go and see the world," I say as I hug him. "For all of us."

"And don't eat all their rations," Pace adds as Alcide hugs him also before practically dancing up the steps to the *Quest*.

Findley somehow got on board while we were talking to Alcide. Maybe he thought I would embarrass him by hugging him. It doesn't matter. I appreciate him as he is. In the end, when it really mattered, he came through for all of us.

"Cast off!" Lyon commands. David and Adam untie the lines, which are then pulled in by two of Lyon's men. We hear the gentle strum of the engine kick on, and the *Quest* slowly rises into the air.

As the currents lift the ship up and away, Pace and I walk hand in hand out on the catwalk. We can still see everyone waving from the decking around the cabin. Lyon, Jane, Dr. Stewart, Zan, and Alcide, grinning madly, Findley, stoic as usual although I know he has to be excited to see the world, and then Levi, standing off by himself, just looking at me . . . at us . . . as the *Quest* floats farther and farther away. And then Levi raises his hand and touches his fingers to his forehead in a salute to both Pace and me before he turns and goes into the cabin.

I hold the dream catcher clutched in my hand and smile. I will put it to good use because I have so many dreams. Dreams for a wonderful future for all of us, as we set about to tame this brand-new world that surrounds us.

The *Quest* slowly turns and heads out to sea. We watch until we can no longer make out our friends on the deck. Pace squeezes my hand, and we turn to go back to the enclave and to the home we hope to build in the ruins of the church. Jonah comes out from beneath the catwalk and stretches before trotting off before us.

Levi offered me the world, but Pace showed me the sky, and for me that is enough. Because my world is here, and I am anxious to see how it all turns out in the end. But still I can't help but turn and take one last look at the *Quest*, which is now just a dot in the bright blue of the sky. Then a flash of yellow catches my eye and Pip darts in and settles on Pace's shoulder.

My world, once hollow, is now endless with possibilities. And my sky is so very blue. But not as blue as Pace's eyes.